PRINCE EDWARD ISLAND SHORES · 1

# Beyond the Tides

# LIZ JOHNSON

## Revell

a division of Baker Publishing Group
Grand Rapids, Michigan

© 2021 by Elizabeth Johnson

Published by Revell
a division of Baker Publishing Group
PO Box 6287, Grand Rapids, MI 49516-6287
www.revellbooks.com

Printed in the United States of America

Library of Congress Cataloging-in-Publication Data
Names: Johnson, Liz, 1981– author.
Title: Beyond the tides / Liz Johnson.
Description: Grand Rapids, Michigan : Revell, a division of Baker Publishing Group,
   [2021] | Series: Prince Edward Island shores ; #1
Identifiers: LCCN 2020058634 | ISBN 9780800737375 (paperback) | ISBN
   9780800740009 (casebound)
Subjects: GSAFD: Christian fiction.
Classification: LCC PS3610.O3633 B49 2021 | DDC 813/.6—dc23
LC record available at https://lccn.loc.gov/2020058634

This book is a work of fiction. Names, characters, places, and incidents are the product of the author's imagination or are used fictitiously. Any resemblance to actual events, locales, or persons, living or dead, is coincidental.

Published in association with Books & Such Literary Management, www.booksand such.com.

21  22  23  24  25  26  27      7  6  5  4  3  2  1

"Once again Liz Johnson enchants us with life on Prince Edward Island. The story of Meg and Oliver resonates as they grapple with their future, their hopes and dreams, and the surprising romance developing between them. Take a ride out to sea with this charming tale. Another winner from Johnson."

**Rachel Hauck**, *New York Times* bestselling author

"In *Beyond the Tides*, Liz Johnson has crafted a hopeful romance that expertly deals with love, loss, and the power of forgiveness. Set against the beautiful backdrop of Prince Edward Island, this is a fun twist on an enemies-to-more love story. *Beyond the Tides* is full of heart, charm, and a couple you can cheer for all the way to the very end."

**Courtney Walsh**, *New York Times* bestselling author

"Meg Whitaker has only a few months to prove to her father that she is worthy of inheriting the family lobster fishing business. Never mind that mal de mer strikes as Meg steps foot on any boat, or that Oliver Ross, an old foe, is out to dethrone her yet again. With poignant self-discovery, Meg comes to term with the past, to the hopes and dreams that were stolen from her. In doing so, she unlocks the door to a future, including love. Liz Johnson has a gift for creating flawed and likable characters caught in a heart-wrenching yet romantic tale. Set on gorgeous Prince Edward Island, *Beyond the Tides* is a perfect summer vacation read."

**Suzanne Woods Fisher**, author of Carol Award winner *On a Summer Tide*

"Prince Edward Island once again comes alive in the capable hands of Liz Johnson. Readers will find themselves deeply invested in Meg and Oliver's journey—one of legacy, love, and the healing power of forgiveness. Rich in beautiful imagery and drenched in heart, *Beyond the Tides* proves that the past you run from may just be the key to discovering a future worth chasing."

**Bethany Turner**, award-winning author of *Hadley Beckett's Next Dish* and *Plot Twist*

# Books by Liz Johnson

**PRINCE EDWARD ISLAND DREAMS**

*The Red Door Inn*

*Where Two Hearts Meet*

*On Love's Gentle Shore*

**GEORGIA COAST ROMANCE**

*A Sparkle of Silver*

*A Glitter of Gold*

*A Dazzle of Diamonds*

**PRINCE EDWARD ISLAND SHORES**

*Beyond the Tides*

For my dad

A good man leaves an inheritance to his children's children.

Proverbs 13:22

# one

Morning had a terrible habit of arriving too early, at least as far as Meg Whitaker was concerned. And it was too fond of adding a chill to the summer air at the shoreline.

She hunched into her oversized sweater and shivered against a gust of wind as a pair of headlights bounced into the red dirt parking lot across from the wharf. Finally. Her dad was already five minutes late, and she had only dragged herself from her bed at such an absurd hour because he'd told her he needed to see her, and this was the only time that Mama Potts could stay with her mom. Besides, after decades on the water, her dad loved this time of day.

As the vehicle rolled to a stop and flipped off its lights, she could see even in the darkness that it wasn't her dad's cherished red truck. This one was baby blue and sported over half a dozen rust spots from more than one harsh winter.

Squinting hard at the truck, she could make out the form of a man sitting behind the wheel. His shoulders were broader than her dad's lanky form, his neck straight like steel. But she couldn't see his features and didn't recognize his vehicle.

He didn't open his door. He didn't turn his head. He didn't move. He just sat there. Staring at her.

Meg could feel the weight of his gaze, every ounce of it. She cringed at a memory she'd tried so hard to forget. Only one other man—well, he'd been a boy then—had ever stared at her so intently that she'd physically felt it. A few days later he'd destroyed her science fair project, her chance at a prestigious fellowship, and all hope of being accepted to Yale.

No way *he* was the one sitting in a truck at her dad's dock at 4:45 in the morning, staring at her through the darkness. He was barely a silhouette behind a windshield. But she couldn't look away. She could only wrap her arms about herself and pray that this man wasn't the one she remembered.

When the low purr of her dad's truck finally reached her on the cement wharf, Meg jerked her head up. The truck's shiny coat glittered even in the low light as he pulled halfway down the narrow lane and parked.

"Sorry I'm late, hon." Her dad's long strides ate up the ground between them until he greeted her with a peck on the cheek. "Your mom had a rough morning."

Meg cringed. She hadn't even thought about why her dad might be late, what he'd been doing in the morning hours that most people still considered night. "How is she?"

"Tired."

They all were. Tired of late nights and far-too-early mornings. Tired of praying for an answer that never seemed to appear. Tired of the mystery illness that was stealing her mom's mobility and very life one breath at a time.

Meg squeezed his big hand, ignoring the calluses from years of pulling in lines and tying traps. "How are you?"

His fingers gripped hers, and his gaze dropped to the space between his feet. "I'm ready to let go."

"Let go? Of what?" Surely not her mom. He hadn't asked

her there to make some grand announcement about how he was throwing away thirty-seven years of marriage because life had become something other than it was supposed to be. He wasn't that kind of man.

He shook his head, his shoulders slumped under a weight she couldn't see.

"Dad?"

"It's too much for me."

She grabbed his elbow. "What's going on?"

He brushed an errant lock of hair back from her face, even as the wind whipped more of it free from her ponytail. "I thought I'd be able to wait until you were married."

What was he talking about? She hadn't had a serious boyfriend in years. And even then they'd discussed marriage exactly once—just long enough for them to both know they weren't ready. They hadn't been particularly in love either.

"Dad." Her voice turned firm. "You're not making any sense. What are you talking about?"

"After you said you didn't want Whitaker Fishing and the *Pinch*, I hoped you'd marry someone who did. Or maybe you'd have kids who wanted it."

"The business?" Her gaze swept over the fishing boats rocking in the narrow dock, sitting low in the water beside the pier. Pale blue and white and barnacle free, *Just a Pinch* had been her father's pride and joy for more than a decade.

The realization sat in her chest, heavy and painful, slipping south with each creak of the mooring lines until her feet were rooted where she stood. He was selling his business. He was selling his livelihood. He was selling her birthright.

Okay, technically he'd asked her a few years ago if she wanted to take over the business. But how could she run a fishing company when she couldn't stomach stepping aboard a boat? She'd never earn the respect of the crew—or enjoy a day at her job. Still, there was something terrifying about the idea that the license her great-grandpa had bought would go to someone without the Whitaker name. Even when everything else seemed unstable, Whitaker Fishing had been theirs.

"Dad! You can't. Not yet."

He held up a hand that stilled her outburst, but it was the calm shake of his head that tore her heart apart. "You said you didn't want it." Confusion seemed to add a question to the statement, his eyes sad. "Have you changed your mind?"

She tried to form a response, but her tongue couldn't shape it. She managed only a slight shrug.

"Your mom needs me now. She can't wait . . ."

There was no need for him to finish his thought. She knew. While the income from the sale would allow them to enjoy the days her mom had left, he really only cared about spending them with her. The money would be nice later. After.

And there would be plenty of money. Lobster fishing fleets were in high demand—mostly because there were a limited number of fishing licenses around Prince Edward Island. They rarely came up for sale, and when they did, they went for small fortunes, and her dad had been approached by brokers many times over the years.

Her eyes swung toward the blue truck. Was that a broker sitting inside?

She quickly dismissed the idea. Brokers on that level didn't drive rusted clunkers. So who was he, and what did he want with her and her dad?

"There has to be another way." But even as she said it, she knew it wasn't true.

"Your mom and I have talked about it. I want to spend every moment I can with her. I've decided to sell." His mouth twisted on the words, his facade beginning to crack, and she could do nothing but throw her arms around her dad and hold him tightly.

"I'm so sorry," she whispered into his shoulder, reining in her own emotions. He didn't need her grief too. He needed her to be strong and sure.

She'd heard fishermen talk of ships in distress looking for any port in the storm. But her mom and dad didn't need just any port. They needed to be able to lean on her in the face of the unknown. She couldn't buckle under her own grief. She wouldn't.

With a gentle pat on her back and a sniff just above her head, her dad pulled away. His long legs carried him back a step just as the glow of the morning sun lit up the ocean where it met the east, turning the water from black to inky blue. "I have to tell you something else." His furry black eyebrows drew together, meeting over his crooked nose.

Her stomach dropped. There was no way this was good news. But what else could he possibly add?

"I'm going to sell to Oliver Ross."

Was there another Oliver Ross on the island she didn't know? Maybe this one was from away. From far, far away. Maybe he wasn't the boy she'd gone to school with or the one she'd actively been avoiding for more than a decade. And it had required some concentrated effort not to run into him since she'd returned to Victoria by the Sea. It was worth it for her sanity.

But when her dad motioned in the direction of the truck, she knew. She knew with utter certainty that he was selling his business to her arch nemesis.

Oliver Ross took a deep breath, squeezed his eyes closed, and yanked on the handle of his old truck. The door swung open with a loud groan. He'd have made a similar noise if he wasn't sure it would just add ammunition to Meg Whitaker's arsenal.

He leaned his hip against a rust spot, and a creak was quickly followed by the soft catch of the door closing. Then all was silent save the morning birds trilling their song and the rolling of the water against the red rocks in the inlet.

He only imagined he could hear the steam coming out of Meg's ears. The thump-thump-thumping was his heart, not the unpleasant rhythm of her toe against the dock. True, her hands had found their way to her hips, and even at this distance, the shadows from the light above didn't hide the fury of her features. Eyes narrowed. Nostrils flared. Pretty pink lips drawn into a thin line.

She was mad. She probably—no, definitely—had a right to be. But he couldn't avoid her forever. He'd been doing a pretty good job of dodging her the last several years. Or maybe she was dodging him. It didn't matter. He'd come face-to-face with her every day if that's what it took to take care of his family, to give them a sure future.

The gravel gave way beneath his first step. Then his second.

He picked up his pace, circling the colorful shanties at the end of the dock and closing the distance before he could come up with a smooth opening line. Or even a bumbling one. So he said nothing.

Whitaker held out his hand, and Oliver returned the firm shake. "Morning, Oliver."

"Sir." He dipped his chin toward the father and then the daughter.

Meg did not respond in kind. Her eyes were stone. He'd seen them laughing once when she was sixteen. She hadn't uttered a sound, but her blue eyes glittered at a joke one of their classmates told. Oliver had wondered just what it took to make her laugh. And then he wondered if he could do it. They were friends. Not close, but they ran in the same circle.

A month later everything changed, and she'd never spoken to him again. That didn't seem likely to change as she addressed her dad now.

"You can't be serious. Why would you sell it to *him?*" She gestured toward him with a dismissive wave of her hand. "There must be a hundred people interested in buying your business. You don't have to settle."

Her words stung like winter wind whipping ice at his cheeks. He steeled himself against a further attack, squaring his shoulders and staring her down. He wanted to articulate every single one of his finer qualities, but the truth was, he didn't know exactly why Whitaker had chosen him. Oliver had been on his crew for six years, and the year before, Whitaker had asked him to take over the day-to-day management of the business. He'd said he needed more flexibility. More time to make sure his wife got the medical care she needed.

It had been an absolute failure. Longtime vendors had called Whitaker directly, interrupting his wife's appointments to question Oliver's decisions. Supply companies had refused to give him the same deals they'd promised Whitaker. Even the local shore buyer had refused to negotiate with anyone but the older fisherman.

Whitaker was too ingrained in the business, and Oliver

had known almost immediately that he would eventually sell. He'd started saving for a down payment, praying that Whitaker would be willing to sell to someone who needed a loan.

Oliver had learned everything he knew from the older man. The week before, Whitaker had clapped him on the back and called him "son." And then he'd given him the best gift in the world. A stable future.

Whitaker pushed his fingers around his frown in slow motion, starting in the middle of his mustache and ending at the point of his chin. "I thought long and hard about who I wanted to pass our legacy on to. Did a fair bit of praying too."

Oliver's stomach clenched at the very suggestion that he might be the answer to that prayer. He'd been called a lot of things in his life—mostly by his dad—but never an answer to prayer.

"At the end of the day, I wanted to sell it to someone I knew I could trust to continue it well. Someone who would follow the rules—the written and the unwritten ones."

Meg's eyebrows jumped to the middle of her forehead. "But, Dad, you know what he did." She waved her hand in his general direction but jerked it back before her fingers could brush against his arm.

Shoving his hands into his pockets and hunching his shoulders—more to have something to do than because of the breeze—Oliver nodded slowly. "He knows." He'd made sure of that on the day he was offered a job as a deckhand.

Her eyes snapped toward him, and he could almost hear a hissed, "No one asked you, boy." But the voice in his head was deeper, meaner than hers. She hadn't even spoken those words to him when they'd faced each other down in the principal's office all those years ago. Oliver had mumbled an unintelligible excuse for his actions. He'd steeled himself against the stinging smack of his dad's hand against the back of his head and the hiss in his ear.

Only it hadn't come, because his dad hadn't shown up that day. Or any day after. He'd been long gone.

Oliver expected an accusation from Meg. But she didn't speak. He couldn't quite read the look in her eyes, but her posture had turned stiff, her arms locked around her middle.

Whitaker held up his hand. "I made my decision with a full view. The past can't be changed, and I don't think he's the boy he once was."

She flinched. Oliver tried not to notice.

He'd been trying not to notice her for more than a decade. It hadn't worked very well in the high school halls either.

"Dad, have you talked with—"

"Your mother and I had a long conversation about this. Several of them, actually." Whitaker slapped him on the shoulder. "She agrees with me about Oliver."

The pinch of Meg's nose and her stumbled step back revealed the betrayal she felt, and a sudden punch to Oliver's gut almost made him refuse the offer. Maybe it should all go to her. Although her dad had said she didn't want it, and she couldn't keep her legs beneath her even in the shallows. But she should still have some say in who took over her family's fishing business.

"There's no way he's saved up enough money to buy it outright," she said.

Whatever inclination he'd had to decline the offer vanished. So he wasn't wealthy, and he'd wondered more than once how he was going to help support his mom and little brother. He was the one up at four every morning, reeling in traps and breaking his back. And if he worked two jobs in the off-season to make sure he paid every one of his bills and his mom's lights were never again turned off, what concern was that of Meg's?

He worked hard, and he'd make sure the Whitakers' legacy wasn't tarnished.

Whitaker's bushy eyebrows lowered over his eyes, his gaze hard on his daughter. "I'm going to give him an interest-free loan. Let him do the job and earn what he needs. He'll pay me back in five years, and then we'll be square."

Oliver patted the folded square of paper in his jeans pocket. He'd worked the numbers, figured out just how many pounds he'd need to sell each season to pay the crew and pay off the loan. The numbers checked out. As long as demand—and the price per pound—stayed high, the license would be his in a few years.

A slow grin inched across his mouth. His mom and Levi would never have to worry about losing their home again.

But the glint in Meg's eyes promised him it might not be as easy as he'd hoped—not that six years of back-breaking labor and the last year of pinching every penny just to make a down payment had been easy. There was a light in her, a fire that made him shuffle back. Her eyes were wild, unfocused. Every breath she took sounded like it had been scraped over gravel.

Then she opened her mouth and ruined his day.

"Don't sell it to him. Sell it to me."

# two

It's not like I definitely want the business. I just don't . . ."

Meg looked up at her mom, who sat on the sofa in the living room of her parents' bungalow. Meg couldn't bring herself to say the words aloud to her mom, even if she'd been thinking them for two days. They sounded so petty even in her own mind. But no one would blame her, would they? Of course she didn't want to see her family's legacy passed along to Oliver Ross.

Besides, her mom wasn't likely to remember even if she did tell the whole truth.

"I know I said I didn't want the business, but I have to save it." She snatched a coffee mug from the dishwater and gave it a hard scrub with the sponge in her hand. "I can't let it just be handed off to you know who. He hasn't . . . He doesn't . . . I can't believe Dad would do this to us."

Meg rolled her eyes at herself. In all fairness, he was doing this for her mom. No one who knew him would ever assign another reason to his actions, mystifying as they were. And she wanted good things for her mom.

But this still felt very much like a personal affront. Even if she knew they would work it out.

Meg sent an encouraging smile in the direction of her mom's hunched form. Her parents had had the same blue-striped sofa for as long as she could remember, but it looked different than she recalled as a child. Haunted. Like her mom's constant presence on the far end was more specter than tangible.

Her mom stared across the room, but her gaze barely made it to the kitchen, stopping short of the sink where Meg stood. "I'm . . ." Her willowy voice trailed off.

Meg held her breath. Maybe this time she'd have something to say. She'd have just the words Meg needed to hear. She'd have a store of wisdom she'd been longing to share.

"What were you saying?"

Meg sighed, plunging her hands into the lemon-scented sudsy water and retrieving another plate. "Nothing, Mom. Just cleaning up the lunch dishes."

"No. No." She shook her head and wiggled her shoulders. "You said something about your dad. And the . . . and the . . ." Her fingers came together in a silent snap, but the word was gone. Forgotten.

The boat. Meg had been talking about the boat. *Ranting* might be a bit closer to the truth, but her mom didn't need to hear any more of that.

The doctors had said it was best not to agitate her. It could make her condition worse. Not that they had any idea what her condition was or what would or wouldn't help it. Maybe agitation was exactly what she needed—something to stimulate her brain.

Okay, probably not.

Rinsing off the last dish in the sink, Meg looked directly at her mom and forced a calm smile. "We were talking about how much Dad loves you and how he's thinking about selling the boat." Her voice remained low and soothing, and her mom's shoulders visibly relaxed.

"The boat. Yes. I told him he should do whatever he thought best."

And he'd thought inviting Oliver Ross into their family business was best. Meg whipped the white tea towel off the handle on the stove but cringed as a sour odor tagged along. She hesitated before pressing it to her nose.

She should have refrained. Her gag reflex nearly took over, and she threw the towel to the ground. It smelled like old eggs.

"When was the last time . . ."

"Hmm?" Her mom tilted her chin up, but her gaze never quite shifted across the room.

Meg searched for a new topic while making a mental note to wash all of the towels in the house before she went home. "Have you had a nap today?"

"No. But that sounds lovely." Her mom pushed herself up and took two steps before Meg even realized it.

Her heart leaping to her throat, Meg sprinted across the room. "No, wait!" she cried. Her mom looked up just as the toe of her shoe caught on the rug. Her knee crumbled, her entire frame falling forward on outstretched arms.

Meg gasped for air, wanting to dive the last few feet but knowing she couldn't risk injuring her mom. Instead, she fell to her knees, sliding like a goalie making a last-period save, praying she could reach her mom in time.

Her mom's weight—light as she was—nearly toppled Meg,

and she managed to keep them both from hitting the ground only by some miracle. Arms wrapped around her mother's slender shoulders, she offered a wobbly, "You okay?"

"Um . . ." Her mom's gaze drifted. "I think so. What . . . happened?"

"Remember?" Meg maneuvered her mom into a standing position. "You need some extra help when you walk."

"I do?"

A lump in her throat caught her off guard, and Meg tried to swallow it. It refused to budge, so she savagely cleared her throat. It remained stubborn. She forced a deep breath in through her nose.

Wrapping an arm around her mom's shoulders, she steered her back toward the sofa. When her mom was comfortably seated, Meg scooped her feet up to the cushion beside her and propped a pillow behind her. Then she pulled a soft throw off the back of the wooden rocking chair and spread it over her mom, tucking it around her shoulders.

"Meggy?" Her mom's eyes fought to stay open but drooped time and again.

"Yeah, Mom?" Her throat felt raw.

"I'm going to take a little . . . a little . . . um . . ."

Meg swallowed the sigh that threatened to escape from somewhere deep inside. Instead, she leaned over and kissed her mom's silky forehead. "Get some rest. I love you."

With an unintelligible mumble, her mom stopped fighting and let her eyes drop closed. Her breaths were so shallow that the slight rise and fall of the white throw was barely discernable.

Only then, when she was absolutely certain that her mom was asleep, did Meg finally gasp against the pain in her throat and the burning at the back of her eyes. Only then did she let the situation wash over her, the sadness piercing holes in her heart.

"Oh, Mom." The words were more breath than voice as Meg sank to her knees, longing to give in to the tears, to the crushing weight of the unknown.

No one had an answer. No doctor could explain why her mom had begun to stumble a few years before. Why even simple words sometimes eluded her. Why she'd stopped making eye contact. Why she had disappeared, leaving behind only a shadow of the vibrant, funny, smart woman she'd once been.

Meg sniffed hard against emotions that insisted on showing up despite their terrible timing.

The rumble of a truck echoed up the drive, and she pressed the palms of her hands to her eyes. Swiping at the remnants of her tears, she jumped to her feet and raced back to the kitchen, to the last dishes left in the sink and the rank towel she'd thrown aside. Scooping it up, she tossed it toward the open door of the laundry room just as her dad entered from the opposite side. Meg plastered another smile in place and prayed that it looked at least partially genuine.

"Hey, Dad." She kept her voice low and nodded toward the sofa and her mom's sleeping form.

He hesitated, his steps halting. When he reached her side, he kissed her forehead. "You still talking to me?"

She squinted up into his face. He'd given her most of his height but not quite all of it. "Maybe. You make up your mind about selling me the business?"

He grimaced, not meeting her gaze. "I'm not sure you know what you're asking for."

21

Okay, that was fair. She didn't really know what it would take to run the boat's day-to-day operations, but she'd learn. It was in her blood, after all. Besides, what she was really asking was for him not to give it to Oliver Ross.

Her lip curled at just the thought of his name. Of his face as it popped to mind. Of his pointed chin and slightly crooked nose. Of his hollow blue eyes. Of his shaggy black hair that matched his heart.

Anyone but Oliver Ross.

And if there was no one else, then she'd figure it out.

"What about school?" he asked.

She opened her mouth for a quick comeback, but the words disappeared. Classes started in six weeks, shortly after the fishing season began. And she couldn't possibly do both. Or maybe . . .

No. Not even she could argue the sanity in trying to juggle both. She couldn't possibly teach her students and be out on the water from before sunrise.

There had to be a way. The fall fishing season only lasted for about two months—from mid-August to mid-October. She had double majored in physics and mechanical engineering. This was merely an equation that needed to be solved.

Except at the moment, her mind couldn't begin to come up with the formula to do that.

"I'll . . . I'll . . . figure it out." She cleared her throat and pushed back her shoulders.

Her dad's frown deepened, his dark eyebrows dipping in the middle. She clearly hadn't convinced him any more than she had herself. He shoved his hands into the pockets of his worn jeans. "I'm still thinking about it. I need to talk with your mom. All right?"

Mom, who hadn't been able to remember the word *boat* just a few minutes before.

Meg sighed. She wasn't going to change his mind by pushing. "I love you. I just don't want to see you make a mistake."

"Huh?" It came out more of a grunt than a question, but she jumped to clarify.

"Selling it to Oliver Ross is a mistake."

Oliver had made a terrible mistake. He never should have told his mom that he was going to get Whitaker's license. He just hadn't figured on Meg Whitaker cutting his line.

"I thought we'd make a whole celebration of it next week. Your favorite supper and dessert," his mom said, her smile competing with the sunshine to fill the tiny kitchen. Hands moving surely and swiftly, she kept her gaze on the simple meal she was preparing. "I've already invited Violet. And your brothers."

Oliver raked a hand down his face and slid it to the back of his neck, letting his chin fall almost to his chest. "Brother," he mumbled. The word wasn't plural.

His mom sputtered, mumbling something to herself.

Looking back up at his mom, he shook his head. "It's not worth making a big fuss just because I might get my own license."

Her stained fingers stilled, the half-peeled carrot in her hand forgotten. "Might?" Of course she latched on to that word. Brushing a gray curl behind her ear, she caught his gaze and held it fast. He had almost a foot and seventy pounds on her, but she'd never backed down.

He wanted to look away. He might have if she had been

anyone other than the strongest woman he knew. Instead, he held fast, staring directly into her face and steeling himself to tell her the truth.

"Oliver James. What is going on?"

He swallowed the bitterness that had coated his tongue since Meg had made her announcement three days before. "Turns out that that sure thing is a little less sure."

Mama Potts turned back to her carrots, dicing them with an extra firm hand.

She'd been named Debi at birth, but he and everyone else in their community called her Mama Potts. It had started when he was six or seven, and she had been delivering yet another homemade clay pot as a gift. One of the little neighbor girls saw the telltale gift bag and called out a greeting to "Mama Potts," almost surely an homage to the teapot in the girl's favorite animated movie.

But at the moment Mama Potts didn't resemble that sweet, round character. Especially as she wielded her knife and narrowed her eyes. "What happened? Did you lose your job?"

His shoulders jerked back. She probably didn't mean for her words to feel like a slap in the face, but how could they not when a lobster fishing job had started all of this?

"No. I mean, not yet. But if Meg Whitaker takes over her dad's company, then I'm pretty sure my employment status will change. Quickly."

Mama Potts's mouth turned down at the corners. "Meg wants the *Pinch*?"

He couldn't hold back the dry chuckle that leaked out. "I doubt it. She just doesn't want me to have it."

Mama Potts's fists clenched at her waist, and her eyes flashed. "She wouldn't dare."

Oliver shrugged a shoulder and slumped into a chair at the kitchen table. Kicking his long legs out before him, he sighed. "She did."

"Well, Walt Whitaker would never be foolish enough to pass his legacy off to someone who knows nothing about the industry. She knows as much about lobster fishing as . . . as *I* do," she said, wagging her finger in his general direction.

He couldn't help but laugh as his mom picked her carrot back up and began hacking at it with her peeler. "I hope not. But you know our history."

Her back to him, she mumbled, "I know that girl can hold a grudge, is what I know."

He grunted. She wasn't wrong. She just liked to conveniently forget that the animosity between them had started with his outburst. He'd been the one to derail her goals. He'd been the one to ruin her project.

"I'm just saying that she should have forgiven you. I mean, you asked."

"Sort of." After a mumbled apology in the principal's office, he hadn't been able to get any closer to her than he had to a rabid fox. Not that he'd tried very hard. Because he'd wanted to be close to her about as much as he'd wanted to be close to said rabid fox.

Mama Potts turned slowly and jabbed a fresh carrot in his direction, the green tops dancing wildly. "You need to fix that. Start with a real apology. None of this 'sort of' business, young man."

Suddenly he was seven instead of twenty-seven, a child getting the tongue lashing he deserved instead of the grown man who had been beating himself up about the same decision for a decade.

"Mom, she won't talk to me. She'll barely look at me."

"It's up to you to fix it. You messed up. You have to own up to it. This avoiding her in Victoria is ridiculous. You sit in the pew behind her at church every Sunday."

True. It was ridiculous. And he was tired of taking her lead. He could fix this. He could make her hear him. He could make her forgive him. Or at least learn to tolerate him.

Before he could tell his mom that, his phone rang, and he looked at the screen. His stomach sank.

Ignoring his mom's motion to put the phone on speaker, he pressed it to his ear. "Hello?"

"Oliver."

There was a hesitancy in Whitaker's voice, and Oliver forced himself not to react.

"I've had an idea. I need to talk with you."

Something akin to hope swelled in his chest, but he refused to buy into it. There was no way Whitaker was going to toss his daughter under the boat. But if it was an outright rejection . . . well, he would have said as much. Right?

Oliver took a deep breath, closed his eyes, and nodded. "Sure."

"Meet me at my place in twenty minutes?"

He eyed the piles of chopped vegetables and the beef his mom had just begun searing. He could be there and back before the stew was done. Probably.

Oliver agreed, hung up the phone, and kissed his mom's cheek. "I'll be back."

"Levi's home, and I won't save you any." If she'd been anyone other than his mom, he'd have waited for her chuckle or the twinkle in her brown eyes. But she wasn't someone else, and he knew she was serious.

The thought of his younger brother eating both of their portions made him stomp the gas pedal as his truck barreled down the dirt drive.

His mom's home and garage sat on an acre of grass overlooking the blue bay, which he hadn't paid much attention to for most of his life. The ocean had just always been there, as close as his right hand. His dad had worked the water. And now he did too. It was his provider. But since he'd fixed up the apartment above the garage and moved into it a few years before, he'd spent more time listening to the sound of the water, the gentle clapping of the waves against the shore.

When Whitaker had taken him on, Oliver had discovered that the sea was so much more than a paycheck. It held a touch of magic. And he wouldn't give it up without a fight.

He didn't slow down as he swung onto the paved road, flying through the barely-there town. The bright red and blue shanties at the end of the dock nearly blocked his view of the gray-shingled pub at the far end of the wharf. But the smell of fried fish from it couldn't be missed. He passed the lighthouse and then turned toward the big white community theater, its windows glowing, the rehearsal running late. It didn't make for much of a metropolis, but Victoria had one thing going for it that night. It took him exactly three minutes to get from his mom's place to Whitaker's.

His truck skidded on the gravel as he pulled up beside the cement driveway of the yellow bungalow. A flash of white fabric in the window beside the front door caught his eye. He didn't have to see her to know that Meg stood behind the curtain.

Now that he was here, knowing what he'd face on the other side of the door, he spent a few long seconds considering turning around and going back for his mom's stew. But sitting there was only giving Meg more ammunition. She could argue that he wasn't sure he wanted the boat. If he wasn't willing to fight for it now, what would make her think that he'd fight for it later? That he'd get up early every morning? That he'd invest in the boat and Kyle, Whitaker's longtime deckhand? Besides, avoiding the inevitable wasn't going to change Whitaker's mind.

Oliver jerked the door open and stepped out, staring straight ahead, shoulders back. In case she was still watching, he kept his stride even, unhurried. Schooling his breathing to follow suit, he reached the door, certain that he looked every bit as calm as he wished he was.

His hand was still raised to knock when the door swung open. Meg stood there, her eyes narrowed and lips pinched. "This was not my idea." It was all she bit out before her dad called from deeper inside the living room.

"Oliver, come in. Let me get you something to drink."

Meg stepped back only enough for him to squeeze past her as he slipped into the rich aroma of shepherd's pie. "No thank you. I'm fine, sir." But the growl low in his belly reminded him that he had to hurry back if he wanted to beat Levi to a second helping of stew. "What did you—" He bit his tongue as Whitaker motioned for him to take a seat in the quaint living space.

Whitaker and his wife sat side by side on the sofa, her gaze on her hands folded in her lap. Meg walked around him and slid into the rocking chair. She crossed her legs and then crossed her arms over her waist.

That left him only one option—the oversized recliner across from the couch, pointed directly at the rocker. Directly at Meg. Her mouth hadn't relaxed, but the hardness in her eyes had eased. And he hadn't even apologized to her. Yet.

Maybe there was hope for them.

Oliver nodded to Mrs. Whitaker as he lowered himself into the chair. "Ma'am."

Her smile was a little lost but still genuine. "Good to see you, Oliver."

Whitaker cleared his throat and leaned his forearms against the worn legs of his jeans. His head hung low, the weight of the decision visibly exhausting him. "I've been thinking about our predicament a lot these last couple days. Seems like there's no easy way about this. I have to step back from the business. And I'm going to hand the reins over to one of you." With a half smile, Whitaker looked at him. "I know I can trust you with my business, Oliver." Then his gaze swung to his daughter. "But it's always been in the family."

Meg blinked her big blue eyes once, the lines at her throat drawing tense. She knew what was coming.

"Still, I don't think Meg knows what she'd be getting into by taking this on."

While Whitaker took a haggard breath, Oliver fought the well of hope that bubbled inside. It wasn't his just yet. Clearly there was more to come. More that had Meg looking like she'd rather have a lobster clamped to her backside than hear whatever her dad still had to say.

"Here's what I propose. I'll wait to make my decision until after this season—during which you'll work the business to-gether."

Whitaker kept talking, but Oliver heard only the ringing in his ears. Three syllables clanging like church bells. *To-geth-er.*

Meg didn't so much as twitch a muscle, and he steeled everything inside himself from reacting too.

He didn't know what was worse—losing the chance of owning his own fishing business or having to work the rest of the summer with a woman who hated him, with no guarantee of getting the business. His fingernails bit into his palms, and only then did he realize his hands had formed fists. Relaxing them one finger at a time, he took a deep breath through his nose and held it. He met Meg's gaze.

Her eyes flashed with something he couldn't quite identify. It wasn't anger or rage or anything he'd expected. But it was fierce. It was fire. And it communicated clearly enough that she intended to win.

He almost nodded to himself, accepting her challenge. They'd both be competing. Meg needed to prove herself a worthy, capable fisherman. Oliver had already proven to Whitaker that he was.

No, Oliver had a different goal. Meg was the one standing between him and his dream. But if he could somehow show her he wasn't the man she thought he was—or the boy he'd been—maybe she'd stop fighting him. Maybe she'd allow him to take over the business. She wouldn't fight her dad's decision or pretend to want a business she'd never shown any interest in.

That had to start with a real apology. But if the fire in her eyes was any indication of her current feelings toward him, it was probably better to wait.

Winning over Meg Whitaker was his challenge. He didn't need her to like him. He just needed her to stop hating him. He had to show her what her dad saw in him. It might take the rest of the season, but he had no intention of losing.

# three

You can't be serious! You've already signed your contract for the school year. I was counting on you."

Meg cringed at the high-pitched squeal coming out of such a tiny woman. Sylvia Tremblay, going on thirty years as the county's high school principal, had a habit of raising her voice an octave or three when upset. And Meg had certainly upset her that morning.

But there was nothing to be done about it except let Sylvia holler, because Meg had already made up her mind. She needed an extended leave of absence. It was that simple. It was that problematic.

She'd spent a week considering every option. There wasn't another. She needed the time off.

"Where on earth am I going to find a qualified replacement?" Sylvia didn't sound particularly interested in hearing a response.

Meg tried anyway. "Maybe Howard could fill in—"

Sylvia's head snapped around so quickly that one of her

gray curls flopped across her forehead. "No. He's retired. Besides, he's not qualified to teach physics."

"But it'll only be a few weeks. Only through the end of the lobster season."

"No."

Meg nodded. She'd hoped one of the former teachers could step in, but apparently there was a history she didn't know. And she wouldn't begrudge Sylvia holding a grudge of her own. "What about a long-term sub?"

Sylvia looked like one of her students, eyes rolling north. "And where are we going to find someone willing to work then? Let alone someone qualified."

Okay, she hadn't fully thought that through. Most of their pool of subs worked other jobs during the busiest season of the year. Actually, most of the town did. Between fishing and theater and tourists, summer and early fall in Victoria were full for everyone. Which was why Sylvia lived and breathed contracts for her teachers.

But Meg wasn't going to give in that easily. Maybe her ideas so far hadn't been great. That didn't mean she couldn't come up with something. Drumming her fingers on her jeans at her crossed knees, she stared through the window over Sylvia's shoulder toward a row of tall pine trees.

"What if . . ." Meg's tongue failed, her idea dissolving.

Clamping her too-pink lips into a thin line, Sylvia pressed her palms against the metal desk between them. She opened her mouth, and Meg's stomach swooped. Whatever Sylvia was going to say, Meg didn't want to hear it.

Bumbling for words, Meg spit out the ones on the tip of her tongue. "What if . . . what if Janelle took my classes?"

Sylvia's eyes narrowed. "And who's going to teach hers?"

And they were right back where they started, except whatever hope Meg had started with had deflated, dispersed like the air in the balloons she used to teach her classes about the states of matter. Staring at her folded hands in her lap, she let out a long sigh through tight lips.

"I'm sorry." She meant it. She was sorry to put Sylvia and her school in a bind. But she was sorrier that Oliver Ross had ever entered her life. If she'd only been born a couple years before, or even a few years later, then her path would hardly have crossed his. He'd be just the man who sat a row behind her every Sunday in the little white church down the road. Nothing more or less.

But regardless of how much she regretted the situation, it couldn't change the facts.

"Can you work with me at all?" Meg asked.

Sylvia's gaze was hard, and even her sagging eyelids couldn't soften the intensity there. Her nose twitched a few times, and she folded and unfolded her hands. Finally she stretched her fingers across the top of the desk next to stacks of binders and cleared her throat. Her voice was raw but strong when she did speak. "I can let you out of your contract."

"What?" Meg grabbed the arms of her chair, needing something to hang on to as the whole world spun upside down. "No. I don't want to be let out of my contract. I just want to delay my start."

Sylvia nodded, but her mouth was firm and tight. "I know what you want. But I don't control the start date of the school year. And *my* students deserve more than a mishmash of instructors to launch the year."

Her words cut, and Meg blinked hard against a sudden burning at the back of her eyes. She'd all but implied that

Meg didn't care about her students. She did. She always had. She wanted the very best for them. And she was the best option for them.

She wrapped her arms around her middle and doubled over, unable to look at her principal while she sorted through the truth of it all. Sylvia was right—the students deserved more than Meg was offering. She sucked in a quick breath, not quite a sob, but not far away from one either. She'd been so focused on doing what she needed to that she hadn't thought about how it might affect everyone else.

The beginning of the year was important—as much for her students as for their teacher. How could she assess where they were if she wasn't there? How could she build any rapport with them if she joined them eight weeks into the semester? How could she set the tone for a great year if she wasn't there?

What a stupid suggestion she'd made. Sylvia was right to refuse her.

Sylvia pushed back her chair, the wheels squeaking across the industrial carpet, and stood. "I'm going to make a phone call from the front office. When I come back, I'll need your decision."

Meg nodded.

When Sylvia reached the door, she paused. "If I have to find a new teacher this year, I'm not going to save your position for next year."

The door closed behind Sylvia with a click, and Meg leaned her elbows against her legs and buried her face in her hands. Through her fingers she inhaled the smell of paper and old textbooks, whiteboard markers and freshly sharpened pencils. So familiar. The smells of school. So much sweeter than the fishy scents of the bay or the smell of sweaty men hard at work.

Was she really going to give up her teaching career—everything she'd worked for the last three years—to take over the family business?

It wasn't even guaranteed to be hers. She was going to have to prove herself to her dad. And to Oliver. Not that she cared what Oliver thought. But he'd never back down, never stop pestering her dad if she didn't show him she could do this.

It would be so much easier just to let it go. Let him have the business. She didn't want ridiculously early mornings and pinching lobsters and feeling nauseous every single day. But she also didn't want to lose everything generations of her family had worked so hard for.

And more than all of that, she didn't want to upset whatever tenuous hold her mom had on reality. What would happen if the Whitakers no longer owned Whitaker Fishing? If their life changed so much that her mom no longer recognized it?

Her memories and her grasp on words were already thin. The doctors had said it wasn't Alzheimer's. They'd ruled out Parkinson's. They'd figured out exactly nothing else. But they'd said to keep her calm, to avoid major changes. Could a change like selling the business send her into a spiral?

Okay, Meg was probably the one more likely to feel out of control. But how could she not, when everything was flying apart?

Besides, if the doctors did finally diagnose the disease that was stealing her mom away, she might need treatment elsewhere. Expensive treatment. There was no way Meg could pay for that on a teacher's salary. And her dad's savings wouldn't last long. Not with Oliver taking five years to pay back the loan. How could her dad not have thought ahead? Why hadn't he planned for the what-ifs?

She wanted to jump in her car, drive to her dad's, and shake his shoulders until he saw how foolish he was being. But she'd sworn to herself she wouldn't be that person. She wouldn't let her own grief spill onto her parents. She'd be the strong one. The tough one. She had to be. For them.

A painful ache started behind her left eye and then shot along her temple until it wrapped all the way around her skull, twisting tight like a vise. Leaning over, she rubbed two fingers against each side of her head, but it didn't help. Nothing eased the pressure building inside her, nor the reality of what was to come.

She had two options. Give up the legacy and risk her mom. Or give up her job and lose her steady paycheck.

Meg had never planned on being a teacher. She'd definitely not expected to love it. But when her dad had called during the last term of her master's degree to say that her mom had fallen more than once, Meg had set aside every one of her dreams and moved back to PEI. At twenty-four, she'd held on to the hope of returning to the University of Ottawa. Now, at twenty-seven, she knew she wouldn't go back.

She'd fallen in love with teaching her high school students, and her dreams were for them much more than for herself. Could she walk away from them now?

She was nowhere near answering her own questions when the door to the office creaked open and Sylvia's shoes shuffled against the floor.

"So? What's it going to be?"

"Um . . ." Meg looked up, fearing her face was as twisted

as her insides felt. Even with her crooked lipstick, Sylvia's gentle smile confirmed that worry.

"Honey." Sylvia pressed her hand to Meg's shoulder. "I want you to stay. And not just because I don't want to have to find a new physics teacher." With a gentle pat on her back, Sylvia strolled around her desk and sat down. "You're a great teacher, but I have to put my school—my whole school—first."

Meg managed a wobbly nod before ducking her head again. Taking a deep breath, she wasn't quite sure what she was going to say as she opened her mouth, but she knew what mattered most. "I have to take care of my mom."

Sylvia nodded. "We'll miss you."

Meg's stomach sank as she pushed herself up from the chair. Now she'd done it. Now she *had* to prove to her dad that she deserved the *Pinch*. She'd just lit her only safety net on fire.

---

Oliver stretched the net across the inside of the lobster trap, securing it into place on the frame. Testing it with a tug of his finger, he nodded. It was strong enough to hold for the season.

Running a hand across the square corners of the wood, he smiled. The lines were as clean and sharp as Whitaker's own traps. Then again, Oliver had spent hours watching the seasoned fisherman build them, measuring and sawing and squaring the wood. Securing the nets and leaving escape routes for the undersized lobsters. Meeting the government regulations.

The stack of finished traps at the end of his table had the

same structure—flat on the top and bottom. They didn't look like the lobster traps sold at antique shops or the ones pictured on the front of the Prince Edward Island tourism brochures. Those traps had domed tops, straight sides, and flat bottoms, the wooden slats of the ceiling curving down to the netted sides.

Oliver should have known. He'd grown up on the island, after all. But he hadn't realized until he'd started working for Whitaker that some fishermen didn't use the traditional traps. Not when the homemade flat traps stacked, stored, and traveled so much better.

Just as he was shifting the trap to attach the netting that would catch dozens of lobsters that summer, the sound of a car approaching made him look toward the road. His mom's home was set off the pavement by a few dozen meters, but the sedan parked at the end of the drive and didn't even approach the house.

He squinted at the tall, slim figure as she pulled herself from behind the steering wheel and straightened her top. Meg. She stopped halfway through adjusting her shorts, her eyes locking on his. He could feel her animosity from there. Could practically see her mentally preparing to face him down.

He wouldn't blame her. After all, he hadn't given her a real apology.

This was his chance. It might be ten years late, but he wouldn't let it slip by. Not when it was just the two of them. Not with the next two months spread out before them. Apologizing was step one to smoothing things over—step one to winning the boat.

Meg's long legs marched down the drive, her arms pumping, neck and back straight. Her blonde ponytail whipped from side to side, and her eyes never wavered.

He dropped his hammer beside the trap, and she blinked. The closer she got, the more he became aware of what she saw, how this compared to her dad's workshop. She'd probably watched Whitaker make thousands of traps in his day. Her dad's tools were all neatly organized around his work space in the garage. She likely hadn't seen a piece of plywood resting on two sawhorses in the yard—a makeshift table. He wished he had a pegboard wall, tools hanging within easy reach, instead of the rusted red metal box crushing the grass at his feet, hammers and wrenches and screwdrivers jumbled together.

He wouldn't have minded a real workspace either, a shelter when there was rain. His dad had had a work shed behind their house when Oliver was a kid. But even now they couldn't afford luxuries like that. At least they had a roof over their heads—a roof no one was trying to take away from them.

"What are you doing here?" He wanted to bite back the words—or at least his tone—as soon as they escaped.

Meg's eyes flashed with something like sadness before she slipped into her steel coat. Armor was what she'd always worn in his presence. "Good afternoon to you too," she said as she reached the grass and closed the distance between them.

He ran a dusty, dirty hand through his hair. It was long and messy, and he shoved it behind his ears. Ears that had always stuck out, had always invited teasing from his buddies. "Right, yeah. How's it going?"

"I've been better." She looked down at his work space, the corners of her eyes wrinkling. Then she took a deep breath through her nose before meeting his gaze again, shield back in place.

"Listen, Meg . . ." This was it—his chance. But his tongue stumbled to get out the words. Finally he offered, "You want to talk about it?"

*Please say no. Please say no.*

They hadn't had more than three civil words for each other in ten years. He couldn't possibly say anything that would help the current situation.

"Well, I quit my job today, so we're stuck with each other through the season."

He wasn't sure what he'd expected her to say, but that wasn't it. There was no going back now. They were stuck in every sense of the word. But the way she hugged herself made him think that she was more upset about the ending of her teaching job than she was about having to spend a few months with him.

He stabbed his fingers through his hair again, dislodging it so that it fell against his cheeks, brushing the collar of his gray T-shirt. "I'm sorry."

Her eyes flashed ice-cold. "About my job or being stuck with me?"

"Yes. I mean, both."

She snorted. It wasn't quite a laugh, but it was rich and genuine and almost made him smile. He'd wondered once if he had what it took to make her laugh, and the warmth in his chest told him it hadn't been a worthless wish.

He picked up the hammer just to have something to look at as he forced out the rest of what he needed to say. "I *am* sorry about your job. And I'm sorry that you're stuck with me." There. That was most of it.

But not enough.

"And I'm sorry about what happened—what I did—to your

science fair project." He looked up just in time to see her grimace, her facial features pulling tight as though she could see the same memory he did.

They'd been in their high school science classroom, big windows letting in streams of afternoon light as teenage Meg carried a cardboard box.

"Where's your project, Oliver?" Mr. Greene asked.

Oliver looked at his empty hands, embarrassed and angry. He turned and ran straight into Meg and her box, surprising them both. Meg dropped the box, and a wheeled robot tumbled to the ground. If she screamed then, he didn't hear it. But when he kicked the robot to the wall, where it exploded into tiny pieces, her cry nearly split him in half.

Every day since, he'd regretted it. Regretted the pain that had built inside him. The release he'd sought. The destruction he'd caused. But he hadn't been able to put into words—still couldn't—the depth of that anger, the source of that pain that had caused him to lash out.

Everyone had said Meg was sure to win the provincial science fair with her robot that could retrieve necessities for the immobile. And it nearly guaranteed her a scholarship to some Ivy League uni in the States.

He had ruined all of that for her.

"Meg, I'm really sorry that I cost you those awards."

Her lips pinched together, her glare unwavering. "Then why did you do it?"

With a shake of his head, he sighed. "Does it matter?"

For a moment, he feared that she'd say it did. Holding his breath, he searched for some explanation. But if he could hardly be honest with himself, how could he be honest with her?

"Just tell me that it wasn't because of Susie Houseman."

"Susie?" He hadn't seen or thought about their old class-mate since graduation. "Of course not. Why would you think it was her?"

Putting her hands on her hips, Meg said, "Does it matter?"

His own laugh caught him off guard. "So what do you think? Maybe we could start over? Begin again?"

A shadow slipped across her face, her eyes turning even more blue. She was silent for so long he thought she might not respond. Maybe she was already planning her getaway.

Finally, barely moving her lips, she whispered, "We'll see."

All right then. They weren't friends exactly, but maybe they weren't enemies either. She hadn't explicitly said that she had forgiven him. But there was a chance. He'd call this a suc-cessful first step. Though the season hadn't even started, he wouldn't quit until Meg had truly put the past behind them.

# *four*

"Good morning, Sleeping Beauty."

Meg scowled at Oliver as she marched down the wharf, shoving her fingers through her hair and yanking it into some semblance of a ponytail. Good mornings started sometime after seven—nine during the summer—and did not begin with an obnoxious honking coming from her phone. Good mornings started with a sweet roll from Carrie's Café, the big blue building across from the theater. They did not include devouring a fried egg shoved between two slices of stale toast while praying Kevin's patrol car was still parked in front of his house as she flew down the street.

And good mornings definitely did not begin with Oliver Ross and his lopsided smirk. Or those ridiculous dimples that had framed his mouth for as long as she'd known him.

"I'm not late." It was the only greeting she could muster this early. And the mocking tone in his words made her put up her guard.

"Never said you were." Oliver let out a breath, nearly a laugh, turning toward the brightly painted shacks lined up in a row where the marina ended. Red and green and orange and blue, they seemed to be their own source of light against the inky sky.

Every fishing license in the area had a shanty packed with gear and supplies. And even though it had all been inventoried and checked before being carefully packed away at the end of the last season, it was time to do it again. Time to make sure that the buoys would float and the ropes would hold. If a mouse had snuck past a trap during the summer and gnawed through a net, setting day was not the day to discover it.

Meg stamped her sneakers against the red-dirt ground and rubbed her hands together. The sun was only a golden halo across the edge of the water to the east, and the wind off the bay was damp and cool. And she was wearing only jeans and a T-shirt. Stupid move. She should have known better.

As he jerked open the door of the deep-green shack that Whitaker Fishing had owned for longer than her lifetime, Oliver's broad shoulders bunched beneath a black sweater. Its neckline had been ripped at the side and sewn back together with lazy stitches. A frayed spot at the hem offered two loose threads that she longed to tug. Worn, but at least it was warm. She assumed so anyway, since he wasn't shivering.

Apparently he noticed that she was. Eyebrow raised, he asked, "You warm enough?"

"I'm fine."

"You sure? I have a jacket in my car."

She snorted. Not so much at the offer—which was surprising—but more at the mental image of wearing something that belonged to him.

No one had ever called her petite. Not when she'd gotten

her dad's height and towered over the boys until almost graduation. But Oliver still had close to six inches on her, plus a lot of years of fishing muscles. *He* made her feel small. Which was calling into question their current power dynamic.

She waved off the offer of the jacket and nodded toward the inside of the building. "Let's just get to work."

He stared at her for a long moment, his eyes shadowed and unblinking. His gaze made the hairs on her arms stand up. Or maybe that was the breeze. *Please let it be the breeze.* She didn't have the mental energy to try to figure him out.

Finally he turned back to the shack and reached inside. Light exploded into the early morning, and she blinked against the harsh, uncovered lightbulb. The morning sun across the bay had a way of embracing the earth, welcoming the day with a gentle invitation into warmth and light. The shanty's single bulb glared like it was as happy to be awake as she was.

When she finally managed to keep her eyes open, she squinted at Oliver, who held out a clipboard, a couple sheets of white paper fluttering on it.

"Do you want to keep tally or evaluate the equipment?"

She reached for the clipboard and pulled the pen from its holder without a word. No need to remind him that she hadn't taken supply inventory since she was a kid. But she'd rather mark a wrong number on her sheet than miss a broken trap or frayed line. She'd let him be responsible for that.

For now, anyway.

He motioned toward a pile of bright green buoys, all painted with large numbers from one to forty-eight, in the same color her grandfather and his father had used to mark their traps. She followed Oliver deeper inside as he ran his long fingers over each marker, calling out only when there was a damaged piece. A broken hook. A faded number. A loose screw.

After an hour, they'd identified three buoys in need of repair, and Oliver had set them to the side, likely to take them back to his front-yard repair station.

"I can take care of those." As soon as she spoke the words, she wished she could reel them back in.

Oliver's furrowed eyebrows spoke his silent question.

Okay, technically she didn't have the tools or expertise to fix the buoys. And she sure couldn't go to her father to ask for his help. But neither was she entirely helpless. She did have a degree in mechanical engineering, after all. How hard could it be to fix a loose screw? Besides, she knew every captain in the area. Surely one of them would loan her a specialized tool if she needed it.

With one hand at his waist, Oliver ran the other through his hair, all the way to its shaggy end. "I suppose. But your dad ga—er—lent me all his tools."

She shrugged as though it was neither here nor there, but the insinuation that her father had already made a decision and had begun passing the business to him brought a sour taste to her mouth.

"How about we look at these"—he waved at the wall of wooden lobster traps—"before we decide? We can figure out who'll take care of what when we know what needs to be done."

She nodded slowly, biting her tongue to make sure she thought through anything she might say before it had a chance to escape on its own. It wasn't that she didn't want to volunteer for her fair share of the projects. After all, they were taking home an equal portion from the catch. But if she took on a job and couldn't figure it out, she'd look like a fool. Especially when there were regulations to abide by and rules she wasn't sure she knew.

She was not about to let Oliver Ross see her looking stupid. Dividing up the projects wasn't exactly in line with her dad's plan to make them work together, but she wasn't worried about that.

She strode toward the 240 traps stacked in neat rows. He followed, pulled a trap down from the top row, and inspected it. The brown wood had faded over the years from the sun and salt water, but it remained strong, its square corners firm and fixed.

As Oliver tugged on the net, her phone rang. With a silent nod, she ducked toward the door. Oliver's eyes followed her even as his sure fingers worked their way over the contraption.

She hadn't realized how musty it smelled inside until she inhaled the sharp tang of the salt water. Stepping from the harsh yellow light into the warmth of the sun, she said, "Hi, Dad."

"Honey, I don't want you to worry."

That was guaranteed an opposite result. "What happened?" She practically snapped the words and immediately felt Oliver's gaze find her. "Are you all right? Is it Mom?"

"I'm fine. I'm with your mother." Her dad's words were thick, exhausted. "She took a little tumble and hit her head."

Her breath suddenly vanished. Her arms tingled and her eyes burned. It took every ounce of her strength just to stay upright.

Still, her words came out even and clear. "Where are you?"

He paused for a long moment, and she could almost see him working through his options. "We're at Queen Elizabeth."

The hospital in Charlottetown. He hadn't told her not to come. He hadn't said they were on their way home. He hadn't said it was no big deal. It *was* a big deal. Everything with her mom was a big deal.

"I'll be right there." She hung up before her dad could object. Or maybe before he didn't. She didn't know which would have been worse.

Her trembling fingers barely fit into her pocket as she searched for her keys.

Suddenly a large hand rested on her arm. "I'll drive you."

Meg shook it off. "I'm fine." She forced out the words, but they didn't even ring true in her own ears. "I can make it." She hoped. The tremors in her hands were increasing, but she had to pull herself together. She had to be strong, especially now. Taking a deep breath, she shook her head. "Really. I'll be fine."

"Please."

The gravel in his tone nearly buckled her knees. Or maybe that was the weight of all the worries that rested on her shoulders. Her mom's health. Her dad's sanity. Her own future.

Steeling her spine, she took a step toward the parking lot, expecting him to stay where he was. "We have to get the inventory done."

"It'll wait." His breath ruffled her hair. He hadn't kept his distance. In fact, he'd gained ground. She could feel his warmth down her back, his presence solid and reassuring.

She hated him a little bit for that.

"Really, I need to go." So why weren't her feet moving? And where were her keys? After shoving her hand deeper into her pocket, she pulled it out empty. She tried the other side and finally laid her fingers on the elusive keys. But when she clenched them in front of her chest, Oliver clamped his big hand over hers.

His narrowed eyes were harder than an iceberg. Bluer too. "I know you're fully capable of getting there. But I can help."

Her lower lip threatened to tremble, and she bit it just to hold it in place. "It's my mom."

"I figured."

"She's . . . she's . . . ill."

He nodded slowly. "I know."

He ushered her toward his truck, opened the passenger door, and settled her into the seat. She felt like a sheep being herded, but she couldn't do anything except try to prepare for what was ahead.

Oliver took several deep breaths as his truck rattled to a stop in the hospital parking lot. Meg hadn't said a single word the whole thirty-minute drive to the city. Neither had she crumbled. She'd sat up straight—her spine made of metal—the whole ride.

But the moment he stopped, she sucked in a quick breath, flung her door open, and raced for the single-story entrance across from them. Oliver barely had time to turn off the truck and close his own door before taking off after her.

He caught up to her just as the glass doors slid open, and she dashed to the simple cream-colored reception desk. "Sandra Whitaker. Where is she?"

The receptionist eyed Meg carefully, then looked around at him. "Are you family?"

"I'm her daughter."

Oliver nodded. That was true—Meg was her daughter. If the receptionist took his nod to mean he was family too, that was fine.

Mama Potts would always be his mother. But Whitaker had given him the support of a true father, probably long before he deserved it. Oliver wasn't about to be turned away. Not if he could be of help.

After a long second, the receptionist typed something into her computer and then pointed down the sterile hallway and mumbled a room number. The light brown walls passed in a blur, the jarring scent of disinfectant not so easy to ignore. It coated everything, erasing the sweet salt of the sea air that had clung to Meg long after he'd locked up the shanty and they'd started down the road.

Oliver followed her as she sailed into a room and then stopped short. Whitaker stood beside a hospital bed, a curtain on the far side dividing the room and blocking the view of another patient. Mrs. Whitaker lay on the bed. She was still and pale and so small beneath the nondescript blanket tucked just below her shoulders, one arm free. A white gauze bandage had been wrapped around her head, a pink spot on the right side.

Meg made no noise except for a tiny gasp.

When Whitaker looked up at them, his eyes went wide— well, as wide as they could beneath his drooping lids and bushy eyebrows. "Megan." He sighed, reaching for her.

She rushed to him, but whatever response Oliver had expected, he didn't see it. Meg didn't fall against her dad or release her emotions. Instead, she patted his back and squeezed his hand on her shoulder, her stiff upper lip never wavering.

"What happened?" she asked.

Whitaker looked back down at his wife. "I was making breakfast, and I heard a terrible crash. She went headfirst into the corner of the nightstand. I didn't even know she was awake." He growled the last, his features pinched. "I had to call the ambulance. There was just so much blood."

"It's okay, Dad. She's going to be all right." There wasn't even a hint of a question in her words, her conviction so strong that even Oliver believed it.

"I think the rug is ruined."

Meg offered him a tight smile. "Mom never liked that rug anyway. Maybe this is her way of making sure we get rid of it."

Whitaker managed a smile then as a young woman in a white lab coat walked into the room.

"Mr. Whitaker?"

Whitaker nodded, his hold on Meg's shoulder visibly tightening even as she patted his hand.

"I'm Dr. Wong. I'd like to talk with you for a few minutes." She eyed Oliver and Meg before adding, "Alone."

"I'd like my daughter to come with me," Whitaker said.

Meg's face paled. "Someone should stay with Mom."

Oliver hadn't planned to say anything, but the words popped out. "I will."

Meg's glare landed on him with all the force of a tidal wave. "I don't think—"

Whitaker cut her off. "Thank you, son."

Meg didn't even attempt a smile, her eyebrows saying more than enough. She followed the doctor into the hallway, their murmured voices too low to understand.

Oliver took the opportunity to really look at the room. It was bland, only the bright lights of the monitor near the head of the bed breaking up the tans and browns and plain old whites. The low moans of the patient in the bed on the other side of the curtain broke the silence. Otherwise all was still.

There was a plastic chair along the wall, and Oliver scraped it across the floor toward the bed, then lowered himself into it. "Hey there, Mrs. Whitaker."

Her hand, pale and laced with veins, opened and closed slowly. Oliver reached out and tucked his fingers into her grip.

"Heard you're having a rough day." He kept his voice low, not really expecting a response. When she squeezed his hand, he smiled. "But you're going to be all right. Your family and these doctors are going to take good care of you."

The corners of her lips lifted in the tiniest smile. Maybe it was real. Or maybe he just hoped she was alert. Either way, he gave her hand another press.

"Mama Potts always says Cows ice cream will fix anything. Broken bones. Hard days. Bad memories." He smiled at the memory of his mom setting a heaping bowl of the sweet treat from the island's dairy in front of him after he lost a tooth in the regional hockey championship, and after he'd gotten stung by a bee as a kid, and after his brother Eli had left.

Okay, maybe it wouldn't quite fix everything.

Mrs. Whitaker's eyes fluttered, and he held his breath. *Lord, let her open them. Let her wake up with nothing more than a headache.*

As she settled, her agitation easing away, her eyes remained closed. She had strange eyes. Whitaker said they'd been beautiful. The most beautiful he'd ever seen. Oliver could believe that. He remembered the light in them, the way they used to shine with life. Meg had inherited the same vibrancy.

But they weren't like they'd been when he was a kid. Mrs. Whitaker's eyes were strange now. Lost. Unfocused. Maybe it was too much to hope that a bump on the head might help them find their focus again. Or that it might lead to an explanation of what was going on behind her lost gaze.

The voices in the hallway rose, Meg's words crisp, drawing his gaze toward the door. "But we have been waiting. We've been on the list to see him for the last year. There are never any openings."

"She's tired of waiting," Mrs. Whitaker whispered.

Oliver swung back toward her. Only slivers of her blue eyes were visible beneath drooping lids, but the strength of her grip on his fingers increased.

"She's scared too," she said.

He nodded, not sure if he should agree. Or even if Mrs. Whitaker would remember having this conversation. In the end, all he could say was, "She loves you a lot."

He could have kicked himself in the rear end for that one. He didn't need to defend Meg Whitaker, and he didn't really want to either. His goal was civility. Maybe a step or two beyond civility toward Meg.

But this was Mrs. Whitaker. He owed her more than he wanted to admit to anyone—let alone to himself. The least he could do was try to put her at ease. With a grin he said, "Give her a pair of skates and Meg could be an enforcer for the Maple Leafs. At least where you're concerned."

The corner of her eyes crinkled. "She's a good girl. She didn't have to come home."

It was his turn to squint at her. What was that supposed to mean? Meg had taken a job at the high school after going to school for more years than anyone could have paid him to study. Her return had practically made the front page of the local paper. "Local Kid Proves Brilliance and Brings It Back Home."

Parents of high schoolers at church talked about how much their kids loved Meg's classes. But no one—including Mama Potts—had ever talked about why Meg had left the capital. Then again, he'd never asked for the details.

One week, church had been the same as it had been for years, with familiar heads of hair ahead of him and little girls wearing hats. The next week, Meg's long blonde hair had hung over the seat right in front of him, blocking his hymnal, as she took her spot in the Whitaker family pew. He hadn't needed to know why. It just was. So he'd figured out how to avoid her. Until now.

And now he wanted to know why. Only he wasn't sure that Mrs. Whitaker could tell him the truth.

Finally he mumbled, "That was nice of her to come home."

Mrs. Whitaker nodded, her head slumping to one side. "It was my fault."

"Oh, I'm sure . . ." He wasn't certain what argument he intended to make, but a sudden shift in her eyes stopped him. They had turned sharp, direct.

"I fell. More than once." She shook her head, a self-deprecating laugh on her lips. "More than a dozen times, probably. Can't exactly remember."

Oliver mustered a smile in response. Her words made his breath catch, but she wasn't looking for sympathy. This was the truth he'd thought she might not know. She knew what had happened, what had landed her in the hospital again. At least for this moment.

"And sometimes my memory . . . well, it's like there's a

blank space where there should be . . ." She shook her head. "More."

"I'm sorry, Mrs. Whitaker."

"Oh, don't be sorry for me." She reached across her thin body and patted his hand. "I remember you. I remember . . . you were a good boy. You took care of your mom and your brother too."

His face burned and he ducked his head, suddenly a seventeen-year-old boy again. Swiping his free hand down the leg of his shorts, he tried not to remember. He tried not to dwell on the kind words, on how they kindled the embers in his chest, unfamiliar and welcome.

"You were so handsome."

The fire stretched from his face to the tips of his ears, and he shook his head, not able to look up from the patch of tile between his sneakers.

"Still are."

"No, ma'am." That was a blatant lie, and he wasn't going to let it slide. Eli had taken his role as the eldest brother to heart and teased Oliver since childhood about his ears. A look in the mirror was enough to remind him of the broken nose that had never healed right. He'd grown into most of his features, but he'd never been the good-looking one.

Everyone on the southern shore knew that Eli was the handsome one—the talented one too. At least he had been ten years before. Levi was the baby and the bookish one, though he'd rarely spoken more than a few words in a row since he was fifteen.

Oliver didn't have any of those traits. He wasn't talented or particularly book smart, but he could reel in a lobster trap. He could balance a ledger, navigate a boat, and manage not to get pinched most days. And the lobsters didn't seem to mind if he wasn't a standout in other areas.

Neither did Whitaker.

He didn't need Meg to think him handsome or smart either. He wouldn't mind if she agreed with her mom on a few other points though.

"Don't argue with me, Oliver Ross." Mrs. Whitaker's slight smile sliced through the sharp edge of her words. With another pat on his hand, she said, "You have kind eyes."

He began to nod his halfhearted agreement when someone cleared her throat behind him. He didn't need to turn around to know it was Meg.

# five

"Why did you do that?"

Oliver whipped around at the accusation in Meg's question as she marched up his driveway. "Why did I do what?" He hadn't seen her since the hospital, since he'd left her with her dad and driven back to Victoria by himself almost a week before.

She stood before him now in his front yard, fire in her eyes. "You know what I mean."

Actually, he did not. He'd done a lot of things since the hospital. Like finishing up inventory on his own, fixing the handful of broken buoys, and buying the materials he needed to replace the six broken lobster traps and replace some frayed line.

Dropping a saw onto his makeshift worktable, he swiped his forehead with the back of his hand. He'd nearly finished the frame on the first new trap, but he stepped away from it. Whatever had Meg up in arms probably wasn't about some new wood and netting. At least he hoped not.

"Seriously, I don't have any idea what you're talking about."

Huffing, she sent a piece of hair bouncing off her fore-head. It settled right back where it had come from, so she brushed it behind her ear. He got the feeling she'd like to brush him aside just as easily. But that wasn't going to happen. Especially when he had so many unanswered questions about why she'd come back to the island and just how much she'd given up to do so.

"With my mom. At the hospital."

He lifted a shoulder. "What about it?"

"You were holding her hand and . . ." Her voice lost steam as she tried to put words to whatever had set her off. Shoulders slumped and head bowed, she sighed.

"How's your mom feeling?"

She looked up, eyes filled with a thousand questions. "She's getting better. Her head is healing."

He knew Meg meant the external injury only. Whatever was going on inside her mom probably wouldn't ever heal. "You've been with her this week?"

She nodded slowly. "Dad is so worn out." He could see the weight of the admission literally push her shoulders closer to the ground. "He can't keep an eye on Mom and take care of the house." Her gaze shot up to meet his. "Please, don't tell him—or anyone—that I said that."

He waved it off. She didn't even need to ask.

Silence hung heavily between them, only the call of the morning birds filling the air. She stared at him, clearly expecting a response. He stared back. Her eyes were wider at this time of day, her chin firmer.

He didn't really think chins changed in firmness, but there was just something stiff about Meg. Something that suggested she was holding herself together and it took every bit of her strength to do it. It dared him to try to crack her shell, to see what softness was beneath.

"Your mom was really good to me when I was a kid."

Of course, by *kid* he meant seventeen. Her kindness had continued after he'd destroyed Meg's robot. In fact, Mrs. Whitaker had never said a thing about it. She had even arranged for her husband to hire him. Any chance of owning the business was entirely because of her. He couldn't not hold her hand when she was alone and scared in a hospital room.

"And she was reaching out her hand," he continued. "I just thought I could give her something to hang on to."

His ears stung at the memory of what Mrs. Whitaker had said to him. He'd never been more grateful that his hair covered the protruding appendages.

Meg sighed. "I didn't know you knew her."

"I suppose there's more than a few things you don't know about me."

Her eyes flashed bright for a moment.

"And I guess there's some things I don't know about you. Like why you came back from uOttawa."

She opened and closed her mouth, a fish without water. Her hands fisted at her sides, her shoulders rising and falling with great breaths.

Part of him wanted to let her off the hook and not press for a response—a tiny part of him. But the majority won, and he leaned forward. "Couldn't hack it?"

Color crept from her neck upward, swallowing each of her facial features until she favored a steamed lobster. That made him grin. Or maybe it was that he knew he'd gotten under her skin. That wasn't exactly conducive to his plan. She wasn't likely to give up the business at this rate. But tomorrow was a new day. Maybe he could make up for it then.

And today she'd accused him of . . . well, he didn't know for sure. But whatever bee had been in her bonnet, she'd definitely thought it was his fault. A turnabout seemed fair.

She let out a tight breath between clenched teeth. "I earned a degree."

"And you had to go all the way to Ottawa for a fancy piece of paper just to teach right here in Queens County? You could have gone to UPEI like everyone else."

Eyebrows meeting above her nose, she said, "Like *everyone*? I don't recall *you* attending uni."

He didn't even wait for her words to land before stomping forward, his hands on his hips, chest out. "I don't recall saying I wanted to waste four years and a houseful of cash."

"I didn't waste four years."

"You were gone six."

She stepped toward him, her posture matching his, elbows bent and shoulders back, her long fingers still tucked into fists. He couldn't help his smirk. Was she going to hit him? Did she think it would hurt? Sure, she was tall, but her hands didn't look much stronger than her mom's had been in the hospital.

Her eyes flashed. "Were you paying attention, Ross?"

"Hard to miss in a town this size." Also, her dad had reported on every one of her accomplishments. Oliver hadn't had much of a choice but to hear about Meg's academic pursuits. Not that he'd minded much. It had been nice to know that he hadn't completely ruined her chances to pursue her dream.

So why hadn't he asked more questions when she'd come

home? Whitaker had been so eager to share her achievements. Oliver hadn't asked why he stopped. Like the flip of a switch, one day had been all about perfect scores on exams, and the next, nothing.

He tried to pinpoint that day, find the exact moment in his memory. They hadn't been on the boat. It had been the off-season.

His gut clenched. Had he been so consumed with his own dream—with securing his own fishing business—that he'd missed something so catastrophic that it had made Meg give up on hers?

"Meg?" His voice cracked, and he sounded like a thirteen-year-old boy for a moment. Clearing his throat, he tried again. "Meg, did something happen with your mom?"

Her labored sigh was nearly as effective as the roll of her eyes.

"I mean, before last week." He stared at his hands for a long minute, seeing the calluses across his palms. "Before she started getting sick."

Meg bent over and picked up a splinter of wood that had been hiding in the grass, a remnant from the nearly finished trap. She turned it over in her hands, letting whatever animosity had been between them drain away. She looked up to meet his gaze when she finally spoke. "You mean *when* she got sick."

He nodded slowly, not quite sure what he meant anymore.

She let out a slow breath, squeezing the splinter in her fist. "She fell. Three times in a week. The doctors couldn't explain it. Dad was . . . worried."

The way she said it, it sounded more like *panicked*. Oliver couldn't picture the staid man riled up. Except about the love of his life.

Meg probably couldn't have pictured it either until she heard it in his voice, saw it on his face. Which was why she'd come home. Oliver didn't have to ask. He knew.

He sighed. "I'm so sorry."

Chewing on the corner of her lip, she squinted toward the water, toward the reflection of the sun, gold against the dark blue waves. They lapped gently at the water's edge, hugging and tugging at the red dirt just beyond the knee-high grass blowing in the breeze.

That water held every one of his hopes for a future that looked nothing like his past. But Meg seemed to see something very different.

"The doctor at the hospital last week said she wants her to see a neurological specialist." She shrugged. "She's seen a dozen of them already." Her gaze shot in his direction but seemed to look far into the distance. "They thought it was Parkinson's for a while, but it's not. It's something else." Wrapping her long arms around herself, she said, "Something they can't identify."

Whitaker, who wouldn't shut up about his daughter, hadn't been as forthright about his wife. Oliver had known she was ill. He just hadn't known she was deteriorating so quickly.

He called himself all kinds of a jerk. He'd been poking at Meg when she'd really left uOttawa to help her parents. Just like her mom had said.

"Listen, Meg, I'm sorry. I—"

"You've been using that word a lot lately. You think it's going to make any difference?"

Clapping a hand on the back of his neck and bowing his

head, he kicked at a clump of dirt. "I don't know. But it's true."

She met his gaze, her eyes distant and cool. "I'm sorry too. I'm sorry that I missed the rest of the inventory."

He shrugged. "It's no big deal."

"Yes, it is." She took a deep breath that moved her shoulders up and down. "We're supposed to be working together. Right?"

"I suppose."

"So . . ."

He didn't follow her thought. "What do you mean?"

"I want to do my part." She squared her shoulders, shoved another rebar down her spine, and stood up even straighter. He hadn't thought that was possible. "I'm going to do my part."

He heard the truth in her words loud and clear—she wasn't going to give up the business. She'd already given up uOttawa. She'd given up her teaching position too. She had nothing but Whitaker Fishing left.

Squinting at her, he tried to find their similarities. Her words sounded so much like his own, but her fair hair hanging over her shoulder contrasted with the black mop on his head. The smooth lines of her nose and easy curve of her mouth were as much like his own rough features as a lobster and tuna.

Nope. Wanting this business was where their similarities ended. Well, the business and stubbornness. Because she had to be all kinds of mulish to hold a grudge for ten years. And she'd done it with ease.

That did not bode well for winning her over.

"I'm sure you will do your part," he said.

"Good." She pursed her lips to the side and twisted her hands into the front of her shirt. "What's my part?"

———

"'Check the boat,' he said. 'It'll be a breeze,' he said."

Meg mumbled to herself as she strolled across the wharf to her dad's boat the next morning. She'd have preferred starting about four hours later, but there was no way she'd let it get back to Oliver that she wasn't up for early mornings. Besides, she'd never seen the water look quite so enchanting, rippling beneath a golden veil. Its gentle fingers crept closer with each wave, shuttling light into the darkness.

"Meggy Whitaker? That you?"

She jerked around at the sound of her name. Little Tommy Scanlan stood about twenty-five meters down the dock on the top rung of the ladder leading to his own boat. He'd inherited his license at the age of twenty-one. Despite the thirty years that had turned him from a skinny boy to a round-bellied fishing elder, the nickname remained. But Meg couldn't bring herself to call him that.

"Hi, Mr. Scanlan."

Little Tommy put his hands on his hips, low and casual. "It true what they're saying?"

The gossip mills generally were true. Only because Victoria was too small of a place to hide much for long. "What are they saying?"

"Your dad selling out?"

She shook her head. He wasn't selling out. He was . . . he was keeping his word. In sickness and in health. That's what the vows said. He'd cared for his wife for a lot of years in health. Now he was doing the other.

Little Tommy shrugged as he climbed onto the wharf,

rocking his boat and the water of the cove. "Well, tell him I know of a buyer if he's interested."

"Thanks, I will." That was what she was supposed to say. What she wanted to say was that he already had one too many people interested in his legacy. But Little Tommy was already out of sight, disappearing into his shanty.

Between the cement jetty and the rocking boats, the water shifted and swayed. She stumbled against the movement she could see and feel in the pit of her stomach, even though the dock remained steady. Everything else seemed unstable.

She held a deep breath, trying to find something unmoving to focus on. She turned until her gaze caught the red-and-white lighthouse in the distance at the mouth of the river. There. Breathe in. Breathe out.

Pressing a finger to the spot behind her ear, she made sure her motion-sickness patch was still in place. She adjusted the copper bracelet designed to put pressure on just the right spot to keep her from tossing her breakfast overboard. Then again, she hadn't eaten anything that morning. And not just because she'd chosen to hit her snooze button a few extra times. Because it was better to get on a boat on an empty stomach. She hoped.

But so far, the empty stomach, motion-sickness patch, and bracelet hadn't made a bit of difference. And she hadn't even stepped foot on the boat yet.

Her stomach took another dive, and she bent over, leaning against her knees. Just as her stomach tried to heave, a large hand thumped her on the back. She screamed. He laughed.

Flinging herself around and forcing her stomach into submission, Meg glared at Oliver. "What are you doing here?"

"You didn't really think I was going to let you check the

boat on your own." He stared at her for a long second before adding, "Did you?"

Well . . . yes. It was her part. She was doing her part. He'd finished inventory without her. She could check the boat without him. She remembered most of the steps from her childhood. How to turn on the engine, check for leaks, stuff like that. How hard could it be?

Maybe her face gave her away, because his suddenly broke out with a smirk. "Do you even have a boating license?"

Her hands fisted at her sides as she marched to the metal ladder and lowered herself onto the *Pinch*, shoving any symptoms of seasickness aside.

Oliver followed her. "You look a little green there, Meggy."

"Don't call me that."

"Ah, but Little Tommy Scanlan said he'd seen *Meggy* Whitaker."

"Yeah, well, you want me to call you Ollie?"

His smirk withered as he followed her aboard. "Not particularly."

"Then we'll call it a deal." She didn't bother with the specifics. She was pretty sure he could read them in her glare.

Oliver ducked his head and nodded toward the helm in the partially enclosed cabin. "Should we take her out for a spin?"

Her stomach threatened to revolt, her hands and knees quivering. She had to get this under control. She had to. She had almost two months of fishing ahead, and if she couldn't stomach it, there was no way she'd win this competition.

"Sure." She forced out the lie. "Let's go."

Narrowing his eyes on her, Oliver turned on the engine, and the whole boat shuddered to life. The low hum drowned out the sound of the waves and of her gasping for fresh air.

"Hear that purr. Just like a cat," he said, petting the silver wheel.

No. Cats were safe and sweet and comforting. This boat was not like a cat.

Maybe once they started moving, she'd be all right. Yeah, she just needed a strong breeze in her face. And this silly patch behind her ear to kick in.

Oliver walked to the dock and freed the ropes that had been holding the boat in place before pulling the round orange fenders onto the end of the deck. The moment he turned the boat away from the dock into the cove, Meg's stomach did more than threaten. It waged a full-on revolution.

Rushing to the port side, she leaned over the edge. *Please don't puke. Please don't puke.* But no matter how many times she repeated the mantra, her stomach still rolled like she was on a dinghy in a hurricane.

"Whoa there." Oliver's hand found the corner of her shoulder, squeezing gently. "You okay?"

Clearly not. But she couldn't admit that to him. Oliver Ross was not going to make her feel any worse today. She would not get sick in front of him. Not today. Not ever.

She pinched the bracelet at her wrist, hoping it would shift to the right spot and hit the pressure point that was supposed to keep her head and stomach—and everything in between—from doing exactly what they were currently doing.

Dragging in a deep breath through clenched teeth, she shrugged off his hand. "I'm fine."

But his hand came back. She could just see it out of the corner of her eye, no matter how hard she tried to focus on the glassy blue surface before her.

He brushed her hair off her shoulder, tucking her ponytail

safely behind her back, his blunt fingers grazing the line of her jaw. Probably an accident. She hoped it was anyway, because it added another sensation she couldn't name to the neighborhood already in revolt.

"If you're going to chuck your breakfast, best not to get it in your hair."

Okay. Definitely an accident. But that wasn't why she shot him a glare that would have made her students shrivel.

His eyebrows lifted as though he questioned the wisdom of going on. "I'd rather not have to smell it for the whole ride."

Using her elbow and most of her forearm, she shoved him back. "I'm not going to chuck my breakfast." She cringed even as she said the words and her head took a carousel ride.

Holding up both hands, he took an exaggerated step away. "Okay, okay."

"I just need a minute."

Oliver said something else, but she couldn't hear it through the ringing in her ears. He sounded like the adults in cartoons. "Wha-whaaaa. Wha-wha."

Her head spun, her heart pounding.

"Meggy?"

"'M fine. And don't c-call meh that." Her tongue felt too thick as she swung her head back and forth. That didn't help anything. Stumbling along the side, hunched low, she bumped against the railing and nearly lost her balance as a gentle wave caught the bow of the boat.

His giant arm hooked around her waist, steady as a tree and nearly as big. The carousel began to slow down, and she hated that she couldn't help but sink into him. Just a little bit. She wouldn't stay for long. She just needed something steady, something stable. And no matter how much she hated to admit it, that's exactly what he was.

If she happened to notice the clean scent of his soap, well, that was just a hazard of being on the boat with him. And if she spent a few seconds wondering how he could possibly smell like sunshine when the sun had only just peeked over the horizon, well, some questions should be pondered. No scientific discovery ever came from not asking questions.

The muscle in his forearm jumped, and his warmth hovered near her ear. "You're all right, Meggy."

She pivoted in his embrace and, putting both hands on his chest, shoved with all her might. "I told you not to call me—"

She didn't get to finish as he stumbled backward. And fell right over the side of the boat.

# Six

Meg threw her hands to her mouth and ran toward the rail as Oliver hit the water, the splash from the impact knocking her back. Shaking off the displaced drops, she leaned forward and peered into the depths below. He disappeared beneath the surface, the bay too dark yet to see even a few inches into the water.

The churning in her stomach disappeared, immediately replaced by an even less pleasant sinking sensation.

"Oliver. Oliver!"

*Please, God. Please don't let me have killed him.*

She didn't always like him, but she didn't want him to drown. And besides, he was supposed to teach her the ropes of the business.

He had to know how to swim. Every kid on the south shore did. It was in their blood, deep in the marrow of their bones. The water called to them every summer—to their dads too, every fall.

So why wasn't he swimming? Why hadn't he surfaced?

Maybe he'd hit his head on the boat. He could be unconscious. Perhaps his breath had been knocked out of him when he hit the water, and he couldn't move.

A million scenarios danced through her head—every one of them more terrible than the one before. It was all her fault.

She was going to have to go in after him. It was that simple.

Grabbing the heel of her neon-orange sneaker, she yanked it off. It landed with a thud on the deck, quickly followed by the second. She barely gave her clothes a thought as she stripped off her sweater. She couldn't afford the drag, especially if she was going to have to pull Oliver from the bay. Her undershirt was plenty decent. At least it would be until it got wet. She shivered as the wind blew hard against her.

Bracing her foot on the railing, ready to jump into the water, she tried again. "Oliver, where are you?"

All was silent until Little Tommy Scanlan's head poked out from the helm of his boat. "Everything okay down there?" he called.

Yes. No. Maybe. She didn't have a clue how to answer him, and she'd wasted enough time. How long had it been? Seconds? Hours?

Shutting down every other thought, she jumped in. The water swallowed her, surrounding every inch of her. It rushed up her nose and into her ears, saturating her clothes and pulling her down, down, down.

She opened her eyes, and they burned. She couldn't see anything anyway, the water murky at best. A beam of light pierced the surface, illuminating every particle in its sweeping path, then disappeared. The lighthouse.

She thrashed about, grabbing and reaching for anything that might feel like Oliver.

*Please, God, let me find him.*

But every grasp of her hands came back empty. Her lungs felt the same. Aching and straining for air.

Finally she hit the bottom, her feet sinking into the red clay. With all her might, she pressed off and soared through the water. When she broke the surface, she gulped in deep breaths, flinging the sodden strands of hair out of her face.

Then she heard it—a laugh deep and rich and filled with humor.

She was going to strangle him.

"Oliver Ross!" She reeled toward his voice and found him hanging from the metal ladder off the side of the boat. "How . . . how . . ."

But any more would have taken breath and energy she didn't have, so she set out to reach him with quick strokes, only to find his hand outstretched to her. Because the weight of her wet clothes was pulling her down—and only because of that—she let him haul her into the boat. Stumbling up the ladder and over the railing, she didn't even look at him. Then she collapsed, her heart thudding against the deck.

"You okay there, champ? You looked like you were trying out for the Olympics."

Rolling her head to see soaking-wet Oliver lounging beside her, propped up on his elbows, did not help her mood. He looked like he was in some kind of cologne commercial— damp hair tousled to the side, all casual and effortlessly sexy. *Not* that he was sexy.

"I was *trying* to save you," she grumbled.

"Aww." He patted the top of her head, and she whipped away from him. "I didn't know you cared."

"Oh, I don't." No need to tell him what she'd really been thinking. "But my dad doesn't need another stress in his life, and for whatever reason, he seems to like having you around."

"Well, next time, don't worry about it. I know how to swim." Sitting up, he reached for his shoes and emptied half the ocean out of one of them and the other half out of the second.

"Yeah, well, you didn't surface, and you were . . ." She pushed herself up and flicked her hand in his general direction, trying to indicate the dark gray T-shirt clinging to every bit of him from shoulder to hip and the dark jeans now painted onto his thighs. If she noticed that fishing had done some nice things for his muscles, she couldn't be blamed for that. Not when they were basically a museum exhibit at this point.

Shoving her fingers through her wet hair, she sighed. "I thought you were at a disadvantage, and you didn't come up."

"Sure I did. I was at the ladder."

Her eyes narrowed. "You saw me jump in?"

He shrugged.

"You heard me calling for you?" Her voice rose half an octave.

He poked a pinky in his ear with a guilty grin. "Must have gotten some water in there."

She wanted to push him in again. And this time she wouldn't dive in after him. "What if I'd drowned?"

His eyes sparked with humor, and she could almost read the truth there. If she'd drowned, he wouldn't have any more competition. But he managed not to say those words, which spared him another dip in the bay. Instead, his mouth shifted into a thoughtful frown. "I'd have gone after you."

Her grunt asked if he was serious.

"Like you said, your dad doesn't need any more stress right

now." He shrugged again. "Besides, the Mounties would have assumed I was guilty. Especially with my track record."

That made her crack a smile. Partially because it was true, and partially because he was making a habit of surprising her.

Oliver pushed himself up, and it wasn't until his shadow swept over her that she realized how late it had gotten.

"Guess we'll have to test her later," he said as he crossed the deck and turned off the engine.

The gentle hum ended, and Meg's skin tingled where it had been trembling only a moment before. She nodded her agreement as she stood, her clothes still dripping and every gust of wind making goose bumps erupt across her body. She could put on her sweater, but it would soak through immediately too. So instead she hugged herself and tried not to think about how warm she'd been when Oliver had wrapped his arm about her waist.

"But we're going to have to go out before setting day. You know—"

"I know."

Setting day was only a little more than a week away. He didn't have to spell it out for her. She'd been away for a few years, but nothing could make her forget setting day. She and her mom had lined up along the wharf with the other fishing wives—or fishing widows, depending on who was asked. She'd cheered and skipped behind the boats weighed low with lobster traps stacked far overhead. Her dad had always turned to wave at her just as he reached the open water, off to set every one of his 240 traps.

For most of the island, setting day was the first of May. For the southwestern shore, it was mid-August. Her dad's license said Lobster Fishing Area 25 between PEI and New Brunswick. Of course, everyone knew that their real zone was much smaller than that. More than seven hundred fishermen shared the area, and every single one of them had an unofficial spot.

Wringing out the hem of her shorts, she said, "We can go out anytime."

He snorted. "Excuse me?"

Flinging her hand in the direction of the open water, she sighed. "You know what I mean. To test the boat. Anytime."

"Sure." The singsong in his voice said he didn't quite believe her.

"And next time—wear a life vest, okay?"

Oliver had moved to the dock side of the boat and was busy putting the moorings back into place. His head snapped around at her words. "I wouldn't have needed one if you hadn't pushed me in." He absentmindedly rubbed at his chest where she'd shoved him. "Caught me off guard." With a chuckle, he added, "Besides, I'm not the one who jumped in on purpose."

"At least I had the forethought to take my shoes off." She held up a sneaker before leaning against the railing and shoving her foot—wet sock and all—into it.

She cringed. He smirked.

But when he reached the dock, he held out his hand to help her up the ladder. She eyed it for a long moment, then slid her fingers into his. Before she could step onto the first rung, the boat rocked, and she clung to his arm for a brief second before dropping her hold. His eyes flashed, but he said nothing more as she scurried up the three steps and they walked around the shanties to the dirt parking lot.

When she reached her car, she opened her door. Oliver stood a safe distance away.

"So, Monday then?"

"That'll be fine."

"Same time?"

She swallowed the groan deep in her throat and nodded.

Just before she slipped into her car, Oliver said, "Oh, and Meg."

"Yeah?"

He pointed to the spot behind his ear. "They take a few hours to kick in. Put it on the night before."

———

Oliver laughed as he wrung his shirt out one more time and toed off his shoes at the side door. Mama Potts would swat him out of her kitchen with her broom if he left mud and water on her clean floor.

But as soon as he stepped inside, he knew she wasn't there. The house was quiet. Mama Potts didn't do silence. Not when she was cooking. Not even when she was going to sleep.

"I got so used to you boys making a racket that I can't barely function without some of my own," she'd told him once when he caught her belting out an Alan Doyle folk song to a shepherd's pie.

There was no noise, no movement in the home. But neither was it empty.

"Levi?"

A soft grunt was the only response.

Figured. His brother was more shadow than man most days. He shared the house with Mama Potts, just the two of them since Oliver had moved into the apartment above the old garage. They were supposed to share meals, but Levi slipped in and out unnoticed most days. As the facilities manager at the high school, he worked odd shifts, whenever the students weren't there. That meant mostly late nights and therefore late mornings.

They couldn't have picked more opposite schedules if they'd tried. Then again, he'd never asked Levi if he'd planned the whole thing. His brother could have been avoiding him for years and just never bothered to say as much.

Levi had never been what anyone would consider chatty. His silence had become more noticeable since their dad left, and since Eli had gotten a better offer and followed their dad's example. That suited Oliver just fine. He had no need to hash out the past or run through the painful memories.

Sure, Levi was the only one who really knew what it had been like back then. They'd packed up their belongings together—what fit in two black trash bags—after the eviction notice had been nailed to the door of the only home they'd known. They'd walked down the street side by side, praying that no one from school would see them.

Well, Oliver had been praying that. Levi hadn't said a word about it since.

As Oliver stepped into the kitchen, Levi looked up from where he sat at the table. The book in his hands was thicker than a door and sported a white library sticker on the cover.

Levi's dark brown eyebrows pinched together, but a quick nod was all he offered by way of a question.

Oliver shrugged. "Had a little mishap on the boat."

"It sink?"

Oliver snorted. "Not quite. Meg Whitaker was there."

The corner of Levi's lip curled, just enough to hint at a joke that only he found funny. "She push you in?"

With another shrug, Oliver nodded.

His brother's whole face lit up, blue eyes flashing with barely contained mirth. Looking at his brother wasn't quite like looking in a mirror, but the similarities were there. Especially when they smiled. Dimples on full display, black hair hanging low over their brows.

Levi closed his book and stared. Oliver didn't continue, so Levi gave him a verbal nudge. "So . . ."

When Levi actually showed some interest in something, Oliver knew it might be their last chance to connect for months. And what were little brothers good for but for harassing older brothers?

Shoving his fingers through his hair and pushing it out of his face, Oliver sighed and fell into one of the wooden chairs. "She got a little seasick."

Levi's face reacted immediately.

"No." He waved his hand to clear Levi's concern. "She didn't actually get sick, but she looked pretty close. I thought I was comforting her, but man, the minute I touched her . . ."

Another raise of Levi's eyebrows and his wide gaze enunciated every syllable of his question. *You touched her?*

"Not like that. Get your mind . . . it wasn't . . . she's *Meg Whitaker.*" He needed to remind himself of that. He'd just been trying to make sure she didn't puke in her hair. He hadn't expected it to be so soft or to have the urge to slide it between his fingers.

Maybe all girls had hair that soft, but he doubted it. He just didn't have much experience in that area. He hadn't stopped working in more than ten years. There hadn't been time for girls. Or even *a* girl. There had been time for keeping a roof over their heads. Then a few years ago, when his mom opened her shop, there had been time to dream of a boat of his own, of a license and business that no one could take away from him.

There wouldn't be time to think about a home—and someone to share it with—until that boat was his. Even when he did think about it, it sure wasn't going to be with Meg.

"I guess I deserved it. I called her Meggy. More than once."

Levi leaned back and crossed his arms, a smug smile falling into place.

"But she thought I was drowning, so she jumped in to save me. So I'm not the only one covered in ocean water today."

Levi kicked his shin under the table.

"Ow! What was that for?"

"Don't be an idiot."

Oliver rubbed his leg. "What? It was just a little bit of fun. She laughed. Sort of."

Levi frowned. "You want the boat?"

"You know I do."

"Well . . ."

"Well, what?" Oliver growled.

"I think your brother is trying to tell you that if you want to earn the boat—and Meg's approval—you can't treat her like she's one of your brothers. And also that you smell like fish."

Oliver jumped to his feet as Violet Donaghy arrived like she owned the place. His mother would throw him back in the ocean if he didn't take the enormous box in Violet's arms, so he reached out for it.

She elbowed past him, setting the box on the table. "Just a few things for the store for your mom. I tried a new design." Her smile danced in her eyes.

Oliver reached to open the lid, but she swatted his hand away. "Not until Mama Potts gets here. And you take a shower."

"I don't smell bad." He hooked the collar of his shirt over his nose, took a deep whiff, and promptly gagged.

"You were saying?" She rolled her eyes and put her hands on her hips.

If he hadn't known her back in school, he'd never have believed she was a year younger than he was. Maybe it was all the time she spent with his mom. Mama Potts had a habit of rubbing off on people, and she'd been rubbing off on Violet for a lot of years, teaching her how to throw pots and craft mugs out of the island's legendary red clay. They'd opened their store almost three years before, selling their pottery and even teaching classes for tourists and locals alike.

"What did you do to Meg anyway?"

"You sure came in sounding like you knew what was going on. Were you eavesdropping?"

Her lifted shoulder said *a little*. "Here's what I know. It's hard to like someone who tricks you. And you need Meg to like you."

Levi shot him an I-told-you-so stare.

Yeah. This was not news. But it didn't make it any easier to know *how* to get her to like him. He'd apologized to mixed reviews. He'd driven her to the hospital when her mom was ill and finished up the inventory on his own. That had not gone over well. So he'd tried teasing her like he would have a sister. Still no go.

"And how exactly do you suggest I make that happen? She's not going to forget that I'm the one who ruined her robot."

"Be someone else," Levi quipped.

Oliver would have returned the shin kick if he'd still been sitting. He settled for a glare across the table, which Levi took without blinking.

"Whatever you're doing, do the opposite."

"Also very helpful. Thank you, Violet." He crossed his arms, which just gave him another whiff of his own scent. At least Meg smelled the same.

When he thought about all of her gorgeous hair soaking wet with salt water, his gut clenched. He'd been . . . well, he hadn't been thinking.

Violet sidled up next to him as close as she dared, given his state. She barely reached his shoulder, but that had never stopped her from being the biggest personality in the room. "I know you don't like to admit it, but you're actually a decent guy."

"Debatable," he said.

"Today's escapades aside, you're a good guy, Oliver. You work harder than any man I know, and every man in town would hire you in a heartbeat."

That was definitely an exaggeration. He could name at least one lobsterman who would rather beat him with a stick than let him within three meters of his boat. But he managed a smile and kept his tone light. "Doubtful. Joe ran me off his property a couple years ago when I offered to mow his lawn."

She swatted his arm. "Joe Herman is eighty-five years old and wouldn't take a nickel he found on the ground. He's too proud to accept help. Doesn't mean he doesn't trust you to do a good job, whatever job you do. Why do you think Walt asked you to buy his business?"

Oliver bit back a glib reply. Whitaker *had* asked him to buy his business. Sure, Oliver hadn't made it a secret that he wanted to own a license one day—he'd been saving for the chance to purchase one. But he'd never asked Whitaker to sell the business to him. And as far as he knew, Whitaker hadn't approached any other buyers.

Violet patted his shoulder, keeping her face and body at a safe distance. "You're a good man, and that's what Walt sees. But that's not enough to win over Meg. You're going to have to do better."

"Better?" He sounded like a parrot. Felt about as smart as one too. He couldn't do better than he already was—except for maybe not making her jump into the water after him.

"Meg's going to see what her dad sees in you soon enough. But that's not going to be enough to make her back off. You've got to make her genuinely like you. You've got to be her friend." Violet's voice turned mocking. "You remember what you learned in kindergarten about sharing and being kind and not pulling girls' ponytails?"

Oliver grabbed her around the neck and pressed her nose into his smelly shirt. That's what she got for being too smart for her own good.

"Forget Meg." Levi chuckled. "Violet's rich."

Her face turned redder than steamed lobster, and Oliver let her go as she tried to wipe off his residue while making a face at Levi.

But Violet did make a good point. He didn't just have to prove to Meg that he was capable. He had to be her friend.

# seven

If she hadn't known that Oliver was standing right behind her, Meg might have enjoyed the deep baritone singing "Great Is Thy Faithfulness." She might even have glanced over her shoulder to see who was there. But she'd seen him as she walked into the white chapel. He'd seen her too. Even when she looked away, she'd felt his gaze follow her between the pews and right to her family's usual spot.

Only there was no family with her today. Her dad had stayed home with her mom.

Mama Potts reached out to squeeze her arm. "Would you like to sit with us, sweetie?" she asked.

A kind gesture. And Violet's smile was more than welcoming. Levi didn't seem to know what to make of it all. But Oliver's frown was more than enough to make her pass.

"I'm fine, thank you."

But she hadn't heard much of what Pastor Dell had said, wondering what people were thinking. Perhaps she imagined the whispers and nudges and questioning looks. Where was Sandra? Where had she been these last few months? And now Walt was missing too.

As the service wrapped up, she knew she'd have to face them. Every biddy poking for news on her mom. Every experienced lobsterman wondering what her dad planned to do for the season and if the rumors of his unusual plan were true.

She wanted the closing hymn to go on forever. At least then she wouldn't have to face them down, answer their questions. And as long as Oliver was singing, he couldn't answer them either.

> Great is Thy faithfulness!
> Great is Thy faithfulness!
> Morning by morning new mercies I see;
> All I have needed Thy hand hath provided—
> Great is Thy faithfulness, Lord, unto me!

As the closing chord on the piano drifted away and Pastor Dell said a blessing over them, Meg hung her head, took a deep breath, and prayed that God's faithfulness covered getting away unnoticed.

She didn't even make it into the aisle before Jeffrey Druthers and Derrick Stewart stopped her. They were an odd pair, Jeffrey so tall he had to duck to get in the church door, Derrick several inches shorter than she was.

"Where's your dad?"

Meg swallowed a retort that it was none of their business and tried for a smile. Before she could respond, Derrick chimed in. "We heard he was selling his license." Hitching a thumb over his shoulder, he added, "To the middle Ross boy, no less."

"Eh, b'y." Jeffrey had grown up in Newfoundland, and its idioms sometimes still popped out. "There's no way he'd do that."

And there was no way that Oliver hadn't heard the exchange. Meg couldn't bring herself to look for him though. Her gaze locked on the wooden planks of the floor right in front of Jeffrey's scuffed brown shoes, and she clutched her purse in both hands before her. Some barrier was better than none.

"Well . . ." She took a deep breath and tried to conjure some form of the truth that wouldn't make her dad look like a fool and her mother sound worse than she was—even if no one knew just how sick that was. "Um . . ."

A hand suddenly slid through her arm, and a sweet voice announced, "Will you gentlemen please excuse us? I need to have a private conversation with Meg."

The men grumbled but nodded as Violet swept her down the aisle. Meg hardly felt her feet touch the ground, so propelling was Violet's force. And they'd only been introduced once or twice.

As soon as they reached the green expanse of lawn, Meg turned to her. "Thank you. Thank you."

Violet looked like she belonged in lace gloves, cooling herself with a Victorian fan, as she smiled reassuringly. Her chic blue dress didn't hold a single wrinkle, and every strand of her rich chestnut hair was perfectly in place, swept up in the back. Freckles didn't dare to mar her porcelain cheeks and regal nose. As princesses went, Violet might have been the closest thing Victoria by the Sea had ever seen.

But fairy tales always had sad beginnings. Violet's was no different. The rumor was that her parents, wealthy real-estate investors in Charlottetown, had died, leaving her a large fortune and no family. Even her smile was condescendingly regal as she led the way toward a large oak on the far side of the grass.

"I heard you might need a hand."

"From . . ." Meg didn't need to finish her question as Oliver stepped from behind the tree. "Oh." So he'd thought she needed to be rescued. She hadn't. She would have figured it out.

"I'm sorry about that." He nodded toward the church door, where a small group of grizzled men had congregated, talking about setting day and the season to come.

"It's not your fault, I guess."

"Some people just can't keep their tongues to themselves," Violet said.

Oliver's eyebrows jumped, and Violet swatted at him.

"Oh, don't go there, Oliver Ross."

Meg watched the exchange with a half smile and a strange knot in her stomach. She'd never seen Oliver and Violet together like this, like siblings, like friends. Quite honestly, she'd never thought about Oliver having friends. But one thing was clear. He had asked Violet to rescue her, and Violet had agreed. Meg was pretty sure it wasn't for her sake.

Violet turned away from him. "I'm going to stand right over here and make sure you aren't accosted. All right?"

"Thank you."

"You're quite welcome." She strolled over to Levi, who was reading a book about three meters away, and chatted at him. He never looked up.

"How's your mom?" Oliver's simple question made her head swing back in his direction.

"I don't know. But the doctor at Queen Elizabeth was able to get her an appointment with a specialist this week. And Dad—"

"Doesn't want to leave her alone. I get it."

She nodded.

"You could have sat with us, you know."

Another nod was all she could muster. How could she explain that the whispers and the stares were easier to take when it was mostly just about her and her family? If they started involving Oliver, she wouldn't have a clue how to respond.

"It took me two washes to get my hair clean yesterday."

His smile was soft but didn't mask the humor in his eyes. "What did you tell Druthers and Stewart about our deal with your dad?"

She glanced over at where they had been, but the group had dispersed. "Nothing." She looked back at him. "But they know Dad was going to sell to you." As soon as she said the words, she saw regret flash across his face, and it made her lungs tight.

"And they know you're involved."

"I don't think so. How could they?"

Oliver dug his toe into the grass. "Little Tommy saw you on the boat yesterday. If he hasn't talked yet, he will."

"Well, it's my dad's boat. Why shouldn't I be on it?"

"Because you never have been before."

Well, that made sense. Rats.

Meg shoved her hands into the pockets of her sundress, and Oliver's gaze dragged over her like he'd only just realized who she was. Ignoring his survey, she asked the question at the heart of the day. "You think there might be a problem?"

Officially they were fishing with a valid license for an approved company. Unofficially there was a code of conduct among fishermen, a gentlemen's agreement of sorts. It ranged from which spot belonged to which fisherman to which boat went out first on setting day. But always it was about integrity. If the collective agreed there had been a breach, she and Oliver would get a warning. If it happened again, they'd be punished. Whatever form that took was anyone's guess.

Oliver's teeth clicked together a few times before he responded. "Whitakers have been fishing these waters for more than fifty years, and I think these old guys aren't going to send out a welcome wagon if there's change."

⁓

Oliver pressed his hand to his stomach, wondering if he should have been the one to put on a motion sickness patch the night before. His insides were in knots, but as he braced his feet against the gentle rocking of the boat, he knew it was unrelated. The water had never made him ill. It had only ever held hope for the future.

A car door slammed, breaking the stillness of predawn, silencing the call of the morning birds. Even the crickets quieted down for a long moment.

It was too dark to see all the way to the parking lot. Too dark to see much beyond his outstretched hand. This was the whispering hour, just before the sun made its first appearance. Just him and his secrets, him and his memories. And God knew he didn't want to whisper about them.

But he wasn't alone any longer. Meg had arrived. He was certain it was her even before her rhythmic stride started down the dock.

He flipped on the boat's light. It pushed away the darkness across the entire deck, and he could see her long arms swinging as she moved closer. When she arrived, her hair shimmered gold in the light. Though pulled back into a messy ponytail, it looked classic, beautiful. He wondered if it was as soft as it had been two days before.

Which only served to remind him of why he'd touched it in the first place.

"Morning, sun—" He stopped himself before he could call her by a nickname she probably wouldn't appreciate.

*Be her friend.*

Holding out his hand to help her on board, he waited for her to take it. She paused on the metal ladder, her breaths audibly quick and shallow.

"Did you put a patch on last night?"

She nodded stiff and short.

"You worried about getting sick today?"

He blocked enough of the light that her face was in the shadow, and he couldn't see her eyes. She didn't have a reason to trust him yet, but he was going to do everything he could to give her one.

"Your dad used to tell me that being on a boat is no different than being rocked in a cradle. Spend enough time on it and it'll put you right to sleep."

Meg cocked her head. "You want me to sleep on the boat."

"No. I want you to imagine it's as safe as a cradle."

"Right." Crossing her arms over her chest, she took a half step back. "And why are you helping me exactly?"

He couldn't give her an entirely honest response. Mostly truth would have to do.

"Your dad wants us to work together. We may be competing for the business, but the winner won't be the person who runs the other off."

Even beneath an oversized black sweater, her shoulders twitched and stiffened. He could feel the tension rolling off of her, the battle between knowing what she should do and what she wanted to do.

That left him only one option. "I'm sorry I'm right about this."

She laughed. It started out as a small chuckle but grew into a beautiful chorus of high notes, the air around them dancing with humor.

It was the thing he'd wondered about since they were seventeen. What would it take to make her laugh? Apparently a little well-placed sarcasm on an early morning was all it took. But man, he felt like he'd just climbed a mountain or caught a season's haul in one day. His heart felt swollen, taking up too much of his chest.

"Aren't you the humble one?" she asked when her giggles finally slowed.

"Well, someone has to be, and I figured it might as well be me." He held out his hand again. "Come on. The sun's about to come up, and I want to show you my favorite spot."

"Your favorite spot? How can you have a favorite spot on the ocean?"

It was his turn to chuckle. "Oh, you'll see."

Finally she took his hand, steadying herself as she stepped aboard. The boat rocked gently, and she stiffened, locking her knees.

"Try keeping your knees bent, like you're ice skating. Try to move *with* the boat."

She nodded and shifted her legs, overdoing the rocking motion, making the *Pinch* rock even more.

"Maybe not quite that much." He stepped toward the helm and started the engine. The boat hummed to life, singing its own song, mingling with the birds and the bugs and the squeaking fenders between the other boats and the dock.

Meg ran a hand down her face and let out a deep sigh. "I know it's coming, so I can't relax."

"But by this point on Saturday, you were basically the same color as that witch in *The Wizard of Oz*."

"I don't think that's a compliment."

"Wasn't meant to be," he said, cracking a smile. "But here's one. You look like yourself this morning. Like you did yesterday."

His gaze swooped from the top of her head to her long, pale legs. She wasn't as feminine-looking as she'd been at church, her dress flirting about her knees and exposing her tanned arms, her hair swept up and showing off all of her neck—all of her beautiful neck. This morning she looked strong, determined, feet shoulder-width apart and hands fisted beside her cutoff jean shorts. The PEI Fisherman's Association sweater had to have been her dad's, dwarfing her frame but declaring that she belonged on the water just as much as he did.

He could show her the same. He hoped.

"You ready?"

She gave a small grunt and hung on to the metal railing as he steered them away from the dock and toward open water. He glanced over his shoulder to make sure she wasn't hanging over the edge before giving the boat more power and picking up speed.

It wasn't like lobster boats were built for recreation. No one was going to ski behind one. But the morning wind off the water combined with their pace made his skin tingle and his eyes water in the best possible way. The air smelled cleaner, clearer, the farther they got from shore. It smelled like possibilities.

As soon as they made it out to the open water, waves—still gentle but larger than in the bay—pitched the boat. He steered them west toward the Confederation Bridge, the rising sun skimming the horizon behind them.

"You okay back there?" he called over his shoulder, his voice rising above the engine's hum.

When Meg didn't respond, he risked a glance over his shoulder. She was more silhouette than figure against the gold, but the wind whipped her hair back and forth, her head tilted slightly to the right.

"Meg?"

"You're right. That's beautiful. I see why it's your favorite spot."

"Oh no." He shook his head as he turned around. "This isn't my favorite spot."

She didn't say anything else as she stared at the rising sun. It was moving fast this morning, and he pushed the boat to stay in the shadows, headed toward a faint halo of light spanning the Northumberland Strait.

More by instinct than by reading his instruments, he knew when to cut the motor and let them drift until they were almost stopped. The tides pushed the bow north, tugging it toward the still visible but distant shore.

"This is it?" she asked, staring into the dimness ahead. "The bridge?" She sounded less than impressed.

"Give it a minute." He hunched over the railing, leaning his arms against the cool metal.

Meg paused a moment and then joined him, waiting and watching. Where the shore had nature's morning song, the only sounds out here were swishing water and their light breathing.

And then suddenly it began. He'd have known the moment

even if his eyes had been closed. Meg gasped, then grabbed his arm as the sunlight touched the point where the water met the piers of the Confederation Bridge.

In silence they watched the sun illuminate the bridge, taking it from the darkness into light, from dark brown to glowing gold against the morning sky. From the island's shore to as far as they could see, it stretched and reached.

The only thing that could add to the moment was the soundtrack to *Star Wars* and a voiceover from the guy who did movie trailers. Since he had neither of those things, Oliver simply watched. When the sun had fully risen, the bridge would be nothing more than thirteen kilometers of scientific wonder, the only physical connection between PEI and the mainland.

But in this magic moment, the bridge glowed.

"How did you find this?"

"Well, the bridge is a pretty big deal around these parts."

Meg slapped his arm, not unlike one of Violet's favorite moves. "You know what I mean. How did you find *this* spot, this moment?"

"Your dad let me take the boat out after I got my license, and . . . this was always my favorite time to be on the water. It's so quiet." He shrugged and frowned. "I just stumbled upon it. Kept coming back."

"And why is it your favorite?"

He bit back another snide comment. Friends were real with each other. He had to be honest with her. And with himself.

"I guess maybe . . . You know how you sometimes have a problem, and you don't think you'll ever be able to figure it out?"

She nodded.

"This bridge must have taken thousands of people to build it. But if God gave some guy an idea for how to span thirteen kilometers of open water, then I figure he can probably show me a way through whatever I'm facing. The bridge reminds me that even if I don't have a plan, God can figure it out."

He didn't look directly at her for a long minute, but out of the corner of his eye, he saw her watching the bridge turn back to cement. The light from her face began to dim until finally she said, "Jean M. Muller." She pronounced it like the French name was supposed to mean something to him.

"Who's that?"

"Jean Muller. He's the engineer who built the Confederation Bridge."

Oliver snorted. "And you know that why?"

"Doesn't every high school girl have a crush on the brilliant mind that made a bridge that spans so much water *and* breaks up icebergs in the strait?"

He couldn't hold back a real laugh this time. "I don't know. I've never been a high school girl—but I tend to think they don't."

Meg's shoulders rose and fell on an exaggerated sigh. "Fine. But I did. I wrote something like half a dozen papers on him and the bridge in school. One year I even did a science fair project on how the bridge breaks up ice."

She probably hadn't even realized she'd said the words *science fair*, but they made him squirm. Partly because he wanted to hear more about her project but couldn't ask. And mostly because all he could see in his mind's eye was the scattered shards of metal and plastic across the science room floor. The remains of a robot.

"You see a problem solved," she said. "I see all the hours of math and physics that went into making that solution."

"I suppose so. But it's kind of the same thing, right? I mean, I may not know how, but I know it got solved. You know how—so doesn't that give you a greater appreciation for the solution?"

"There are a lot of things that need solutions." She said the words under her breath, but they required no interpretation.

"Ready to go back?"

She nodded as he flipped the motor on and steered them in the direction of their dock.

"You have to admit that was pretty cool," he said after a long silence.

"That almost made getting up at four in the morning worth it. Almost."

Oliver grinned to himself. "Well, get used to it. Now that you can stomach the water, you'll be up early every day."

She pressed a flat hand across her stomach, and her eyes grew wide.

"What happened? Forget to get seasick?"

She licked her lips, her eyebrows bunching together. "I think maybe I did. But I feel good."

"Well, now that I know we won't have to hold back your hair while you get sick . . ." He let his thought trail off as he really looked at her in her bright orange shoes and casual clothes. "Meg, do you have anything to wear on the boat?"

She looked down at herself, swiping her hand over her sweatshirt. "What's wrong with what I've got on?"

"Everything."

# eight

Meg squeezed her mom's hand but didn't get any response. "Mom," she whispered. "Did you hear that?"

Her mom turned in her direction but didn't make eye contact. And she hadn't said a word all day. Meg met her dad's gaze over her mom's bowed head, and he offered only a grimace. Mom hadn't heard anything that the doctor with fancy degrees wallpapering his office had said. Or at least she hadn't understood any of it.

Meg wasn't sure how much she herself had understood. But the bottom line was clear. The stiffness in her mom's legs was getting worse, her balance dissolving. And her best chance for a diagnosis—and maybe a cure—was a specialist in Toronto.

"But the last doctor we saw said we should try to keep things normal, not take her away from the places she knows or do anything out of the ordinary," Meg said. "She's easily upset."

From where he sat on the far side of a large wooden desk, Dr. Rubinski's mouth drew into a tight line, and he folded his hands in front of him. His white lab coat pulled against his shoulders as he leaned forward. "That's the best advice you could get at the time. But she needs a full scan and workup. We don't have the resources to do that here, and my colleague in Toronto is one of the best neurologists in the country."

Meg nodded, but her heart screamed that there had to be another way, a better way for them to fix her mom, to turn her back into the woman she'd been. Meg squeezed her fingers again, but there was still no reaction.

Sometimes her mom just wasn't there. And how scary it would be to become alert in a strange place.

As Meg and her dad stood to leave, the doctor's deep voice interrupted, and they dropped back into their chairs. "I want to help you manage your expectations."

The words were anything but hopeful, and they stole her breath.

He closed his eyes before lifting them again. "Even with a diagnosis . . ." He shook his head as though he'd given up. The white flag of surrender.

What was the point of going to Toronto then? She wanted to demand that he give them something more, something helpful, but her mom was already slumped in her chair.

"We should get her home," Meg said.

The doctor's frown remained, the truth clear. "I'll have my office manager call and set up an appointment for you. We'll try to get her seen soon, so you may have to travel on short notice."

"That'll be fine," Meg's dad said. He turned to his wife and helped her up, tucking her under his arm and ushering her from the bright natural light of the office into the flickering fluorescents of the medical complex hallway. The white walls were bare, the brown carpet fresh. But all Meg could focus on was the glass door exit. Everything else disappeared as she trudged beside her mom, afraid to reach for her, terrified her mom wouldn't respond—or worse, wouldn't know who she was.

The doctors had ruled out everything they could. But without a diagnosis, no one knew what symptom might appear next, which part of her body might be the next to shut down.

Meg gasped for breath, but the air didn't fill her lungs. She tried again, but she was broken. She finally stumbled outdoors, into the sun and trees and open spaces. They surrounded her, and if she still couldn't get a deep breath, at least she could fake it. For another minute.

She held open the passenger door of her dad's truck as he lifted her mom into the seat. With a gentle pat on her leg, Meg tried again to reach her. To no avail.

She closed the door, swallowing a silent sob. *Keep it down. Hold it in.*

Her dad didn't need to see her lose it. He couldn't handle anything else. She wouldn't put him through anything else.

Wrapping her arms about his waist, she whispered, "The doctor in Toronto will help."

"I know. Just . . . take care of the business while I'm gone."

"Of course I will. You take care of Mom. All right?"

Her dad's face broke for just a moment. One second he was the strong man she'd known her whole life. The next his face contorted in a pain without words.

"Oh, Dad. It's . . ." She held him tighter, wishing she could finish that sentence. But she didn't know if it was going to be okay. And she wouldn't make a promise she couldn't keep. "We'll get through this."

When she looked up, big tears dripped down his face, falling off his chin and onto his shirt. Her eyes burned, and she blinked furiously to keep her own tears in line.

*Be strong. Be strong. Be strong.*

She repeated the words again and again until her spine was just a little straighter, her muscles solid enough to carry every fear and heartache her dad couldn't. That was her job. Carry the weight.

He sniffled and swiped at his eyes with the back of his hand. "You're a good girl, Megan. I thank God that you're mine."

Oh, rats. She couldn't hold it together much longer.

"Love you too, Dad. You should get Mom home."

With that, she raced to her car, flung her purse inside, and threw herself behind the wheel. The temperature difference inside the closed-up sedan made sweat trickle down her back as she rested her forehead against the steering wheel.

*Be strong.*

But no amount of repeating that phrase could make it so. A hiccupped sob escaped from deep in her chest, from the place where it hurt to breathe. Wrapping her arms around her waist, she curled over on herself and let the tears she'd been fighting slip to freedom. One splashed on her leg, another landed on the steering wheel.

This was the first time—the only time—she'd allowed herself to cry about this. And it had to be her last.

Suddenly her phone chimed, and she whipped her head up, looking for her dad's truck. But it was gone—probably long gone. At least he hadn't seen her break down.

Grabbing her phone, she found a text from Oliver.

I'm in town. What time do you want to meet?

Oh, what had she been thinking when she told Oliver she'd meet him in Charlottetown? He said he needed some new gear, and he'd offered to show her what the rest of the lobstermen wore too. She knew she'd be in town for her mom's appointment. She just hadn't counted on being such a mess.

Flipping down the sun visor, she took quick inventory. Red-rimmed eyes, glassy from tears that had smudged her mascara. The tip of her nose had turned pink, and she had to bite her bottom lip to keep it from trembling.

All in all, not her best look. And she wouldn't have cared if . . . well, she just didn't need Oliver asking all of his questions about her family and her mom's health and her own mental state. Because right that minute, her mental state felt about as solid as mercury.

She started to text him that she couldn't make it. But a little voice in her head reminded her that she didn't have time to waste. Setting day was less than a week away, and most lobstermen weren't her size. If she had to order something, it could take weeks to arrive.

And then what? She'd have to wear her sneakers and shorts. She didn't see the problem with that, but when she'd suggested as much, Oliver had looked like she'd said *semiformal*. While they weren't best friends, he wouldn't point her in the wrong direction. After all, like he'd said, the winner at the end of the season wouldn't be the person who drove the other away. That's not how her dad worked, and Oliver wouldn't risk it.

At least, she didn't think he would.

She deleted the half-typed message and replaced it.

How about now?

"How about these?" Oliver held out a pair of Carhartt pants, long and lean and plenty tough to last a season. They matched the three pairs already hanging over his arm.

When Meg cringed, he immediately knew his mistake. His pants were straight and a little boxy, the stiff canvas material about as form-flattering as a garbage bag. They were utilitarian. Functional. They were not for making anyone look their best. And truthfully, he'd never thought about it before. He hadn't been looking to impress Whitaker or Kyle, the longtime deckhand. And he sure wasn't looking to impress Meg with his sense of style.

But it would be a shame to put her long legs into a circus tent like those pants, so he shoved them back onto the shelf of the general store. All the while, Meg flipped through a row of hanging sweaters and water-resistant jackets, her gaze not quite focused.

"You'll need something warm. A couple sweaters probably. And some sturdy pants."

She nodded but didn't look at him.

"Do you see something you like?"

She nodded again, her eyes focused somewhere past him on the far wall of gear and tackle.

"What's that?"

Meg's only response was a silent dip of her chin.

Oliver pressed a hand to her shoulder as he whispered, "Meg?"

She literally jumped, both of her feet leaving the ground. She headed for the nearest rack of sweaters, so he wrapped his hand around her arm and pulled her toward him, catching her about the waist with his armful of pants.

She crashed into him with a loud whoosh of air and an embarrassed laugh. "Sorry."

She tried to push away, her hands small against his chest. But something about the worry lines around her mouth kept his hand locked in place. A chunk of her hair had fallen into her face, and he only then noticed it wasn't pulled back in its usual work ponytail. Everything inside him wanted to brush that strand behind her ear, to find out if it was as soft as it had been on the boat, let himself get lost for just a minute. But he refused to give himself permission, even a fraction of an inch.

"Hey. What's wrong?"

"Nothing. I'm fine. I'm good. I was just . . . thinking."

"Thinking, eh? Must have been something pretty important."

She met his gaze then, intense and fiercely controlled, and shook her head. He knew she wasn't being honest with him. But he couldn't bring himself to push her. Not this time. Not when Violet's voice kept ringing through his mind.

Stepping back, he released her waist and held her shoulder at arm's length. He grinned as he made eye contact, hoping it reached every corner of his face. "You have a very important decision to make."

"I do?" Her voice was barely a squeak.

"Yep." He nodded toward the shelves at her back. "You've got to choose between a tent and a burlap bag."

Her mouth opened and a tiny chuckle popped out, sweeter than the call of a wood thrush. The corners of her eyes crinkled, and the stress around her mouth eased until her lips were curved and wide. "Are those my only two options?"

"'Fraid so."

"Not at all." The other voice spoke over his, loud and assured.

Oliver turned around to see a woman taller than Meg and almost as broad as he was. Her tan skin was dark as leather but looked soft as down. She wore shapely jeans and a flannel shirt tied in a knot at her waist. But she wasn't looking at him, her gaze for Meg.

"Kelsey Sanders," she said, holding out her hand. "Your first season?"

Meg took her hand and shook it quickly. "That obvious?"

"It always is when the men try to take the women shopping." Her side-eye landed directly on him, a clear indictment that he had been tried and found wanting.

Meg's eyes grew round and filled with questions. "You work a lobster boat?"

"Only the best out of Tignish. Twenty-two seasons."

The season for the small fishing community on the northwest shore had long come and gone, as it had for the rest of the island. "What brings you all the way to town then?" Oliver asked.

Kelsey gave him a surprised look. "A sale, of course." She held up two long black pairs of . . . not quite pants. They were too skinny for that, but they immediately caught Meg's attention.

"Do you wear leggings on the boat?"

With a wave of her hand, Kelsey led the way to the back corner of the store, a corner Oliver had never explored before. Tucked behind the boots and the changing rooms he'd never needed to use, three silver racks held a slew of clothes. Softer, gentler clothes.

"Your boyfriend's right," Kelsey said.

"We're not—"

"I'm not—"

He and Meg stumbled over each other to correct Kelsey's assumption, but she didn't seem to care one way or another. With a flick of her wrist, she waved them both off. "You're going to need something sturdy. This is a good brand, and these utility leggings are the best. Stretchy but thick enough so . . . you know. And the knees are reinforced. Plus they have pockets."

Oliver was pretty sure they were talking in some sort of code. Didn't all pants have pockets? But Meg was fully engaged, nodding every few seconds.

"Get a few pair. You'll have to wash 'em every day."

"Will they last?"

"Yep. At least a season. Maybe more."

Meg pulled three pairs off the rack, held them to her waist, and tucked her hand into one of the pockets. Her expression was exactly the opposite of the one she'd made when he held up the circus tent. "So soft," she muttered to no one in particular.

"One in every color then?" Kelsey asked, already grabbing the hangers out of Meg's hands.

"I suppose I won't have time to come back to town once the season starts, will I?"

Kelsey shook her head, the light catching a few gray hairs among the mass of pale brown folded into a braid. She tossed the pants toward Oliver. Without a word she was telling him to hold them. It wasn't unlike the guys he'd seen carrying their wives' purses. Meg's small black purse hung across her body on a thin strap, so her hands were free. And as long as he kept holding her things, he supposed they would remain so.

This was not how men shopped. And it definitely wasn't a side of himself that he'd show to Whitaker, unless he wanted a few elbows to his ribs the next morning. But maybe it was a side that Meg needed to see. Something had been bothering her since she walked into the store, all tight-lipped and lost gaze.

If he could help Meg prepare for setting day—even if his entire role became carrying the items Kelsey pointed out— then he'd do it. So long as Whitaker and Kyle, Little Tommy, and all the others from Victoria by the Sea were far from sight.

Kelsey helped Meg pick out a few sweaters and under-shirts and socks that wouldn't fall down into her boots. Then she led the way to a narrow wooden case along the back wall. It was filled with fancy little boxes adorned with purple flowers. Little silver tins sat open on the top row. Whatever was coming out of them smelled like heaven, like wildflowers in heaven.

"Stock up on this. It's expensive but worth it," Kelsey said as she pulled three boxes off the shelf and tucked them into the crook of her own arm.

Oliver leaned forward, trying to read the fancy lettering on the box, drawn in by the scent. No one had ever shown him this stuff before. No one had bothered pointing out the back corner, for that matter.

Meg flipped a box over, and he physically recoiled at the sticker on the bottom. At thirty dollars, the tin should have been made out of gold.

Meg scooped up three boxes of her own and turned to walk away before Oliver got his question out. "What is it?"

Kelsey made a pitying face that his mom had many times before. "Oh, honey. It's face cream." She patted his cheek.

"You know what the wind and waves do to a paint job. Your skin is even more delicate."

He and Levi had repainted their mom's place the year before, and the seaside wall had been a mess of chipped and cracked paint. They'd had to scrape it off completely before applying a fresh coat.

He rubbed his cheek where Kelsey had patted him. It wasn't exactly soft, and his whiskers were a few days old. But it wasn't too bad. Then again, he was six seasons into a lifetime, and he had no desire for his skin to turn the color *and* texture of cowhide.

"I'll take one of those." He snatched a box from the shelf and added it to the pile on his arm. Both Kelsey and Meg shot him raised eyebrows, but he shrugged. "What? I like to take care of my skin."

Before either of them could respond, someone behind him cleared his throat. Oliver turned slowly and had to drop his gaze several inches to find the man responsible. He was a slender man, barely reaching Oliver's shoulder. The wispy brown hair combed across his forehead was likely intended to cover his receding hairline. It wasn't successful.

But it clearly didn't matter what Oliver thought. Not when the man was looking at Kelsey as though she'd hung the moon and every star. She giggled like a woman half her age and reached for his outstretched hand.

"Are you ready, honeypot?" he asked, a hint of an Irish brogue dancing through his words. His eyes glowed like gold in the sun, and he pulled her hand to his mouth, pressing a gentle kiss to it. "I couldn't wait another minute to see you."

"Oh, sweetheart. I'm sorry to keep you waiting." Kelsey tugged him to her side, looking down at him with love in her eyes. "I was just showing my new friend what she'll need for the season."

"From Summerside?"

Meg shook her head at the same time Oliver said, "Victoria."

"Aye. A lovely area."

Oliver agreed but got the feeling that Kelsey's love couldn't care less. He had eyes only for her. Their shared gaze was practically tangible, and Oliver glanced over at Meg to find her holding back a smirk.

After what seemed an hour, Kelsey finally looked up at them. "Excuse us. We're newlyweds, and . . ."

"Enough said." Meg held up her hand and waved them off. "Thank you for your help. And congratulations."

The bride and groom walked away hand in hand, and Oliver wasn't sure how to follow that up. All he could really wonder was if that's what love was supposed to look like.

His parents had been just about the opposite—no joy between them, no care for the other, no desire to spend time together. If he didn't know better, Oliver might have thought that was the reason his dad left. But he could still hear the seething murmur in his ear and the stinging smack across his cheek that reminded him exactly why Dean Ross had walked out on their family.

And the memory made it hard to breathe.

"Well . . ." Meg nudged him with her shoulder. "Boots?"

He managed a shallow breath and followed her to the seats in the footwear section. "Yes. I know about boots." Plopping onto the padded bench, he set his stuff and all of hers to the side.

After trying on and modeling half a dozen rubber muck

boots of varying heights with nonslip soles, Meg settled on a pair she liked. Then she sat beside him and held out her arm.

Oliver handed over the things she'd chosen, and she clutched them to her chest. But she didn't make a move to get up. Instead, she stared into the store, her gaze once again distant, lost somewhere in the future or the past. Certainly it wasn't in the here and now.

"You want to talk about it?" he finally asked.

"No."

"All right."

She heaved a great sigh, the tip of her pointed chin dipping until her hair fell around her face in a golden curtain. "My dad's going to need our help."

He opened his mouth to tell her that Whitaker already had whatever he needed, but her lifted finger stopped him.

"My mom is . . . We saw a specialist today."

His stomach dropped. He already feared the worst, whatever that might be—a drawn-out illness with endless treatments, a terminal diagnosis, or more of the unknown. He waited for Meg to fill in the blanks, but she didn't speak. "What did he say?"

"She needs more tests, more specialists, more scans." Throwing her head back, she clicked her tongue. "I don't know why they think more is going to help her. No one has been able to help her in years. But suddenly this doctor in Toronto is going to have a diagnosis." She didn't even try to cover the frustration in her tone.

He could fill in the blanks himself. "Your dad is going to be out of town for a while." No question mark. No question.

When she looked at him, little lines puckered between her eyebrows and her teeth sank into her bottom lip. He'd never seen her look so vulnerable, so delicate. Everything inside him wanted to throw their things on the ground and pull her against him. He just wanted to protect her, eliminate every bit of her pain.

Which wasn't exactly normal, given their history.

He gripped his new pants a little tighter against his chest and tried to show the right facial expression—understanding and empathy.

"We don't know when yet. It'll be short notice, and I just need for my dad to be . . ."

"Free to focus on your mom."

"Yeah."

He nodded.

"Like completely free. Like we need to field all of the calls and orders and everything."

There was an unspoken request too. They couldn't go to Whitaker with anything. If working together wasn't working out, they'd have to figure it out on their own.

He stared at her, watching the way her bottom lip wiggled back and forth as she worried it, waiting for the animosity that had been between them to bloom. It didn't.

Because they had to do something big. Together.

# nine

Oliver couldn't sleep. Like a kid on Christmas Eve, he lay awake, eyes wide open, feet twitching in his bed. He kicked off his sheet then pulled it back across him, flopped over, and pressed his face into his pillow. Pinching his eyes closed, he shut out the light of the moon coming through the window in his one-room apartment.

Still awake.

A lot of the lobstermen slept in their shacks, close to the dock. Oliver only lived a kilometer away, and he usually got better sleep in his own bed. The cots in the shanties didn't extend past his ankles and barely fit his shoulders. He'd rather sleep on the cement floor. Since his bed was an option, he'd taken it.

But he hadn't gotten better sleep in his own bed that night.

Long before the alarm on his phone went off, he rolled off of the firm mattress, stumbled to the bathroom sink, and splashed cold water on his face. Staring into the mirror, he told himself the truth. "You can do this."

He took a deep breath and ran a hand through his shaggy

mane. He hadn't bothered flipping on a light, and the moon made the room glow, his pale eyes with it.

This wasn't his first setting day. But it was his first as the captain of the boat, his first with an untried, inexperienced hand. One who happened to have an equal say in everything.

*Lord, let her be easy.*

Everything else about setting day burst with excitement and required his focus. He just needed Meg to leave all of her ornery temper and sharp tongue on the shore.

He threw on his work pants, a T-shirt, and two sweaters before shoving his feet into thick wool socks. After pulling on his muck boots, he lined his pockets with protein bars and bags of peanuts.

He snagged his keys and his wallet before racing out the door and down the rickety wooden steps behind the garage. The main house was still dark, but a shadow on the other side of the kitchen window promised that Mama Potts was awake. He was almost to his truck when the kitchen door flew open, and a disembodied hand held out a paper towel–wrapped sandwich.

"Eat something before you go."

"Yes, ma'am." He jogged over to take it from her, and she stole a kiss on his cheek.

"I'm proud of you, Oliver."

Her words carried an unexpected weight, a million reminders of all the reasons she might not say that. He hadn't always been worthy of her pride. Not after Meg. Not after he'd failed to provide for them. Not after Mrs. Whitaker had started bringing them groceries.

A sudden lump in his throat made it hard to respond. He shoved half of the grilled cheese-and-egg sandwich into his mouth and mumbled a thanks around it as he backed toward his truck. Swallowing the mass of spicy cheese, he said, "See you later."

"Wouldn't miss it," she called with a wave.

He slammed his truck door, and his tires spit gravel as he sailed down the empty black road. The world was deserted this early in the morning. Smart people were still in bed. But as the wind whipped through his open window, he'd never felt more wide-awake. The cool air carried the scent of salt water and freedom. The ocean. He purposefully kept his radio off on these early morning trips to the dock. A chance to listen to the waves, to hear what the water might say. It whispered this morning, an invitation to spend time with it. A welcome to the season, a welcome back to the sea.

The birds were quiet, as if they too knew the day belonged to the tides and the waves. And as he pulled into the parking lot, the clouds split and the moon shone on the water. If the golden bridge by the light of the sun was his favorite thing in the world, the silver ripples of the moon's glow in this very spot were his second. He enjoyed them for a long moment until he stepped onto the dock and saw two men standing in the shadows next to his boat.

Okay, technically it wasn't his boat yet. But it would be. It could be—as soon as Meg realized that this wasn't the life she wanted. That even if she conquered her motion sickness, the early mornings and hard work were never going to change.

When he got closer, he recognized Little Tommy Scanlan and Jeffrey Druthers, whose boats were on either side of his, still empty. They hadn't even begun to stack their lobster traps on the back end. And somehow he didn't think they had been waiting for him just to have a friendly chat.

"G'morning," Oliver said, crossing his arms over his chest. "Something I can do for you gentlemen?"

Little Tommy's eyes were beady and dark, and he scratched at his graying whiskers. "It's true then. You're captaining Whitaker's boat."

He wanted to have a quick retort and a witty remark. All he really had was the truth. "I suppose."

Druthers frowned, his bushy mustache failing to cover the displeasure that lurked in every other feature of his face. "Are ya buying in then?"

"Nothing's been decided just yet." That was true too. Let them infer what they would.

"You know what yer old man did, right?" Little Tommy asked.

His chest tightened at the reminder that Dean Ross had run out on them just before the season started. He hadn't just run out on Mama Potts and his sons. He'd run out on a perfectly good job on a fishing boat and a captain who'd been counting on him.

The conclusion was clear. They expected him to be just like his dad.

"Don't think you need to worry about that. I've been working Whitaker's boat for six years."

Druthers waved his hand, dismissing the number and all that it represented. "Yer dad worked mine for nearly ten." Crossing his arms over his overalls, he leaned forward. "Cost me near a third of my usual profits that year. Had to train a new hand on the fly and replace all he took."

Oliver had no response to that. Every bit of it was true.

So long as he was just a deckhand, no one had seemed to mind that he was working on a boat. But if he owned one—if he was an equal with the other fishermen—well, they might not be willing to bear it.

"You know there are rules, boy," Little Tommy said. "And punishment for not following them."

Oliver dropped his arms to his sides and squeezed his fists. Everything inside him wanted to ask just what rules they thought he would break. He knew the written ones—the laws that limited the number of traps he could set and the regulated area he could fish. He knew the days of the season. He knew the requirements for sustainability and throwing back females with eggs. And he knew the size minimum.

He knew the unwritten rules too. How fishermen didn't mess with another boat's haul. How a license for the area didn't mean he was free to fish the whole area. How the first boat left the harbor at six in the morning on setting day every year, and from their small dock, Druthers led the way.

"Yes, sir. I'm aware of the rules."

What Oliver didn't know was if he'd done something to deserve the aforementioned punishment. Or was this entirely about the sins of his father?

An uneven gait joined them on the dock. *Curr-thump. Curr-thump.*

He knew before turning around who the steps belonged to. Meg, who was still learning how to walk in her muck boots. Meg, who had barely begun to earn her sea legs.

Meg, who somehow twisted his insides tighter than a rope.

The two experienced lobstermen cringed and curled in on themselves.

Maybe this wasn't only about him. Maybe it was about having a *her* around too.

Meg stopped at his side, gripping two steaming paper cups

of coffee. She held one out toward him, and he took it, curling his chilled fingers around the warmth. "Figured it's going to be a long day. Got you a double-double at Timmies."

He nodded his thanks. Two creams. Two sugars. Just how he drank his Tim Hortons coffee. She'd had to drive over to the head of the bridge to find the open shop, and he savored the rich flavor of his first drink.

She eyed the men across from them with a narrow gaze. "I didn't know you'd be here."

It wasn't even close to an apology that any good Canadian would offer if they didn't have coffee to share. And Oliver loved it.

"Just watch yourself out there," Little Tommy said as he and Druthers shuffled toward their own boats.

Meg took a long sip from her cup before saying, "What was that all about?"

"Guess maybe they aren't so happy that your dad's not going to be here." No need to tell her they weren't thrilled that Whitaker was thinking about selling to him. Or that they didn't seem particularly fond of her.

Let the old guys get used to it. He and Meg had a job to do. In a minute.

He took his time sipping the coffee, staring out at the open water as the warmth trickled through his middle and to the very tips of his fingers.

"What would you have been doing today?" he asked, risking a glance in her direction. She wore a heavy sweatshirt, the hem of her plaid flannel shirt sticking out halfway to her knees. The black leggings that Kelsey had recommended made her legs look longer than usual.

"Besides cheering on the boats from the wharf?"

He jerked his eyes up and nodded.

"Lesson plans, I guess." There was a longing in her words that he'd never heard from her before.

"You like making lesson plans?"

She laughed out loud—a pop of noise overtaking the sound of the waves and the creaking of the rocking boat. "About as much as getting a tooth pulled." She sipped and let out another sigh. "But I like teaching. I like the students, and I like seeing them get something they didn't before."

"And you gave all that up for early mornings and smelly fish."

She shoved his shoulder. "And I don't plan to regret it."

By the time Kyle Mulligan arrived, Meg and Oliver had filled the back half of the boat with lobster traps stacked taller than she was. Meg paused to mop her forehead with the sleeve of her sweatshirt. She bent over, resting her hands on her knees and taking a few deep breaths.

"Doing okay there, rookie? Your patch working?" Oliver asked as he leapt onto the dock.

She closed her eyes as the boat swayed, waiting for the discomfort. But her stomach stayed put and her head didn't go on a fair ride. "Just fine."

Oliver had already reached Kyle, clapping him on the shoulder and smiling. Even in the yellow light of the overheads that pooled on the dock, she could see the deckhand return the smile.

She tried to force one of her own but couldn't make her muscles do it. She already wanted to be back in bed. Back at school. Back where she wasn't the rookie.

Then again, she didn't have a job there any longer. She'd closed every door but this one. This was her only option. And it wouldn't take long to get the hang of it all. She just needed a little practice.

Ignoring the twinge in her back as she pushed herself up, she clomped across the fiberglass floor and shinnied up the ladder.

"Meg Whitaker. So it's true." Kyle reached out his hand and nearly shook hers right off. "Oliver here told me, but I couldn't believe it. You're here for the season?"

She managed half a smile and a jerky nod.

Kyle's grin was wide, his salt-and-pepper mustache stretching across his face. "I bet your dad is awful happy you're carrying on the family name."

Oliver's shoulders visibly twitched, and Meg didn't quite know how to respond. "Happy to be here." She didn't add the *I guess* that crossed her mind.

"What happened at the school? The kids too much for you?"

She chuckled. "No. Just . . . wanted to help out my dad."

Kyle smoothed his mustache with his knuckle, the brightness in his ruddy face dimming. "I was sorry to hear." He paused for a long moment, seeming to weigh how much he should say. "It won't be quite the same without him."

Kyle and her dad had been working the boat together for more than thirty years. Other deckhands had come and gone, but Kyle had been her dad's first hire, the most stable.

Her gaze swung to Oliver and back to the barrel chest of the man she'd known since she was a child. Why had her dad offered to sell his business to Oliver? Why not Kyle?

She had to bite her tongue to keep from blurting it out.

The dock was beginning to fill up with hands loading traps and buoys and buckets of bait, and it wasn't the time or the place to ask. But she made a note to herself. Something had made her dad choose Oliver when Kyle had been standing right in front of him, and she wanted to know what.

"If I'd have known you were starting so early, I'd have been here an hour ago. Thought I'd be here earlier, but Mrs. Mulligan, she always says that setting day is no day to skip breakfast. She did up a big feast—salmon quiche and hot scones. I swear, she was baking all night." Kyle rubbed the overalls covering his round belly. "Woulda been rude to refuse, eh?"

Oliver patted his own flat stomach. "I couldn't wait to get here, but right about now I'm wishing Mama Potts had sent me with a second sandwich."

The sun was only just beginning to paint the morning sky a pale gray at the horizon, erasing the stars with its power. They couldn't have been working for more than two hours. Meg had thrown a frozen egg thing into the microwave and shoveled it in on her drive to the wharf, but now she felt hollow too, a low ache in her belly. Which growled loudly the minute that Oliver plucked an energy bar from the pocket of his pants.

He raised his eyebrows in question. "Hungry?"

She shrugged. She'd make it the rest of the day. She'd be fine.

But when he reached into his pocket, pulled out another bar, and held it out to her, she snatched it like she hadn't eaten in weeks. "Thanks," she mumbled as she clawed the wrapper away and chomped into it.

Kyle's laugh echoed, drawing the attention of at least a few others in the area. "It's good to keep your strength up. You're going to need it."

After their early-morning snack break, they set about loading the rest of the traps, carrying them from the shack to the dock and then passing them to Kyle on board. He loaded the boat with the precision of an architect, threading the traps together to fill every nook and cranny.

Meg wanted to believe that she and Oliver had been just as efficient, but Kyle was built like a moose and twice as strong. Even as she struggled to carry one awkward trap, he tossed their gear around like plastic buckets on the beach. Their boat was fully loaded before the others on the dock, sitting low in the water.

"Well, well. She looks pretty good."

Meg whipped around at the familiar voice, her dad's lanky frame leaning against the front of his truck in the parking spots opposite the dock. An immediate question popped to mind, but she bit it back, refusing to ask about her mom. "What are you doing here, Dad?"

"You didn't think I'd let you head off on setting day without cheering you on, did you?"

"Walt!" Kyle called from the boat, offering a sharp salute and a quick nod of his head.

Her dad returned the gesture with a lazy hand. "Looks good."

"It won't be the same without you out there," Kyle said.

Her dad's gaze dropped toward her. "You're in good hands."

Suddenly his features blurred, and she swiped at her eyes. Ridiculous. There was no reason she should be crying. Except that it was great to see her dad—just for a moment—in the setting he loved, with people who respected him.

He was giving all that up.

"Where'd you find that getup, kid?" her dad asked. "You fit right in."

She ran her hand down her leg and popped the stretchy fabric before wiggling her booted foot. "Um, Oliver took me shopping."

He snorted. "Oliver? *That* Oliver?"

The very one who strolled down the dock from the shack, several lengths of line hanging from his shoulders. "She said she was going to wear jean shorts," Oliver said without preamble. "Figured you wouldn't take kindly if I let her catch her death out there."

"I think you're right. Her mother and I are pretty fond of this girl."

The early morning glow had reached over the horizon and all the way to their little alcove, and Meg raised her hands to her cheeks to cover the pink there. Dads. Embarrassing their kids since the dawn of time.

Still, she wouldn't have wanted it any other way.

She smiled at her dad. "I'll stop by later today, all right?"

"You think you'll have the energy for that?"

"Why wouldn't I?"

Famous last words. She'd watched her mom take care of her dad during lobster season for years. She should have known better.

They were second to head out to sea—one of the unspoken rules of Victoria's harbor. They waved at the local families lined up and down the jetty, Oliver at the helm and Meg and Kyle on either side of him. There wasn't anywhere else to stand, so she held on to the dashboard with all of its beeping, blinking gadgets as the wind whipped around her. She'd pulled her hair into a braid, but already wisps had escaped. She shoved them out of the way, closing her eyes and lifting her face into the wind. It smelled of life and vitality.

"Feeling okay there, kid?"

Without even looking at Oliver, she waved one finger in the air. "First, no one gave you permission to call me 'kid.' My dad has special rights." She waved another finger. "Second, I feel absolutely perfect."

Okay, so her knees were a little wobbly, and she'd rather sit than stand as they flew across the waves in the wake of Druthers's boat. But her stomach hadn't threatened an all-out uprising. As far as she was concerned, that counted as a victory.

Oliver's deep chuckle carried over the hum of the boat. "What about Kyle?"

"What about him?"

"Can he call you 'kid'?"

She leaned around Oliver to get a good look at the man who had been her dad's right hand for years. His big brown eyes wrinkled at the corners, humor deep in each line.

"Yeah. Kyle gets a pass."

Oliver tapped one of the screens in front of him while pursing his lips to the side. "That seems a little unfair. What if Kyle doesn't even *want* to call you 'kid'?"

She shook her head in mock seriousness. "What can I say? I don't make the rules."

His laughter was deep and scratchy but melodic. It almost sounded like he was out of practice. Like he hadn't taken time for humor. Like he wanted more excuses for joy. But he said only, "This is our spot," as he cut the engine and let the boat drift.

Whatever hint of humor had played across his face disappeared as he put his hands on his hips, took a deep breath, and let it out through tight lips. And in that moment, she knew. He felt the weight of responsibility like she didn't. Not yet anyway.

But she would. This wasn't just her dad's legacy. This was all of their livelihoods.

Kyle moved first, practiced and certain with his steps. He grabbed a cluster of traps and lined them up on the edge of the boat. Before he could get the second straightened, Oliver scooped up a handful of sour-smelling herring and tucked it into place. Lobsters would crawl through the netting to eat the tasty fish in the trap's kitchen and then get stuck when they tried to crawl out. With any luck, two or three might find their way in each day.

Meg stood watching for a long moment before finally grabbing a bright green buoy and attaching it to the long rope connected to each of the six traps.

When each trap was baited and marked, they shoved all of them overboard. The cool water splashed into the boat, sloshing beneath her muck boots. At least she wasn't wearing sneakers. Oliver steered them to the next spot and the next and the next, where they repeated the actions until Meg could do them in her sleep.

By the time all 240 traps were set, all she could think about was cozying up in her bed, closing her eyes, and dreaming of anything but the smell of herring.

Only she'd promised her dad she'd stop by for a visit.

# ten

"Do you need anything, Mom?" Meg called over her shoulder as she tossed a load of towels into the washing machine. She waited for a moment, hoping, wishing, praying. Her mom sat tucked in the corner of the sofa on the far side of the room, her eyes open. But from the laundry room, Meg could see just how little her mother actually saw.

There was no response except a short knock on the side door, followed immediately by the groan of it opening.

"Hey there." Oliver had let himself in like he belonged in this home, like he was the one who had grown up under this roof. At least he wiped his feet on the mat before ambling past her into the living room.

His hair was damp and clean, and he smelled like soap. Much more pleasant than the herring he'd spent the morning digging through. And his skin glowed even beneath his five-o'clock shadow.

"Been using that face cream?" Her question surprised even her, and she clamped her lips closed as he turned toward her.

His mouth pulled into a half smile as he rubbed one big palm up and down his cheek. "What gave me away?"

She shook her head and mumbled, "Nothing," as she poured laundry soap into the tub and turned it on. The rush of water and cranking of the machine covered her silence—and apparently his footsteps. When she looked up, he'd made his way to the rocking chair near her mom. He sat with a strange grace for someone his size, and she couldn't look away as he reached for her mom's arm and gave it a gentle squeeze.

"Hey there, Mrs. Whitaker." His voice was soft, his tone low. "How you doing today?"

Meg held her breath, somehow praying both that her mom would respond and also that she wouldn't. It wouldn't be fair, not when Meg had spent so many hours talking to her and had gotten so little.

Oliver leaned forward, his elbows on his knees, and glanced up. Meg dropped her gaze and stared at her idle hands. She had to do something, if only so she didn't look like she was watching him. She turned on the kitchen faucet, poured in dish soap, and filled the sink. But the clinking dishes didn't drown out Oliver's words.

"We missed you this morning at the dock. *Just a Pinch* looked good as ever, all washed up and shining in the sun. She did a good job today, and we got all our traps set, right where Whitaker likes them."

Meg snapped her gaze up. Was he talking about her or the boat? Did it really matter?

Given the bitter taste in her mouth, apparently it did.

"She still rides smooth on the water. You should come out on her sometime."

He was talking about the boat then. Good.

*So why are you jealous?*

She was *not* jealous that he'd complimented a lobster boat. But it wouldn't kill him to say that she'd done a good job too. She'd kept up with him and Kyle both. Although she hadn't volunteered to shove her gloved hand into the bait bucket, she'd been useful. Even if she'd been moving a little slow by the time they pulled back into the dock.

She couldn't help the annoyed breath that escaped, and Oliver's questioning side-eye followed. This time Meg met his gaze, refusing to look away.

Maybe it was the look on her face or his mind-reading skills. Either way, he said, "You'd have been proud of Meg today too. She worked hard. Fishing's in her blood."

See? That wasn't so hard.

Except it didn't make sense. There was no good reason he would compliment her, not if he wanted the business as much as she did. And he did, she was sure of that. Maybe he figured whatever he said to her mom would never be repeated—couldn't be repeated.

Her chest burned, and she pressed a sudsy fist to her sternum. It didn't help. There were too many reminders that what she had was only temporary. That everything was going to change. Soon.

"Where's Whitaker?"

She blinked quickly to clear her mind and figure out if Oliver was talking to her or her mom. His gaze squarely in the direction of the kitchen, she decided he was asking her.

"On the phone in the office."

Oliver nodded.

"Did you need something? I figured you'd be getting to bed early after our day today."

He snorted. "It's four o'clock in the afternoon."

Right. Yes. Comparing the way he looked to the way she felt, she was the one in need of a nap. But her dad had always said it was better to push through the day. Otherwise she risked not being able to fall asleep when it was time.

She squared her shoulders and took two deep breaths. Then she gave her tired limbs a pep talk. *Keep going. Just a little longer.*

"You want to come join us?" he asked.

As if she needed an invitation to sit with her own mom.

"No. I have some more work to do." She spun around, looking for another chore, something else that would help her dad out around the house. Her gaze stopped on the fridge, and she swung it open, looking for supper. A pot roast sat on the second shelf, and there were potatoes in the pantry. But her mom would have a hard time eating that.

She decided on a simple creamy potato soup, soothing and warm. Just like her mom used to make it. Only her mom hadn't had a heavy blue gaze following her every movement. The weight of Oliver's stare made her motions stiff and her fingers fumble the potato.

"Do you need a hand?"

He was right by her side, his breath shooting sparks down her spine, making everything inside her tingle.

No. No. No. Not okay.

She spun around and waved the potato in his face. "What are you trying to do?"

"Help you make some supper?" He was so much closer than she'd thought, so close that she could see the thread of blue in his plaid flannel shirt that exactly matched his eyes. So close that she could count the freckles on his cheeks and smell the lavender scent of his face cream. So close that she could feel his warmth all the way across her body.

She stumbled back and bumped into the counter next to the stove. "No. Not that." She laid her potato down. "This . . . Why are you pretending to be so nice?"

He shrugged. "Maybe I'm not pretending."

"Ha." It came out as more of a dry cough than a laugh, but it still made his dimples appear. And boy, did they show up, lighting his face, making his eyes sparkle and his lips twitch.

"Maybe I'm just a nice guy who wants to be your friend." He leaned forward, closing what little gap had been between them.

"Unlikely." It struck her why that was so true. "Not with the business on the line."

Still so close she could feel his breath on her skin, he whispered, "Maybe I'm not the same guy you knew before."

"Or maybe you're exactly the same guy."

He stepped back, and she let out a breath she hadn't realized she'd been holding.

His smile bordered on a smirk, but there was a kindness in the tilt of his head. In the way he'd made sure she was prepared for the season. In the way he'd treated her mom.

She wanted him to be the same guy who'd kicked her robot into the wall and watched it fly into a thousand pieces. She knew what to do with that guy. She'd been practicing for ten years.

She didn't have a clue what to do with this Oliver, with the one who was slowly sneaking into her thoughts. The one with the broad shoulders and—it had to be admitted—the eyes that could stop traffic on Route 1. The one who picked up a peeler and a potato and swiped the skin off in long, sure strokes.

"What are we making?"

She turned around, standing by his side at the counter. "Creamy ham and potato soup."

He raised his eyebrows in a playful salute. "My favorite."

She shook her head and groaned to herself as she dug a pot out of the cupboard by the oven and plopped it onto the stove. She took the peeled potato and diced it into small pieces along with a ham steak from the fridge.

Before long Meg stirred as Oliver poured a milk and flour mixture into the water that held onions, ham, and potatoes.

"Smells good in here."

Meg smiled in her dad's general direction but kept her eyes on the simmering pot. "Hi, Dad. How's Aunt Ruth doing?"

"I'm not sure. Didn't talk long before the hospital in Toronto called."

She dropped her wooden spoon, which splashed into the pot and sent drops of their supper sizzling across the hot surface of the stove. "What did they say?"

Her dad shoved his hands into the pockets of his jeans and hunched his shoulders. Everything inside her wanted to curl up and return to another time. She didn't care when. Just so long as there was no more illness and she didn't have to watch her mom deteriorate.

"They have an opening at the hospital this week," he said.

"*Thi-is* week?" Her voice cracked, and a firm hand rested between her shoulder blades. She wanted to shrug it away, but she had a feeling Oliver's support was keeping her upright.

This should be good news. Her mom was going to be seen by one of the best neurologists in the country—in the world. This is what they needed to find the truth, to get a diagnosis.

But a slithering voice in the back of her mind whispered the truth. *Maybe you don't want to know.*

Knowing was all well and good when there was a treatment plan, a cure. But what if there wasn't one?

Rocking back on her heels, she leaned into Oliver's hand, felt his forearm down the length of her spine, and just tried to breathe.

"We have to leave tomorrow."

She choked on another gasp. "Okay."

They could decide not to go. They could stay put right there in Victoria. Only she wasn't free to ask them to do that, to beg her dad not to leave when the entire world was shifting. That's not how their family operated or what her dad needed. She was better than her desire to fall apart.

Pushing herself away from Oliver's hand, she squared her shoulders.

*Say it. Just get it out.*

"I'll help you pack."

———

Some fishermen got their fill of the sea in the early morning hours, the salt water spilling into their boats and rocking them back and forth. Yet Oliver had been so busy watching Meg the past few days that he'd missed it. Not that he hadn't enjoyed watching Meg—what with her shaky sea legs and hesitancy with the merchandise. But he was determined to stop watching her and start enjoying the job again.

She clambered on board, those black pants she'd worn every day since setting day hugging her legs in all the right places and drawing his gaze whether he liked it or not. Okay, he was determined to watch her *less*. Enjoy the wind in his face and the smell of clean air more.

She passed out the three coffees she'd brought, and Oliver thanked her with a quick nod before she wandered off.

Kyle thumped him on the back. "'Mornin' to you, Captain." He tipped an imaginary hat. "I've a good feelin' about this one."

Oliver cringed at the title. Technically Whitaker still owned the *Pinch*, and until the ink was dry on the contract, Oliver wasn't about to call himself the captain. He glanced toward Meg, whose face was the same as it had been every other morning at this time—stiff and pinched. She gave no indication that she'd heard Kyle's remark or of her thoughts on it. But as much as he wanted the title, it could just as easily be hers.

She looked like she could pilot this morning, arms crossed as she stared out to sea. The sun was almost up, but the lights on the dock illuminated her. Hair pulled back, braided, and roped into a knot at the nape of her neck, she was practically a Viking princess.

Less. He was supposed to be looking at her less.

Jerking his gaze back to Kyle, he tried for a good smile. Kyle smirked and shook his head.

So he wasn't quite as stealthy as he'd hoped. Sure, Meg was beautiful. Didn't mean he would ever—*ever*—act on that. There were plenty of other things to focus on.

Druthers's boat coughed once and then growled to life, breaking through the soft birdsong and sending fine ripples back against the shallow waves. Without so much as a wave, Druthers pulled away from the dock and set out for the open water.

There'd been no sign of Little Tommy's boat when he arrived forty-five minutes before.

Oliver turned on the engine, and Meg whipped her head in his direction. "Ready?" he asked.

She pressed a finger to the spot behind her ear where she'd stuck a little patch and nodded.

He didn't ask Kyle. He was always ready.

As they rolled over the small crests, Oliver closed his eyes. Just him and the sea. Just him and a vast ocean before him. Technically New Brunswick was only a few kilometers away, but for him, there was nothing but water.

Whitaker had once told him that this moment in the morning, before the work had begun, was his quiet time with the Lord. A still moment when all the other noise of the world disappeared until there was only the Creator and the created.

Oliver wanted to wrap himself in the moment. It was warmer than a parka and twice as comforting. He could just breathe it in. Despite the brisk wind and sharp spray off the water, it felt like home. It felt like security.

The last time he'd felt anything remotely like this was his sixteenth birthday. Mama Potts had made his favorite pie from peaches she'd picked herself, and the sweet scent of cinnamon and sugar had permeated the whole house. Back when they'd had a house. Back when he'd happily shared a room with Levi.

Back when he couldn't imagine losing any of it.

His eyes flew open. He was so close to losing all of it—everything he'd worked for, everything he'd prayed for—again. He couldn't let that happen.

He licked his lips, recoiling at the salty tang and forcing his mind back to the work at hand. Pulling up to their first buoy, he reached for the gaff only to see that Meg had already picked up the long staff with the hook on the end to scoop up the floating marker. Like she'd been doing it for years, she grabbed the rope, fed it into the electronic hauler attached to the stern of the boat, and reeled in the line.

When the first trap of the cluster popped to the surface, Kyle reached over to help her pull them onto the narrow counter attached to the edge of the boat. But even with the help, the strain of the work tugged on Meg's features. Her mouth turned tight, the tip of her nose wrinkling. After the traps were lined up, she dropped her hands to her sides, flexing her fingers a few times before digging into the trap's parlor to see what they'd caught.

There he went again, watching her instead of doing the work.

Opening up the closest trap, Oliver found two brown lobsters. Their shells wouldn't turn the famous red until they were boiled, and these two seemed just about the right size for the pot.

Seventy-seven millimeters. That was the magic number. Any smaller and the lobster got tossed like a bath toy back into the water per governmental regulations. Too much bigger and it had been alive too many years, its meat too tough to enjoy—no matter how much butter sauce was served on the side.

He whipped out his reverse pliers, slipped a rubber band on the tip, and squeezed the tool open. Then he picked up one of the unlucky crustaceans, flipped it over to check for eggs, and slipped a band on each of its claws.

With his metal gauge, he measured from the back of its eye sockets to the point where the tail began. One lobster was right at seventy-seven and the other just a millimeter more. Perfect. He tossed them to Kyle, who tucked them into little compartments in the bottom of the plastic crate at the stern. It would hold more than a hundred pounds by the time they filled it up. And with any luck, they'd fill at least two or three that morning.

As he moved to the next trap, he glanced at Meg, the reverse pliers in her hand trembling against the pressure of the band around it. Suddenly the pliers snapped closed and clattered to the deck with a metallic chime, followed almost immediately by a nonmetallic thunk.

Meg screamed and dropped to her knees, holding a writhing lobster in one hand and the claw it had dropped in the other. She looked up at him, her eyes wide and unblinking. He had a feeling her lower lip might have quivered if not for the way she'd sunk her teeth into it.

Squatting down before her, he pursed his lips to the side, trying to decide what he should say. What she needed to hear. "Guess he didn't have a good grip on his claw." Scooping it up, he waved the pincher like a hand, shooting for a smile and settling for a grimace.

"I know. They drop their claws when they're scared. I didn't mean to . . ." She nodded to her pliers and squeezed her hand by way of explanation.

She wasn't the first deckhand to drop her tool, and he nodded in understanding. Her little friend wriggled again, flapping his tail against the underside of her forearm. She screamed but held on tight, twisting out of reach of his other claw as she shoved it to arm's length. Right in Oliver's face.

He gasped, jerking away but not fast enough. Pain sliced through the tip of his nose. His pulse thundered in his ears, accompanied by visions of losing his entire nose to the angry lobster. And he might have if Kyle hadn't slipped a band on it and taken it out of Meg's grip. His mustache didn't quite cover a smug grin as Oliver dabbed at the blood on his nose with the back of his glove.

Meg, on the other hand, received a gentle smile and a firm hand on her shoulder. "You should have seen Oliver his first season. You're doing just fine."

She blinked then, her blue eyes nearly glowing with the praise.

He should have said that. He should have said something—anything—kind.

Maybe he was supposed to be watching Meg a little less. But he couldn't ignore her. All of his hopes hinged on her. On helping her succeed. On helping her see that this wasn't the life she wanted.

On helping her see she had a choice.

# eleven

Everything hurt.

Everything.

Meg tried to throw off the light blanket, but her shoulders and arms screamed in protest. She remained wrapped in cotton.

Okay. Maybe it was smarter to try to roll over first and slide out of bed.

She pushed her foot against the mattress and immediately decided she'd rather lose her whole limb than try that again. Her body didn't work anymore. It was that simple. But that didn't fix her problem.

Her alarm kept chirping, and church wouldn't wait. She'd sworn she just needed to rest her eyes for a minute. They'd had a good morning, more than three hundred pounds of hard shell before eleven. Back home with plenty of time to get ready.

She'd just needed a tiny little nap before late church. That's what her dad had always called it. Some of the lobstermen called it seasonal church. Either way, Grace Community had adopted a schedule of starting their service at two during lobster season.

Pastor Dell was fond of joking that God's love wasn't dependent on whether they made it to church every Sunday, but his might be. At this point Meg wasn't entirely sure she would be able to make it to any church service ever.

She tried to pull her blanket away from her chin, but her fingers refused to grasp. Or open, for that matter. Her hands were basically immobile claws after grabbing and throwing traps most of the week.

*Get up. Get up. Get up.*

The chant in her head didn't make it so.

She had to. God might not mind if she stayed in bed, but there was no way the rest of the lobstermen in town wouldn't talk about her absence. Oliver would absolutely notice that the pew in front of him was empty. And word was bound to get back to her dad.

By sheer force of will, she rolled herself from bed and dragged her feet across the fluffy rug, onto the hardwood floor, and into the tiled bathroom. Her feet barely registered the change in flooring, but at least they had some feeling. That was more than she could say for the rest of her body, which felt only pain, could register only the torture of muscle movement.

Somehow she managed to turn the shower on and waited for it to begin steaming before stepping under the spray. It didn't help. She couldn't lift her hands above her elbows.

Well, who needed to get clean? And another day of unwashed hair wasn't the end of the world. It could be camouflaged in a messy bun. Reaching her hair proved to be harder than she'd anticipated, and finally she bent over, tipped her head forward, and threw a scrunchie around her hair.

By the time she wriggled into the least constricting piece of clothing she owned—a shapeless gingham sundress—

and glanced in the mirror, she didn't have time to care that she looked almost as bad as she felt. Her growling stomach, however, refused to let her leave the house without at least a protein bar. It was one of the nasty, gummy ones that Oliver always had on the boat, but it was better than going hungry. And she was always hungry these days.

By the time she reached the little white chapel of Grace Community Church, the parking lot was full and the double doors were closed. She parked along the side of the road, pulling off into the grass and praying she could beat Kevin and his parking tickets outside after the service.

She hobbled up the steps and waited outside the big wooden doors. Taking a deep breath, she closed her eyes and forced herself to be silent and still for just a moment. Silent and still wasn't a guarantee that all eyes in the sanctuary wouldn't turn in her direction. But anything less was a guarantee they would.

She opened the door, and the last notes of "Amazing Grace" drifted out.

Oh, great. Whenever they sang "Amazing Grace," it was the last song before Pastor Dell stepped up to the podium. She couldn't wait. And she couldn't let her displeased muscles dictate her speed. Sucking in a quick breath, she forced herself down the center aisle at a quick pace.

*Left. Right. Left. Ri—ow, ow, ow.*

She grimaced but kept going, ignoring the weight of every gaze in every pew that she passed. As she fell into her family's row, she caught one gaze with her own. Oliver's eyes were clear and filled with concern.

"You okay?" He mouthed the question just as Pastor Dell invited the congregation to open their Bibles.

She nodded quickly, spun toward the front, and held as still as possible.

Oliver spent the whole sermon trying not to watch Meg shifting in the pew before him, but every twitch of her shoulders and strain of her neck was all too familiar. He could almost see the cringe on her face with every movement. And he knew if he didn't do something about it, he'd be risking more than he could afford to lose.

Whitaker had never said it, but he wanted Meg to succeed. He'd wanted her to want to carry on his legacy all along. That was no secret. And now that she'd finally shown an interest, Whitaker wanted her to enjoy it, to have a successful season.

Which left Oliver little choice. He had to help her.

But if he'd learned anything about Meg Whitaker in the last week, it was that she didn't want help. Or at least she didn't want help from him. She seemed plenty happy to work with Kyle—they were pretty much doing the same job, after all. However, the minute Oliver offered to lend a hand, she put on her hard shell.

This was different though. This was about survival. And no one survived without a few tips and tricks. Like the right clothes, the right gear, and the right creams.

He stuck his elbow into Violet's side just as Pastor Dell began his closing thoughts. Violet let out a little yelp, and Meg froze. The Harts behind them probably did too. He shot Violet a hard glance.

"What?" Violet mouthed. Her hands were folded in her lap, but her eyebrows were not nearly as pious.

He nodded toward Meg's back, and Violet shook her head, clearly not understanding.

"Sore." He said the word on a breath, and her eyebrows dipped together. She made a motion with her hand like it was a kite soaring on the wind.

He shook his head and glanced up at the pastor, who was still going. Oliver squeezed his own shoulder, mimicking a massage while sending a pointed gaze in Meg's direction.

Violet still didn't get it, her face crinkling up like he was crazy. Finally she rolled her eyes at him and turned back toward the front just as Pastor Dell started to pray.

Oliver tried to focus on the words, but it was hard to do when his eyes kept opening, his gaze landing on the messy knot of golden hair before him. He imagined he could smell her soap from his seat, but that couldn't be real.

Suddenly the sanctuary filled with voices, and everyone around him had risen. He jumped up as Meg stiff-legged her way toward the aisle. He wanted to grab her hand, hold her in place. But he didn't dare touch her in her current state. Instead, he reached around Violet's back and snagged his mom's elbow.

Mama Potts leaned forward to see down the row, her head tilted in question.

"Meg looks . . ." He kept his voice low but ran out of words. How to describe her condition without alerting the wagging tongues to her pain. She didn't need anyone else thinking they couldn't hack it. There was enough doubt between Little Tommy Scanlan and his buddies to make the season harder than it had to be.

Oliver knew he could do the job. He could run the business.

But he had to prove that to the other crews. And he couldn't do that if he lost a man—or in this case, a woman.

Mama Potts frowned, her eyes narrowing.

He gave a hard nod toward the center aisle and Meg's hobbled steps. Mama Potts turned, and even though he couldn't see her face, he could see the moment she recognized what he had been trying to point out. Waving a hand in his general direction, she slipped past Levi and chased Meg down.

"Where's she going?" Violet asked.

Oliver allowed himself a little grin. "To make sure I don't lose a deckhand."

Mama Potts's voice was too low to carry over the hum of the room, but her eyes were kind as she talked with Meg. She nodded several times and pointed at her own neck and back. Meg's deflating sigh said it all. Help had come.

There. Good deed done. He'd helped Meg solve her problem. At least one of them.

The knock on the kitchen door later that afternoon nearly made him spit out his iced tea, and Oliver was still choking when he got to the window. He brushed back the lace curtain to see Meg standing outside, her arms hanging limp at her sides, her face a tight grimace of all things painful. He was sure everything ached.

Opening the door, he leaned an arm against the frame. "Meg."

"Oliver." She matched his tone, her eyes holding a bit of reserve. "Is Mama Potts around?"

He shook his head, squinting into the sagging sun. "She had to run over to the studio. Her kiln is in a bad way again."

"Oh." Meg hung her head, the lines around her mouth deepening.

"You want to come in? I think she left the muscle cream on the table."

For a moment he could have sworn she was going to say she'd wait outside. But finally she said, "All right."

A gentleman probably would have held the door open for her to lead the way in, but he figured it might take a few weeks for her to make it inside, so he marched into the kitchen and stared at the empty table. Putting his hands on his hips, he did a slow turn until he spied a small glass jar on the white-tiled counter. Its pale contents and metal lid would have made most people think it was some sort of lemon jam. No one would make that mistake again if they spread it on toast.

Not that he'd done that more than once.

With her slow stride, Meg made it into the house just as he picked up the cream and held it out to her. "This should do the trick. I use it the first week of most seasons until my muscles remember what it's like."

Her gaze raised from the jar, her chin still low. "You use this?"

"Sure." He crossed his arms and felt the familiar pull of his back muscles relearning their job. He stayed active all year long, but the first week of the season was the hardest. He'd given her everything to prepare except Mama Potts's famous muscle relief cream. "Figured you could use the same. After all, I'm using that face cream." He rubbed a hand over his cheek. "Makes my skin feel brand-new."

She laughed, a stiff chuckle that kept everything safely in place. But still, he'd made her laugh. That was twice in a month. It wasn't exactly a trend, but he'd take what he could get and be thankful for it.

Meg held up the jar. "I tried ice packs and heating pads. I even turned on my electric blanket and wrapped up in it like a cocoon. I still hurt. Everywhere."

"I know the feeling. This'll work."

"Tell Mama Potts thanks." She unscrewed the lid and lifted it to her nose, inhaling deeply. She sighed.

He knew that feeling too, like somehow just the smell of eucalyptus and mint could unwind a body's insides. The scent alone was a relief.

He didn't have another second to dwell on the familiar aroma as the jar slipped from her loosened grip. She reached for it but jerked to a stop halfway, and he dove to catch it before it could shatter on the floor. Grabbing it just in time, he held it up with pride.

Meg was hunched over, hands on her knees, breathing in shallow gasps.

"Whoa. Meg. You all right?"

"Sure." Only she didn't look up, couldn't seem to move.

He set the jar on the table and shuffled her into a chair. When she finally looked at him, her face was red, her eyes glassy.

"Tell me it gets better," she whispered.

"It will. I promise." He nodded toward the still-uncovered jar. "Do you have someone to help you get your back and shoulders and all the hard-to-reach places?"

"Of course . . ." Her voice trailed off. "Actually, no."

Her mom and dad were in Toronto, and Meg lived alone. He knew that and shouldn't have asked.

"Let me help."

Her eyes flashed bright, then grew stern. "No thanks. I'll manage."

"You can barely move. Don't be stubborn."

This time her eyes flashed with fire. "I'm not being stubborn."

"Really. And what would you call this?" He pointed at her stiff chin and rigid neck. "Are you being relaxed and casual?"

"Kind of." She grimaced.

"Okay, so what happens when you get home and can't reach the part of your back between your shoulder blades?"

"It doesn't hurt."

"Liar," he said on a laugh.

"Fine. Okay. Help me. Please." She nudged the jar toward him, and it stopped in a patch of sunlight filtering through the kitchen window.

"If you insist. But just know, you're going to have to wash these clothes and your sheets twice to get the smell out."

"Will I be able to lift my sheets?"

He scooted his chair behind hers and pulled the cream to within arm's reach. "Yep."

"Then do it."

He dipped his fingertips into the translucent cream and scooped up a small amount before rubbing his hands together. It was cool on his skin, tingling and soothing. It made him feel both alive and tranquil in the same breath. He stared at her pale back for a long moment, noticing the freckles between the skinny straps of her dress, watching the shallow rise and fall of her breathing.

Then he pressed his hand to the back of her shoulder, and the whole world was on fire.

Her skin was taut and strong and smoother than her face cream. And he was touching her.

That wasn't the point. It couldn't be the point. But somehow it was.

He tried to focus on the motion, watching as his thumbs ran the length of her shoulders and then glided up the sides of her neck. He reached to the outline of her dress but never further, rubbing the magic cream until it disappeared into her skin. Her chin dipped forward. He stole another scoop of cream and massaged it into her upper back, right where he knew it hurt the most. Around and around he rubbed it in, pressing into the knots until they released their hold.

Meg gasped and then let out a soft hum of approval.

Goose bumps broke out across his arms. He closed his eyes. Fought for a breath.

Only then did he realize his nose was nearly pressed to the nape of her neck, buried in the sweet smell of her. She'd left her hair in a knot on top of her head, and the little hairs that hadn't stayed secure in the band tickled his face, whispered soft promises, and put terrible ideas in his head.

Like, would it really be so bad to press his lips right there?

———

*"Let me help."*

It was all so innocuous, so simple. He was just going to help her reach the places that she couldn't. But *this* was not harmless.

Everything inside of her quivered as his enormous hands kneaded and rubbed what ached. It was like he knew the sore spots, knew where to press to make her let go of control. His fingers spanned nearly all the way across her back, somehow able to work both her shoulders and the spot in the center of her back at the same time. Strong and agile.

The pressure of his thumbs forced her to let out the breath she'd been holding. It came out on a moan.

Her ears burned, her face flashing hot. At least Oliver couldn't see her expression. And he didn't stop, so maybe he hadn't heard. Or maybe he just understood.

She bit her lip to keep any other potentially embarrassing sounds from escaping. But it didn't do much in the way of wrangling her wayward musings.

Mama Potts's cream made her tingle everywhere he touched her. But another thought snuck in. That sensation might have nothing to do with the cream and everything to do with the man rubbing it in. It was too terrible to imagine.

He worked first her right arm and then her left, his body warm at her back. He was always warm. Even on chilly mornings before the sun came up, she could sense him on the boat. A beacon. A fire.

That's what his touch felt like. A warm fire on a cool night, a lazy Sunday after a long week.

No. That wasn't right. She wasn't supposed to think that.

He was not a warm fire. He was four o'clock alarms and lobster pinches.

His thumb hit a twinge by her left shoulder blade, and she nearly whimpered.

So. Good.

She was going to have to pay someone to do this next time. No way could she rely on Oliver Ross to massage her unmoving muscles. But for this minute, she couldn't bring herself to pull away. His fingers were strong, concentrated. He honed in on the knots in her back like he had a radar right to every single one of them. And when he pressed into them, she felt like a limp noodle. Even worse, she couldn't bring herself to care.

His hands dipped from her shoulder toward her elbow, well into the places she could reach on her own. A tiny voice in her mind told her to pull away, to grab the cream and go home.

She told it to shut up.

This was heaven, and his fingers worked miracles.

But suddenly they stopped. She wanted to whimper. Couldn't he keep going? Just another hour. That was all she asked.

His chair scraped along the floor until he could have looked directly into her face. He didn't though. Thank goodness. Head bowed, hair like a curtain over his cheeks, he tugged on her right arm. She gave it willingly, and he pulled and kneaded the muscles from her elbow to her wrist and back again.

When he wrapped her hand in both of his, her mouth went dry, and she could only focus on their connection. His hands were tan and strong, his knuckles thick but nimble. Her fingers looked tiny in comparison, fragile and weak. But when he pressed his thumb against her palm, rolling it back and forth, she felt like she could take on the world.

He slipped his fingers between hers, squeezing their hands together palm to palm, and her gaze shot up. He was already watching her, and their eyes locked.

Something like lightning zipped between them, up her arm and straight to the base of her neck. She tried to swallow but couldn't manage against the cotton in her throat.

His pale blue eyes flashed so bright that she could see a darker ring of blue around his irises, and his Adam's apple bobbed. If the swath of black hair sweeping over his forehead and across his left eye bothered him, he didn't show it. He didn't even flinch. He just kept staring at her, locking her into place.

And making her stomach dive straight through the floor.

Everything inside her screamed that this was wrong. Whatever she was feeling wasn't how it was supposed to be. Sure, she hadn't wanted to strangle him in a while. Maybe they'd even developed an uncontentious coworking relationship. Perhaps they were even approaching mutualism—each benefiting from the other. But this . . . awareness . . .

She squinted at him, trying to block out the curve of his broad shoulders.

Nope. She did not like this one bit.

But her traitorous hand didn't budge.

At least not until someone cleared their throat.

Meg jumped to her feet like she'd sat on a firecracker, her entire body at once languid and on high alert as she spun toward the kitchen door.

Violet stood there, one hip cocked to the side, her hand resting on her waist. "So . . ." She dragged the word out, filling the silence. "What have you kids been up to? It smells like . . ." Her nose twitched and her lip curled.

"I have to go." Meg hobbled for the exit, stopping only when Oliver called her name.

"Forget something?" He held up the jar of muscle cream.

She didn't reply, only stumbled back to him, took the miracle in a jar, and moved as fast as her stiff legs could carry her into the fresh evening air. The door wasn't quite closed behind her before Violet began teasing Oliver, her voice singsonging a childhood taunt.

"It wasn't like that," he said. "I was just helping a friend."

Sagging against the pale exterior wall of the cottage, Meg sighed.

Right. Friends. Barely friends. Definitely *just* friends.

# twelve

*Be cool. Be cool.*

Meg felt like one of her students before a big presentation. Only she wasn't facing down a classroom full of her peers. She was going to have to face Oliver after all that had happened the day before.

She hadn't meant for it to go that far. Clearly not.

And really, nothing had happened.

Except for the terrible ache in the pit of her stomach every time she remembered how she'd very nearly thrown herself at him. How could she not when he'd basically given her the ability to move again? It wasn't like she'd tried to kiss him or anything. But those sounds she'd made. Ugh.

A monster in her belly tried to claw its way out, and she clamped a hand on her stomach as she slammed her car door shut with her hip. Leaning against the side of the car in the early morning air, she took three deep breaths. She could do this. She didn't have much of a choice.

Except running away.

Which felt like an entirely logical response at the moment.

There were so many pros to leaving. No more 4:30 alarms. No more fear of getting seasick, even with the patches. And no more Oliver Ross.

She didn't have a job to leave, other than her dad's business. And Oliver was more than capable of running it on his own. Sure, he'd get the whole thing at the end of the season. But she wouldn't even be around to care.

Except she did care.

The monster inside stopped clawing and started gnawing, persistent. She couldn't walk away from this business, from her dad's legacy, from her mom's stability. Even if it meant seeing Oliver every day after such utter embarrassment.

And it did.

"Morning, kid."

Meg jumped at the greeting, forcing a smile into place despite the hour and the direction of her thoughts. "Morning, Kyle."

He lumbered toward her from the opposite side of the small gravel parking lot, his gait stiff but familiar. "How you doing today?"

She nodded as he reached her side and touched her shoulder. His hands were the size of bear paws, and he had enough potential energy to level her. But his grip was surprisingly gentle, fatherly, as he pulled one of the coffee cups from the paper tray she'd set on her car's roof.

"I'm okay. How about you?"

"I get to work a boat with a good captain and the prettiest deckhand I've ever seen. I'd say I'm better than I deserve."

Her face flushed at the compliment, but the heat faded when she realized that he'd again called Oliver the captain. "Kyle, can I ask you something?"

He nodded and motioned for them to walk toward the trail that led around the shanties, their bright colors muted in the dim morning.

She followed a step behind as she tried to frame the question. "Were you upset that my dad didn't offer to sell to you?"

Kyle's laugh was rich and booming, bouncing through the still of the morning and echoing off the shanties and shacks. "Would you have tried to take it off my hands if he had?"

"Probably not." Like a kick to the shin, the truth hit her. There was no *probably* about it. "But aren't you angry? I mean, Oliver's only been working for my dad for a few years. And . . . and . . . how can Dad be sure he'll carry on the legacy well?"

Kyle stopped walking, the toe of his boot digging into the ground as he scratched at his short hair. "Well, your dad did talk to me about his plans a while ago. Said he was thinking of selling." His lips twitched. "Guess he never really offered it to me, but that was my chance to speak up. And I didn't. Know why?"

She shook her head.

"I didn't want it. Still don't." He took off for the dock, leaving her behind.

She raced to catch up, big boots clomping after him. "But why? It's a good business."

"It is. It's also a lot of work. I like to work hard, but I don't particularly want to be responsible for every trap, every line, and every government regulation." He looked ready to spit on that last one. "You know that he has to report every lost trap and overboard tool? He has to worry about the weather and the environment, lobster prices and the economy. That's too many worries for this old mind. I'm just grateful to have a job and a captain who worries about them so I don't have to."

Meg stopped twenty meters from *Just a Pinch* and worked through what he'd just said. All of those worries, all of those concerns. Oliver was carrying them. They were supposed to be dividing the work equally. But she hadn't taken on anything more than the boat work, and he hadn't said a word about the other things.

She marched up to the boat, climbed on board, and walked right up to Oliver. "I want to do more."

He turned slowly, his eyes narrow and gaze heavy as he plucked the coffee cup from the tray.

She immediately remembered why she had seriously considered making a run from this whole island. And why—given their last encounter—her words could have been taken poorly.

His brows rose slowly, but the rest of his features remained still. His slightly off-balance but strong features—the crook in his nose and wide mouth. All these separate pieces, which on their own were imperfect, came into focus. And the thing she'd been refusing to admit to herself became clear.

Oliver had turned into an attractive man. A very attractive man.

But there was a fight in his eyes, an easy-to-read battle over how to respond to her.

She shoved away her other thoughts and rushed to beat him to it. "I mean with the business. I want to do more with the business. You're doing all sorts of things that I'm not."

He glanced toward the steering wheel, a new confusion filling his eyes. "Like navigating?"

"Yes." She bit her tongue. Stupid. She wasn't licensed to drive a boat. "No."

He tried again. "Like baiting the traps?"

"No." She shook her head so hard that her headband nearly came loose. "Not the bait." She could smell it already, even with a lid on the bucket. Or maybe that was the scent of fish parts seared on the back of her nose for all eternity. She was happy to leave the baiting to Oliver and sometimes Kyle. "Like the stuff off the boat. Like working with the shore buyers or the . . . I don't know . . ." Her eyes darted in Kyle's direction at the stern. He hadn't bothered to even try to mask his amusement. "Like the government?"

"You think I spend a lot of time with the general assembly at Province House?" He laughed and straightened an imaginary tie. He dropped his hands over his gray sweatshirt, a string of holes in the collar and another at the hem. "Think I'd fit in there?"

"No."

"Well, you don't have to be so blunt about it."

Her stomach dropped through the bottom of the boat. "I'm sorry. I-I-I didn't mean—"

He stopped her with a wink and a raised hand. "Relax, Meg. I'm only teasing."

She sighed. Of course he was teasing. And if she'd had any sort of bearings, she'd have known that immediately.

"I'd have found a different line of work if there was any chance I'd have to buy a suit."

"But what about . . ." Again she looked to Kyle, who was barely holding back the laughter shaking his shoulders. "Regulations?"

"I read them every year. Same as every other fisherman on the island. If the PEI Fisherman's Association makes a bad policy, I'll do the same as everyone else. I'll put on my Sunday best and go to a meeting to speak up."

"You would?"

His chin ticked to the right. "Of course I would. Without these waters, we'd all be out of a job, eh?"

She nodded slowly, taking in the truth. He'd become a man she barely recognized, regularly surprising her. And making her surprise herself.

Strangely, though, she'd forgotten for a few minutes how awkward this interaction should have been. But it wasn't. Not when he had a disarming habit of putting her at ease. Or at least distracting her from what had preoccupied her before.

"I want to help."

He shook his head. "I've got it covered."

She grabbed his forearm, and his muscles twitched beneath her grasp. But she didn't let go. "I'm not asking. This is an even deal. I'll do my share."

He looked into her eyes for so long she was pretty sure he could see her soul. She stared right back at him.

Finally he nodded. "All right. Next time there's an extra-fishing situation, you're on it."

She nodded curtly, let go of his arm, and said, "It's getting late. Shouldn't we be on the water by now?"

He chuckled and mumbled something about who was the boss as he pointed them toward the open water and another day of fishing.

---

Morning had a terrible habit of arriving too early on a lobster boat. And the earlier it arrived, the earlier the nights did too.

Meg could barely keep her eyes open past eight most nights. And she'd fallen asleep on the sofa in her little apartment yet again. But an insistent chirp tugged her toward consciousness. She swatted at the phone at her side. Just five more minutes.

Cracking one eye open, she saw her dad's face across the screen. Grabbing it, she answered with one swipe of her thumb. "Dad?"

"Hi, kid."

"Dad." She sighed his name, the only word she seemed capable of getting out. She wanted to ask about her mom, but the words lodged somewhere in the back of her throat. "How's the *Pinch*?"

Seriously? He'd been in another time zone and meeting with doctors for almost a week, and all he could do was ask about his silly boat. No, not silly. It had been his livelihood, his trusted friend, for more than thirty years. And right about now it was probably the only thing that didn't feel like it was falling apart.

"She's good. Still floating."

He let out a booming laugh. "Glad to hear that. I wondered if you and Oliver would go at it and send her to the bottom of the bay."

"No. I've been a model team member."

"And Oliver?"

She wanted to rat him out. Problem was, he didn't have a habit of making mistakes. And he was more than a little good at his job. "He's been . . . surprisingly helpful."

"Helpful?" His tone turned skeptical. "How?"

"Oh, you know. Finding work clothes, seasickness patches, his mom's magic muscle cream."

Her dad sighed. "Megan, I should have thought of those things."

"No. It's all right." She rushed to reassure him. A heaping

dollop of guilt was the very last thing he needed. "I've been fine. He's showed me all the secrets. That's why you set me and Oliver up to work together. Right?"

He didn't respond right away. "I didn't even think about what a toll this would take on you. You must be exhausted."

"Not at all." Well, that was a lie. There had to be some sort of middle ground that was honest but not quite the brutal exhaustion that made it hard to lift her arms or carry a takeout tray from Carrie's. "I mean, it's hard work, and I'm sleeping really well. But I'm okay. And Mama Potts's muscle cream . . ."

"It's magic, isn't it?"

"You knew about it?"

He sighed again. "It should have been the first thing I gave you."

"She took care of me. She saw me at church. I must have had all the telltale signs of a new fisherman."

He chuckled. "Barely able to walk. Stiff movements. Hunched shoulders."

"Exactly."

They fell into silence. Meg knew she needed to ask the question that hadn't been addressed, but she couldn't bring her mouth to speak it. If it was good news, surely her dad would have started with that. And if it was anything else, she didn't want to hear it.

"I'm sorry I didn't do better by you, kid. I'm so proud of you, and I should have—"

"No, Dad. Don't worry, you left me with Oliver and Kyle. You left me in good hands." As the words sailed out, she realized she meant them.

"And you and Oliver?"

She rubbed her eyes, clearing the last bit of her nap from them. "We're . . . we're . . ." She wanted to say they were getting along. Despite herself. Despite the bitterness that she'd carried for so many years. She wanted him to be every bit the angry, unrepentant teenager. She wanted to have every reason to hold on to the hurt. Because at least that gave her something to hold on to.

He just wasn't that guy anymore.

"It physically hurts me to say this," she said, pressing a hand to the middle of her chest, where it burned. "But he's a really decent guy."

Her dad let out a sad chuckle. "But you still want the business?"

"What I want is to not lose our family's history. And maybe our future."

"Whoa. That's pretty deep for a Monday night."

It was her turn to laugh, this one filled with real humor. "I can't help but feel like everything's changing, and I want to hold on to something stable."

"Oh, sweetheart. Everything is changing. But the truth is that lobster fishing isn't stable. Never has been. It ebbs and flows more than the tides. One year might be a good haul, the next enough to put a business under. In thirty years captaining the boat, I never once had a sure season."

Meg leaned forward, pulling the red fuzzy throw blanket from the back of the cushion around her shoulders and hugging it beneath her chin. "But it always felt so certain. You went out every morning, worked so hard. Tucked me in every night. Like clockwork."

"You must have been six or seven the year we almost had to sell the whole thing. We had a terrible haul. Couldn't catch a hard shell to save my life, and even if I had, the price had fallen to next to nothing." His voice dropped, pain lacing his words. "I barely made enough that season to pay Kyle and had to cut my other deckhand. Thought we were going to lose the house and all of it."

Meg swallowed the lump in her throat, trying to remember if she'd felt her dad's stress or her mom's worry. But even in those lean years, she'd known nothing but love. They'd sheltered her. She could do nothing but the same. She just had to know what she was sheltering them from.

"Dad, what did the doctors say?"

He coughed and then paused for a beat. "They're pretty sure it's something called"—papers rustled, and she was sure he was reading it back to her—"progressive supranuclear palsy. PSP."

A lump materialized in her throat in the time it took him to say three little letters. "I've never even heard of that. What does that . . . mean?"

"The doctor said there's some damage to nerve cells?" He said it almost like a question. Like he didn't want it to be true or he couldn't remember what was real.

"What caused it?"

He sighed. Springs on the other end of the line squeaked, and she could picture him sitting on the corner of the bed, resting his elbow on his knee and his head in his hand. "They don't know."

"But there must be some sort of cure or treatment, right? They have some ideas for helping her?"

He was silent for too long. Plenty long enough for her to know that answer.

"Dad, she's going to get better. She can beat this thing."

Her mom was strong. She'd had to be to face PEI winters and summers as a lobster widow. She'd taught Sunday school for years and never complained when the kids were bratty. She'd cared for their family and made Meg believe there wasn't anything she couldn't do.

Yet the playback of the last few years flashed through her mind. Every stumbled step. Every fall. Every time her mom couldn't make eye contact or find the word she wanted to use. The stiffness in her arms that made lifting a fork to her mouth a trial.

She knew the truth before her dad said it.

"It's progressive, sweetie. It's going to get worse. She's going to get weaker and lose even more control. They tested her balance and vision and . . . it's not good."

"Is it—" Her throat closed, and she couldn't get a sound out. Maybe if she didn't ask, she wouldn't ever have to know.

Her dad knew what she meant, because he'd been asking the same questions. "*It's* not terminal."

The disease wasn't, but something would be. It was clear in the words he didn't say. Meg's mom was only going to get worse, and eventually there would be a complication, a symptom, that would take her away. She was dying.

Unacceptable.

"There are other doctors we can see. A second or third opinion. There has to be something more we can do."

"We're going to bring her home and love her with everything we've got."

Meg didn't hear anything after that. The ringing in her ears and stinging in her eyes shut out everything else. Everything had changed, and she didn't have anything left to hold on to.

"You're here early." Oliver smiled in Meg's direction as he climbed aboard the boat and clapped his hands together against the blustery winds.

He was always the first to arrive, Meg generally dragging in a few minutes after 4:30. She wasn't particularly chatty on most mornings, but she outright ignored him on this one.

"Sure is cold out today."

She shot him a narrowed gaze. "You think?" Her tone was sharp, slicing, and altogether foreign. Especially after Sunday afternoon. He was pretty sure they'd finally put the past behind them. Maybe not best friends, but she'd become less hostile. At least since she'd sent him swimming for no good reason.

"Whoa." He held up his hands in surrender. "Someone get up on the wrong side of the bed?"

She dunked a mop into a bucket of soapy water and sloshed it onto the deck—even though they'd thoroughly cleaned the *Pinch* after dropping off their catch the morning before. "What side of the bed I get up on is none of your business."

He tried for a soothing smile. "I just meant . . ." Well, he wasn't entirely sure what he meant, but as he looked closer at her, he wondered if she'd slept at all. Dark circles shadowed her eyes, which were rimmed in red. The tip of her nose was pink, though that could be from the cold weather. And a perpetual frown tugged at the corners of her mouth.

He reached to touch her arm, but she jerked away from him. "Meg? What's wrong?"

"Nothing. Just here to do my job and then go home."

Apparently they were right back in the past.

Oliver scrubbed his hands down his face, clawing at his eyes. They'd been making progress. "So you're mad at me again?"

"You know that I am." She didn't even look up as she splashed water on his boot.

"I know that you *were* mad at me, but . . ." He stepped away from the wild arch of her mop. "I thought maybe, after everything that's happened, I thought maybe we were . . ."

She looked up then, just long enough for him to see the flare in her eyes that suggested her mind had wandered to someplace beyond his intent.

"Friends," he rushed to clarify. "I thought we were becoming friends."

Not that he hadn't thought about what it would be like to kiss her. But only once. Maybe twice.

She began to shake her head—her long braid flopping over her shoulder, loose strands whipping across her face—but stopped midway through the motion. Her brows narrowed, her whole face scrunching up. She turned her face toward the dock light, and only then did he notice that her eyes weren't just rimmed with red.

"Meg?"

"What?" Her word snapped sharper than a lobster claw, but the immediate jerk of her shoulders confessed that she wished she hadn't been quite so harsh.

He was tempted to return to the dock and wait for Kyle to arrive, but he couldn't ignore the tiniest crack in her shell. Sliding to her side, he towered over her but didn't touch her. "Meg?"

She sighed this time before responding. "What?"

"Why are you mad at me?"

"You know why." Her gaze never wavered from the deck beneath his feet.

"Why are you *still* mad at me?" Clearly something had come up to remind her of that awful day, the moment he'd lashed out with all of his own anger.

She poked the center of his chest. "It's none. Of. Your. Business." Then she crumbled like her bones were giving up. Her face twisted, and she squeezed her eyes against something he couldn't see.

The wind picked at her hair, taking first one strand and then a second, playing with them, brushing them against her cheek. Oliver had the strangest urge to tuck them behind her ear, to brush his thumb against the smooth line of her cheek and move them into their place. Maybe it was all he could set to rights in her life. But it was something.

She beat him to it, shoving her fingers through her hair, sliding stray pieces into her messy braid. She might have known he was about to touch her. Or perhaps she just needed something to break the tension between them.

There was always tension, but this was different. He couldn't put his finger on exactly why. Maybe it was because for the first time, he wanted to fix whatever was wrong for her sake.

Before—when they'd first started working together—he'd just been trying to quash the animosity, to make the situation manageable. To make sure Whitaker knew he was the best man for the job. Oliver still wanted that with every fiber of his being. And he wanted Meg to never hate him again. If it wasn't too much to ask, maybe he even wanted her to like him.

But since he didn't have a time machine and she probably wouldn't be going to Yale on some science scholarship anytime soon, he'd have to settle for getting her to accept his apology.

Risking her wrath, he stepped so close he could hear her harsh breaths and see her fists trembling around the mop handle. She stiffened immediately.

"I'm really sorry that I ruined your robot."

"It wasn't just a robot." Her gaze fixed past his shoulder, somewhere near where the sun would soon crest the horizon, splitting the fog and heralding the morning.

His gut twisted. "I'm sorry I ruined your life. Can you . . ." It was stupid to ask, but he had to try. "Could you ever forgive me?"

Her eyes swung back toward his face, meeting his gaze. The fire was gone, replaced by something deep and volatile, thick black clouds hanging heavy. "I don't think so."

"Why?"

She didn't pause before spitting out her answer. "My mom is dying. I have to be mad at someone."

# thirteen

Meg couldn't believe the words that had flown out of her mouth—or how brutally honest they'd been. Her knees gave out, and the mop fell from her grip, clattering to the deck. She was sure she would follow it all the way down. Until big arms scooped her up and pulled her against a wall of soft knit.

She wanted to push him away, to never let him see her pain. But the moment her hands reached his chest, she collapsed into him, her face buried in the center of his sweatshirt.

His arms snaked around her back, holding her close. Holding her upright. The only thing stable in the whole crazy-awful day.

Or two days?

Time ran together, lines on the calendar blurring. There was only the time before—when she had hope—and the after. Her dad's words repeated in her mind. *"It's going to get worse."*

The tears started afresh, washing down her cheeks and

soaking into his sweatshirt. She hiccupped a sob that was muffled against him. Still he held her. He didn't move, save for one thumb that made a slow circle across the middle of her back. He smelled of laundry detergent and mountain spring soap. And he felt like an unmoving rock even on a moving boat.

He didn't tell her to stop or to quiet down. He didn't twitch with an eagerness to let her go. He only held her.

Which made her cry even harder. When she tucked her hands beneath her chin and curled into him, the wind couldn't get her. But the storm was inside.

"I'm so-orry." Her voice broke, but it was so muffled against his sweatshirt that maybe he hadn't heard.

His hand spread wide across her back, his fingers long and strong and digging in just enough to tell her he didn't mind holding her as she fell apart.

"I didn't mean . . ." To snap at him? To lash out at him? To hold her grudge for so many years? Yes, all of that. But how could she explain when she couldn't breathe without the air catching in her throat? When every word physically hurt?

Slowly he unwound his arms, and she clung to his sweatshirt. If he pushed her away, he'd see her face streaked with tears, red and splotchy. Eyes squinted with pain and lips pinched in grief. He'd see the very worst version of her.

But maybe that wasn't really the worst. The harsh words and stinging vitriol weren't who she wanted to be. The version of her that clung to old resentments was so much worse.

Even so, she didn't want him to see her like this just now. But when he raised his hands, he didn't push her away. Instead, he cupped her cheeks and smoothed back her hair, whispering softly, "You don't have to say anything right now."

It wasn't a pardon for her sins but a reprieve for an aching heart.

Oliver rested his cheek on top of her head, his thumbs trailing back and forth across her cheeks, wiping away the evidence of her meltdown and making something inside her chest unwind until she could take a deep, unstilted breath.

She risked a step away, and he dropped his hands to his sides, a gentle flex to his fingers before they relaxed. But that was as far as her gaze would go. She couldn't meet his. Not yet.

"Um . . ." He shuffled his feet, and she knew what he wanted to ask.

She also knew her own limits, so she said only, "Mom and Dad are coming home."

"All right. Are you up for going out today? Kyle and I can—"

Her gaze flashed up to meet his then, his blue eyes warm and knowing. "I want to."

"All right." He nodded quickly. No argument. She had the sudden urge to hug him.

Boots stomped on the end of the dock, and they both blinked, their solitude broken. "Thank you," she whispered as slamming car doors and boat engines filled the morning.

He merely nodded before picking up her mop and bucket and preparing for the day ahead.

Meg had never been inside the church when it was quiet. Every Sunday morning the sanctuary nearly vibrated with voices that reached to the top of the white steeple. Children's laughter and shushing mothers. Toes tapping and hymns ringing.

As she snuck into the old building, she heard none of that. There was only the evening light shining through the western windows, illuminating dust motes in beams that fell across worn wooden pews. A rough-hewn cross hung at the front, over a simple podium made of the same boards as the rest of the floor. Not ornate. Not modern. But her sanctuary nonetheless.

She made a move to sit in the last pew, but her feet wouldn't let her. They knew the way they'd walked every Sunday for most of her life. So she tiptoed down the aisle and slipped into the seat she'd always known. Oliver wasn't behind her. Not that she'd mind it if he was.

He'd been by her side the entire day. Not hovering, just . . . there. Steady. Solid. He'd held her and let her soak through his sweatshirt. And he'd said absolutely nothing to Kyle, who had squeezed her arm, asked if she was all right, and taken her at her word that she was.

Oliver knew the truth. She was far from all right.

Hanging her head, she stared at her hands folded in her lap. They were tan and rough, and she ran a thumb over the calluses at the base of her fingers. They had changed too. Why shouldn't the rest of her world tilt on its axis?

"Meg? Is that you?"

She jerked up, straightening her shoulders and turning toward the familiar voice. Pastor Dell's words were always gentle but filled with conviction.

"I didn't expect to see you here this evening. I was just about to go home." Despite his words, he strolled from the back of the room toward where she sat, his dark brown gaze taking a quick survey of her.

What he saw couldn't be impressive. She hadn't showered

or changed, and she ran her hands quickly over her wind-blown hair. There was nothing to be done about it. Or about the baggy sweatshirt stained with sea and sweat and what she'd termed lobster juice. Oh, she so did not belong there.

Pushing herself up faster than her aching muscles liked, she said, "I'm sorry. I shouldn't be here. I'll go."

He'd reached her by then and put a gentle hand on her shoulder. It was too much weight to bear, and she fell back into her seat, into the grooves she'd worn into this very spot.

"Not at all. Stay as long as you like."

He sat in the row in front of her, propping his knee on the seat beside him and his arm on the back of the bench. He didn't ask if he could sit with her, he just did.

"I like to sit in here when it's quiet too," he said. "It gives my mind space to think." He stared up at the open beams of the ceiling, a soft smile in place. He looked like he belonged in this place, with his glasses perched high on his nose and a knit cardigan sweater covering his sloping shoulders. He was soft and kind, but she couldn't ever remember talking to him alone before. That didn't stop her.

"My mom is sick."

His smile flickered and went out. "Your dad called and told me they were going to be out of town for a few weeks. That he was taking her to Toronto for testing. Have you heard from them?"

She nodded, but when she opened her mouth, all that came out was a near sob. Her lower lip quivered, and she couldn't make the sounds she wanted. Her mind played on repeat the conversation with her dad.

Had it only been the night before? Had she only been carrying this weight for less than a day? It felt like a steel plate had been welded to her chest, permanently impeding every breath, making every step more difficult.

Suddenly her eyes flooded, and she dipped her head, pressing the heels of her palms against the deluge. "I'm sorry," she managed. She felt her entire body tense, knowing he was going to pat her shoulder and say, "There, there" or something equally ineffective.

But he didn't. He didn't reach for her or move in any way. His breathing continued softly, and he didn't seem put off by her tears.

"Grief is such a strange thing. It ebbs and flows like the tide, lying in wait only to roll in when we least expect it. I suspect that's how it'll be with you and your mom for a while." He paused. "A long while. And while it's fresh, the tide won't go out. It'll sit and stir on the beach, always there. Always evident."

When she peeked up, he was looking at his folded hands, so she stared at him through watery eyes. "But I have to get it under control."

"I'm not sure that's up to you at the moment."

"I have to be strong."

His gaze swung to her then. "Well, who said that?"

"I mean, I need to be there for my dad. I have to help care for my mom. I can't be . . . I can't be another drain on them. Not when Mom is . . . Well, this disease is just going to steal more of her every day."

Pastor Dell's eyes narrowed, intense and focused. She brushed some imaginary lint off her sleeve to have anything else to look at.

"Whatever made you think that grieving with them would be a drain?"

Without an answer, she shrugged. It had always been the truth. She could give up her education. She could move and care for them. She could even carry on the business for them. But she couldn't let them see her tears. She couldn't add one more hurt to their already heavy loads.

"You know, people come to tell me their heartaches. A lot. Broken marriages. Addictions. Prodigal kids." He sighed as though recalling the worst of the stories he'd heard. "I do my best to point them to the encouragement found in God's Word. I spent years memorizing Scriptures for just those moments. I've got hope and encouragement ready for every situation." He rapped his fist twice against the back of the pew. "But sometimes in the midst of the worst pain, it's hard to hear the truth. Sometimes when the pain is too loud, all we can hear is the person crying with us. And that sounds a lot like love."

———

By the time they'd unloaded their catch with the shore buyer, cleaned the boat, and prepared for the next morning, Oliver could barely drag himself through the kitchen door. The smell of Mama Potts's roast filled the entire house and made his stomach growl. But he was pretty sure he couldn't raise a fork to his mouth, even for the tender meat.

"Hurry and wash up. Supper's almost ready," Mama Potts called from the kitchen before he'd even managed to toe off his boots. They clomped to the floor, and he was tempted to follow them, instead crashing a shoulder against the white shiplap wall.

"You trying to tear my house down?" she yelled.

"No." It was the extent of his vocabulary and the length

of his stamina. For the life of him, he didn't know why. He'd worked hard every day of his life. He hadn't gotten up any earlier than usual. And he'd eaten every single one of the snacks in his pockets.

The only thing that had changed was Meg. But it didn't make sense that holding her while she drained every last tear onto his sweatshirt would leave him so depleted. He hadn't minded the holding her part. And it was past time he was honest with himself. He actually rather liked holding her.

Sure, she was a little prickly sometimes. But now he could see it all for what it was. A shield. An empty attempt to protect herself from pain.

But the pain had gotten in anyway.

He felt it too. To a much lesser degree, he was certain. But that pinch in his chest every time he thought of Mrs. Whitaker hadn't gone away. And every time he wondered what Whitaker would do without the love of his life, he had to swallow a lump in his throat.

"Ollie?"

He cringed, still sagging against the wall. His mom hadn't called him that in twenty years, and he wished he could wipe it from her memory.

"I'll be right there." But he was stuck in the short hall, memories of Mrs. Whitaker splashing across his mind's eye. At church holding Whitaker's hand. Inviting him to join them for supper after a day on the boat. Delivering groceries and homemade bread to Mrs. Finnick's basement, where he'd lived with his mom and Levi after the eviction. Mrs. Whitaker had patted his cheek, and he'd nearly jumped out of his skin, craving her kindness.

He'd destroyed her daughter's dreams the next day.

Yeah, he knew a thing or two about shields and armor and how they didn't work.

In her favorite gingham apron, his mom strolled around the corner, a giant two-pronged fork raised in one hand and a knife in the other.

He held up his hands in surrender.

"Hon, are you feeling all right?"

He nodded, but his swallow stuck in the back of his throat.

"Are you sure?"

"Just tired." He pushed himself up, ignoring the way the room spun. But he couldn't cover the stumble in his steps.

She rushed toward him, dropping the knife, which clattered to the floor. "Levi," she yelled over her shoulder as she wedged herself under his arm. He had almost a foot on her, but her arms squeezed him like he was still a child.

"I'm fine, Mom. Just tired." His stomach sloshed back and forth, bile rising in the back of his throat. Maybe he wasn't just tired.

His brother arrived as silently as he lived. Without a word Levi wedged himself under Oliver's other arm and basically carried him toward the living room. Oliver shuffled his feet along and let them propel him right onto the sofa. His head fell to the thin pink pillow against the armrest, and his stockinged feet hung off the other end. He closed his eyes for half a second before his mom pressed her palm to his forehead.

"You have a fever."

"No, I don't." The shiver that raced down his spine might have had something else to say.

"Don't argue with me, boy."

He cracked open one burning eye to see her standing right

before him, hands on her hips and a pinched line where her smile usually was.

Her nose wrinkled. "And you smell like sour fish."

"Smell like har' work and a job," he slurred.

"You can't . . ."

He was too tired to argue anymore, so he closed his eyes and the rest of the world disappeared.

⁓

When Oliver woke, the sun had set, and the only light came from the lamp in the corner of the room. A heavy quilt covered him, and he shoved it over the back of the sofa, sweat sticking to his face and down his back. He wanted to rip off his extra sweatshirt, but that required moving more than he was willing to at the moment. And despite the absence of the scent of supper, his stomach growled.

"Hey there, sleepy."

He opened one eye and peered across the room to find his mom rocking in her oversized recliner, an open paperback in her hands.

"Hey." He sounded like a grouchy monster from a kids' show.

"So that's your new plan for winning arguments. You just pass out on me." She closed her book and shot him an affectionate glare.

"I'm sorry." His voice cracked, and he pushed himself up. The room took a quick spin, so he plopped himself right back onto the pillow.

"Are you hungry?"

He grunted, and she got up, returning a few minutes later with a bowl of steaming soup and a glass of water. Perfect.

Only he wasn't sure he could eat the soup lying down. And lapping the water like a dog wasn't going to work either.

He pushed himself up again, slowly this time, giving himself a moment to acclimate. Then another small movement and a short break. By the time he made it upright, his feet firmly on the floor, the steam on the bowl had disappeared. But the living room and all of its furniture held steady. A nice change.

He reached for the bowl, cupping his hand around the hot pad beneath.

"I'll put your water over here." His mom slipped one of the clay coasters she'd made closer to the edge of the end table.

He nodded as he sipped at a spoonful of corn chowder. It was salty and soothing and tingled at the back of his throat. It wasn't a fancy homemade soup, just something from a can with more broth than shreds of chicken or corn. But it tasted of comfort. When all they'd been able to afford was food from a can, corn chowder had been his favorite. There'd been no money for crackers then, so no need for them now.

He set his spoon down and took a swig of water. "Thanks." He sounded more like a human this time.

She stood before him, staring at him with a strange intensity, only the sound of her breathing and his slurping soup between them. "What happened?" she finally asked.

"I don't know. I just felt *off* all day. I thought maybe it was . . ." He couldn't get the words out past the memory of holding Meg as she'd sobbed in his arms.

His mom sat on the cushion beside him, her apron gone, revealing the stained jeans she'd worked in that day. She patted his arm. "Did something happen on the boat?"

"Just . . ." He wasn't sure how much he should say. It

wasn't really his news to share. Of course, once it was out there, the truth would make the rounds through Victoria faster than lightning. "Meg heard from her dad last night."

"Oh no." The smooth lines of her face crumpled. "It's not good news, is it?"

"No."

Mama Potts got up and paced the living room, her hands twisting at her waist. "I knew it wasn't good, the way Sandra has been hanging on to Walt's arm. She's barely walking on her own. But I was praying I was wrong."

Setting down his empty bowl, he leaned his elbows on his knees, folded one fist inside the other, and stared at a patch of tan carpet. "Mom, I don't know what to do. Whitaker's been like . . . well, you know."

She continued her march, head shaking and eyes focused on another time or another place.

"I don't know how to help. I feel like I have to do something. Something more than what I'm already doing."

"What are you already doing?"

"I'm—that is, Meg and I are—handling the business. I've made sure that he doesn't have to worry about anything. I'm getting all the phone calls and checking all the messages. I'm dealing with the shore buyer and managing the books. I want him to be able to spend as much time with Mrs. Whitaker as he can."

"And what about Meg?"

He opened his mouth, then closed it. He took a long drink of water. "What about her?" She was Meg. He'd handle the business for her. He'd take over 100 percent of the details. He'd even hold her while she cried.

But he already knew—she didn't really want that from him.

174

"Is she getting to spend time with her mom?"

Again he played fish, words escaping him as he tried to form them.

His mom plopped down next to him, this time closer than before, and patted his knee. "Honey, I wish more than anything in the world that you didn't know what it's like to lose a parent."

His shoulders tensed, and he shook his head. "It's not the same thing."

"Not exactly, maybe. But looking back . . ."

He moved his knee away from her touch and put his face in his hands, squeezing his eyes shut. He didn't want to look back at anything.

She sighed. "We don't talk about your dad much."

"For good reason. You taught me if I didn't have something nice to say, I shouldn't say anything at all."

"I did." Her words were slow, contemplative. "But it wasn't all bad. Without your dad, I wouldn't have gotten three beautiful sons."

He snorted into his hands. "You mean two good-looking sons and a—"

"Oliver Ross." Her voice cut sharper than the knife she'd dropped earlier. "Eli is still my son. And I love him."

"Yeah? When's the last time you watched the Rangers play?"

She stiffened, and he wanted to punch himself in the face. What kind of a jerk changed the subject to something that hurt his mom worse than the subject of his dad leaving? Him. Yep. He could be almost as much of a buffoon as Eli when he tried.

"I'm sorry, Mom." But he didn't want to talk about his dad. And he sure didn't want to think about how often he missed the guy. If he could have regrets about a bully and a cheat, well, Meg would be in a world of hurt when she lost her mom.

He pushed himself to the edge of the seat. "I should get to bed. I've got an early morning."

She stood before he could. "You don't think you're actually fishing in the morning, do you? You just passed out on my sofa a couple hours ago."

"Who else is going to do it?"

"Kyle can handle the boat."

Pressing his hands against the cushions, he forced himself up on semi-steady legs. When he looked down into her eyes, he saw the worry there.

"Dad took everything from us," he said. "Our home. Our stability. Our reputation. This is my chance to get it all back. And I'm not going to give up."

# fourteen

Oliver survived the following morning. But just barely. The next was only slightly better, as he was pumped full of vitamins and all the home remedies Mama Potts could cook up. He managed to stay on the *Pinch* and haul in his traps. As far as he could remember, every single one of them had had bait when they dropped back into the water. And he hadn't fallen in with them. That had to count as a win.

That they'd hauled in more than two hundred pounds both days was as good as he could hope for.

By Friday morning, he was mostly on the mend and thankful that Meg hadn't given him a second look since she'd fallen apart in his arms. He wanted to tell her he wasn't embarrassed and she shouldn't be either. But maybe it wasn't about how she'd cried in front of him. She could just as easily have been distracted by everything going on with her mom or preparing for her parents to return that weekend.

Kyle, on the other hand, had been shooting him strange glances most of the week. Oliver had shrugged it off as lack of sleep, and no one would argue with that. Not with their hours.

"How you feeling?" Kyle asked, thumping him between the shoulder blades.

Oliver let out a wheeze. "Perfect. Happy to have a floating boat."

Kyle let out a belly laugh that turned heads from several other boats around them.

"What's so funny?" Meg asked as she joined them, passing out tall cups of coffee.

"Ma'am." Kyle gave her a mock bow.

Oliver smiled his thanks—and hoped he'd remembered to acknowledge her earlier in the week.

If knowing the regulation trap size and navigating the *Pinch* were his jobs, Meg had taken on the role of coffee distributor. Not that she couldn't have done something else—in fact, she did a lot of other things. It was just that the coffee she brought from Tim Hortons was so far superior to his own burnt sludge that he couldn't turn it down. She'd brought it every day for almost two weeks, and he prayed she'd bring it for another six.

Pressing the plastic lid to his lips, he sipped, the liquid burning over his tongue and down his chest, heat radiating to the tips of his gloved fingers. Bitter, but not too much. Silky smooth. A touch of sweet cream and sugar. "Mm-hmm."

For the first time in days, she returned his smile. "I'm glad you like it."

Kyle drank his like a shot of whiskey, downing it in one tip of his head and then chucking his cup into the trash bucket. Meg cupped her hands around her coffee, sniffing at the steam that escaped the small hole in the lid. Her lips curled up at the corners, a tiny dimple tucked into her cheek.

"Your folks coming back from away this week?" Kyle must have noticed too.

Her smile faltered, but she forced a brave face back on. "I'm not sure Toronto really counts as away."

Kyle raised an eyebrow. "Don't argue with your elders, kid."

She laughed then. "Fair enough. Yes. They're coming back *from away.*"

Kyle clearly wanted to ask another question—probably the same one Oliver did. But there were some things still off-limits. Like how her mom was doing. Like how her dad was holding up. Like if she was about to crack under the pressure of it all.

Instead, Kyle cracked a joke he'd heard on the wharf, and Oliver walked toward the helm and turned on the engine. It purred to life, and he sipped his drink while he checked the instruments and set their coordinates into the GPS.

This had become their morning routine—coffee, ribbing each other, and preparing for another haul. A simple tradition before they stocked up on bait and headed out for the open water. Oliver didn't mind it. As much as he'd hated the idea of her being on his boat at first, it hadn't been terrible.

He just had to figure out how to make her not *want* to stay. Let her know she could run the business but make her hate the very idea. Or maybe make something else more appealing.

He wasn't sure how to do that. And he wasn't any closer to coming up with an idea by the time they reached their first buoy. At that point, he only had the brain space to concentrate on what was before him.

They hauled in the cluster of traps at the first buoys without incident, save for a higher-than-average number of undersized lobsters, which were tossed back into the water. "Next year," Kyle said as he chucked one more overboard.

Meg had gotten good at snagging the buoys with the gaff, and she worked the hauler like she was part machine herself, threading the rope into it and pulling the traps right to the port side. She grabbed two and Oliver the other three, and they settled them onto the counter. They cleared them out, baited them, and shoved them back overboard.

The air was still and quiet as they approached their fourth marker, Oliver watching the GPS panel.

"I don't see it," Meg called from behind him.

She'd never said that before, and it made his stomach fall to his boots. She had to be wrong. They'd put their traps down right here the day before.

He looked over his shoulder at Kyle, who shook his head. Oliver narrowed his gaze. They had to be wrong. Maybe a wave had blocked the view of the bright green floater. He joined Meg at the rail and squinted across the flat surface of the water. Even their boat caused only a ripple in the glassy surface.

He crossed his arms and frowned. This made no sense. Buoys floated, but not far when they were attached to a cluster of traps sitting on the ocean floor.

Grabbing the binoculars from beside the wheel, he scanned the water from the boat to the horizon in long, sweeping motions.

Nothing.

"What happened to it?" Meg's question carried a heavy note of concern, the same kind that twisted his insides.

"Could be the rope broke."

Kyle snorted his disagreement, and Oliver couldn't blame him. The industrial ropes they used didn't just break. And if a rope had frayed, they'd have noticed it the day before or the one before that.

*Punishment.*

The word popped into his head, but he shoved it away just as quickly. They hadn't broken any unwritten rules. There would be no reason for another fisherman to cut their line, no matter what threat Little Tommy Scanlan had made. Punishment only followed a crime. And no one on the *Pinch* had committed one.

"What are you thinking?" Meg asked, jerking him from his thoughts.

He squinted across the water again. "Nothing."

It was her turn to snort. If a little more feminine than Kyle's, it still got the message across. "We lose five traps, and you're not thinking anything?"

"Well . . ." He closed one eye and stared at her through the other. "We have to report lost equipment to the authorities." The government kept track of litter in the fishing areas but didn't penalize licenses unless they made a habit of it. This was Whitaker Fishing's first offense in Oliver's six years on the *Pinch*.

Meg's eyes flashed bright in her pale face, despite the frown still tugging at the corners of her lips. "I can do that. I'll do it as soon as we get back to shore."

"All right. I'll show you exactly where we're at."

She followed him toward the control panel, and he stepped to the side so she could see the simple GPS. Pointing at the flashing light, he said, "This is us." Then he pointed to a list of coordinates. "And these are all of our drop points. Every one of our forty-eight clusters."

"Hey!" Kyle's call whipped them both around. "Look over there."

Oliver followed the line of Kyle's finger to the opposite

side of the boat. There was the bobbing buoy, bright against the gray of the morning water. He steered the boat toward it until they were close enough for Meg to reach it with the hook, but it was on the wrong side to put it into the hauler.

Hand over hand, all three of them pulled the wet rope in. There wasn't a cluster of traps on the end, only a small stone.

Oliver felt it like a slap in the face.

"Still think it broke?" Kyle asked.

No, there was no pretending that now. Their line had been cut, their traps most likely left on the bottom. And it posed just one question.

"Who would do this?" Anger laced Meg's words, and she crossed her arms over her gray sweater.

*Punishment.*

"Someone thinks we've broken a rule." It was the only explanation Oliver could muster. Still, he racked his brain and could come up with no offense worthy of this retribution. Letting out a slow breath through tight lips, he pressed his hands to his hips and looked around once more. But the offending ship and its captain had their own traps to check. They'd long since gone.

They worked the rest of the morning in relative silence, communicating only through sparse grunts and monosyllables. By the time Oliver navigated them back into the harbor, their catch unloaded, his feet felt like they weighed a hundred pounds each.

He secured the boat and trudged off it after Meg and Kyle. That's when he saw Little Tommy standing beside his own vessel, securing it to the dock. Oliver's feet flew across the wharf until he was only inches from the older man's face.

"Why'd you do it?"

Tommy blinked slowly, his features revealing nothing of the crime he'd almost certainly committed. "You best be careful, boy." He gave Oliver a little shove on his shoulder, despite the six inches and thirty pounds separating them. "I don't care fer yer tone."

Oliver didn't budge. If Tommy hadn't cut their line, he sure knew who had. "Why'd you cut our line?"

"I don't like what you're implying."

Oliver's chin ticked to the left, his fist clenched and trembling at his side. "I'm not implying anything. And I don't like what you're *doing*."

Tommy took a tiny step toward him. Throat clenched so hard that the veins nearly popped, he grunted, "I ain't doing nothing. But now I'm tempted."

Oliver could barely hear the threat for the roaring in his ears. Louder than the ocean had ever been, a rush of blood surged through him, almost knocking him to the ground. It stirred a fire in his gut that he hadn't felt in years. A familiar chorus.

He didn't deserve this boat or this business.

But he did. And he was going to show Little Tommy Scanlan just how much.

His fist was nearly to his shoulder when two hands wrapped around his forearm, right beneath his bunched-up sweater. They were lean and delicate and cool, dampening the fire that Tommy had stoked.

Oliver looked down just as Meg smiled at him. Gentle. Soothing. She took an exaggerated breath through her nose, her motions broader than they should be. Then she turned that same smile on Little Tommy.

"Mr. Scanlan, it appears one of our lines was cut, our traps lost."

His furry eyebrows joined to make one black caterpillar right above his nose. "You don't say. That's a shame."

"It really is. Especially when it's hurting my father."

The sunspots on his forehead disappeared into deep ridges, and he crossed his arms over his stocky chest, tucking his hands beneath his armpits. "How's that, now?"

Meg tilted her head in Oliver's direction. "Well, you know that Oliver and I are working the business for him this summer. He's made no final decision about selling his license."

A sweetness Oliver had never heard before danced through her words, her smile matching every sugary syllable.

"I don't suppose you saw anyone go out last night or leave especially early this morning? We'd sure like to know who cut our traps."

Tommy's pale green eyes darted toward Jeffrey Druthers's boat tied in front of the *Pinch*, but he shook his head. "No. I didn't see no one. But I'll keep my eyes open."

"Thank you." Meg lifted one hand from Oliver's arm and gave Scanlan a little wave. "Tell your wife I said hello."

He grunted and stalked away, his angry footfalls echoing back to them.

Oliver couldn't look away from Meg's profile and the perfect line of her lips. "I wasn't planning to hit him, you know," he said as he pumped his fist.

She jumped, pulling away her other hand, a tangible absence in its wake. "No, of course not. I didn't . . ."

But he was pretty sure she had thought he was going to. After all, *he* wasn't entirely sure what he'd been about to do—planned or otherwise.

She didn't wait around for a confession or any sort of change of heart. "You think he did it?"

"I think we've broken new rules, and no one outside Victoria cares that the *Pinch* has a new captain and first mate."

"First mate?" She flashed a row of straight white teeth at him, spinning on her toes in his direction. "You've never called me that before."

"Yeah, well . . ." He hadn't meant to call her that now. But if she was intent on taking on her half of the job, he'd give her her due. "You've got a call to make about some lost traps."

"All right. What are you going to do?"

"I'm going to find the jerk who cut our line."

Meg hadn't turned into an early bird in the span of a couple weeks, but neither could she stay awake past ten most nights. Her lids felt heavy and her muscles were slow to respond to everything.

Still, she trudged up the road to the harbor that night, the only sign of life the intermittent beam of light gliding over the water. Even the Lobster Barn's windows were black against its gray-shingle siding at the far end of the wharf. The angled parking spots reserved for customers were empty, every last one of the old pub's regulars at home for the night. The parking lot by the shanties was empty too. Oliver had probably left his truck at home. Maybe he hadn't even left yet. Maybe he'd allowed himself more than a couple of hours of fitful sleep before dragging himself back to the boat.

But she had no doubt he would join her. If he wasn't already there.

The dock was empty, the boats silent save for the rhythmic creaking of the inflated fenders. This time of night was a different kind of dark. In the morning, even hours before the sun rose, there was a promise of light. At this time, that promise wasn't even a whisper on the wind.

Thick clouds rolled across the sky, blotting out the moon and hiding the stars.

She found her way from the road down to the dock more out of habit than out of sight. The lamp at the end of the row of boats before the pub left only a puddle of light. Tiptoeing down the way, she held her breath as she reached the *Pinch*, knowing it too out of muscle memory.

Suddenly a bright light flashed in her face, and she jerked her arm up to protect her eyes. The light disappeared in a split second but left her blind for a long moment.

"What are you doing here?" Oliver. Of course.

"Same thing as you, I guess."

"Night fishing?"

She snorted, rubbing her eyes with the heels of her hands until the flashing slowed. "Funny." By the time she could make out his figure—hands on his hips and feet squarely on the deck—he'd turned off his flashlight.

"Seriously, Meg, what are you doing here? We have to be on the boat in a few hours." He sounded an awful lot like her father.

"Seriously, Oliver. I could say the same to you."

He sighed, dropping his hands to his sides and relaxing his shoulders.

"We agreed that we were going to share the responsibilities. Remember?"

"And you reported the lost traps and I'm taking care of whoever lost them for us." He grumbled something under his breath just as a gust of wind rocked the boat and cut through both of her sweaters.

She couldn't fight the shiver that raced down her back as she wrapped her arms around her middle, hunching against the chill. Maybe it hadn't been smart to leave her apartment without a coat. But once she was on the boat, she'd be more protected from the biting wind.

"That division of labor is hardly equal. Besides, I want to be here."

Shoving a hand through his hair, he sighed. "You're freezing already, and it's going to be a cold night."

"Then let me aboard so I can warm up."

He hesitated as though he was going to argue the flaw in her logic, but finally he stepped aside and reached out to help her step down. She took his hand, automatically leaning into his warmth, wishing he'd hold all of her cold parts with his radiator palms.

She pulled away the instant that thought materialized. Holding herself as tight as she could, she turned in a slow circle. "So what are we doing out here?"

"Waiting."

She raised an eyebrow but realized a second later that he couldn't see more than her silhouette. "For what?"

"For someone to show up when they shouldn't." He motioned toward a dark spot on the deck along the port side. "Care to join me?" He lowered himself, then patted the seat beside him. Whatever was on the ground muffled his movements, and she shrugged. Couldn't be worse than standing in the wind.

Kneeling, she touched the dark spot, which turned out to be some sort of cushion. Then she settled in next to him, pulling her knees up under her chin. "Nice setup. Where'd you get it?"

"Nicked it off Mama Potts's patio furniture." He put a finger to his lips. "Shhhhh."

She chuckled, scooting just a little closer to him. Not so close that they were touching, but close enough that his body heat made at least half of her feel like it might not go numb. Close enough that she could smell the crisp, clean scent of his shampoo and the subtle hint of lavender facial lotion. She thought it was her own cream until she remembered that she'd failed to put any on after her shower. She opened her mouth to ask him how he liked it, but he spoke before she could.

"How'd you know I'd be here?" he asked.

"You said this morning that no one outside of Victoria cares that my dad is thinking about selling. The only ones who do are right here, in our harbor. If you were looking for him, I figured you'd start here."

He chuckled, and she could almost feel the vibration through the fiberglass deck. "Smart."

"I know."

He laughed out loud at that, and it felt like a shot of espresso straight down her throat, warm and piercing.

They settled into the silence then, the boat rocking gently. All she really needed was a blanket and a lullaby. The cool air seeped through her jeans, and she hugged them a little tighter.

"Here." Oliver didn't ask permission before tossing his heavy jacket over her extremities.

Immediately her shivers stopped. "Thank you. But won't you be cold?"

He turned his head toward her. Maybe her eyes were adjusting to the darkness, or perhaps she imagined it, but she could almost see the slightest uptick of the corner of his mouth. Of his perfectly formed lips. The rest of his face might have been filled with imperfections, but his lips were regal. Full. Perfect. Unmarred by the chafing wind.

Not that she'd been noticing or anything.

She looked away, pulling his jacket closer to her chin and snuggling into its warmth.

"I guess you'll have to share if I get cold too."

"Oh." She grabbed the coat by its collar to hand it to him, but his paw clamped over hers before she could move.

"Kidding, kid. I'll be fine."

It was supposed to get down to eleven or twelve overnight— lovely weather with the sun shining. But without even the light of the moon and the air heavy with water, it would soon be too much. "I'll share."

"You're going to share my own coat with me?"

"Well, when you put it like that . . ."

She could practically feel the grin radiating off him when he nudged her shoulder with his own.

"So have you seen anyone out here?"

"Yeah."

Her shoulders tensed. "Who?"

"You."

Her laugh broke free, and she shook her head. "Right. Except me."

"No." He leaned back against the boat, stretching out his impossibly long legs and crossing them at his ankles. "I haven't seen or heard anyone else."

He kept his voice low, and she wondered if he was worried that someone else would hear them. But the very air seemed a blanket that protected them, kept their presence a secret. They'd hear someone approaching long before they'd be heard themselves, so she leaned back and stretched her legs out next to his.

"Did my dad teach you to do this?"

"This?"

"Yeah." She freed an arm and swept it across the breadth of the boat. "How to catch a thief."

He shrugged and chuckled. "I guess not. Never had a reason to go looking for someone before. But it's something he would do if he was here. He'd protect his business."

True. Her dad would have done anything to keep the family legacy alive. He wouldn't have flinched at sleepless nights. So why would he make a poor choice about who would take it over?

"When's your dad getting back?"

She pushed her own questions out of her mind and focused on his, despite the clench in her gut at the change of direction. "Next week. Dad called this afternoon. They decided to stay in Toronto for a few more days. Do some touristy things."

"That's good. Make some memories."

She nodded. "Listen, about my mom and dad . . ." Well, that wasn't quite right. It wasn't exactly about her parents. It was more about the last time she and Oliver had talked about them, and how they hadn't talked about them at all since then. About how she'd fallen apart in his arms and then barely spoken to him since.

"Everything . . ." he started, then paused. "Well, I know it's not all right. I mean, any new news?"

"Oh, no. Nothing like that. It's just that—I mean—I didn't mean to . . . I'm sorry I was so angry with you. You didn't deserve it. Not like that."

"Huh." He grunted, and she had a feeling that a stiff breeze would have knocked him over. That wasn't altogether surprising, given how long she'd been angry with him. "So you're not mad anymore?"

She shook her head, letting her chin rest on her chest as she thought through the truth. "I'm still mad. Just maybe not at you. I'm mad that I'm losing my mom. I'm mad that there's nothing I can do about it. I'm mad that half the time I don't think she even remem-bers me." Her voice caught, and she swallowed down a hiccup.

His hand slipped beneath the coat and squeezed her knee. "I know."

Ugh. How could he be so sure that he understood? What made him an expert?

"When my dad left, I felt a lot of the same things."

Oh. Right.

"Mostly I was mad at my brothers," he said. "I was mad at the world. I was mad at God."

She snuck a peek at him out of the corner of her eye. He'd dared to speak the words that she'd been afraid to, to admit the truth that had been bubbling deep inside but never named. "You were?"

He squeezed her knee again. "Oh, so much." There was almost a note of laughter in his voice, as though admitting it was a lifted weight.

"Is that why you kicked my robot?"

He lifted his face toward the sky. She matched the direction of his gaze, searching for a lone star and finding two sparkling side by side. "In part."

She surprised herself when she pushed. "Then why?"

"Do you think kicking something would make you feel better?"

Letting it slide that he hadn't actually answered her question, she thought about his. "I don't know. But it couldn't hurt anything but my foot."

He chuckled. "Or, you know, if you kick something important to someone else."

"I suppose." Her smile dimmed, the memory of that loss paling in comparison to what she knew now. "How do you deal with it? How do you say goodbye to your parent?" Saying the words aloud made her tremble, and he slipped his hand from her leg to her shoulders, pulling her into the hard angles and firm lines of his body. She sank into him, dissolving whatever barrier she'd erected between them.

"I don't know. I never got to say goodbye."

"Oh, Oliver." The regret in his tone made her temples ache, and she wrapped her arms around his waist in a quick hug— for once to comfort him instead of the other way around.

"It's okay. *I'm* okay."

"But don't you regret it?"

"What? His choices? His actions?"

She nodded into his shoulder, his cable-knit sweater soft against her cheek.

"I went to bed one night and woke up the next morning, and he was gone. His part of the closet was empty, his boots next to the door up and vanished. Every morning I'd get up and see his plate in the sink, crumbs from the eggs-and-bacon sandwich my mom had made him before he went out on the boat. That morning, there was no plate."

"I'm so sorry."

Leaning his cheek on her head, he whispered softly, "Me too," before letting out a short breath.

There was a weight to his words, a regret that she couldn't

deny. She wanted to ask him what he wasn't telling her but didn't want to interrupt him.

"Mostly I'm sorry that I don't have any good memories with my dad."

"None?"

"Maybe when I was really young, but . . . he was a hard man. A bitter man. Even so, if I'd known he was going to disappear from my life completely, I think I'd have tried to make some happy memories, some moments I could look back on."

"What would you have done?" It was none of her business, but she'd never heard Oliver talk this much in her entire life, and the low timbre of his voice surrounded her, warmer than any blanket. It settled low in her chest, more soothing than his mama's miracle muscle cream. He knew where she hurt because he hurt there too.

"I don't know. Never thought about it." His dry chuckle didn't hold much humor. "Guess I figured it wasn't worth stewing over what might have been. What about you?"

"What about me?"

He lifted his shoulder. "What kind of memories are you going to make with your mom?"

"I guess I'm already doing everything I can—taking care of her and Dad."

"Really? Seems more like you're picking up after them."

She jerked away from his embrace, nearly falling off the seat cushion, her heart thudding against her ribs. "What's that supposed to mean? I'm doing what they need me to do."

"And that's great. But are those the memories you want to look back on? When she's gone, will remembering that you did the dishes and folded laundry fill you with joy?"

"You . . ." She stared into his shadowed face, ready to lash out. But she wasn't mad at him. She was mad at . . . at . . . "It's what they need."

"Maybe so. Or is it what you need to tell yourself to keep some distance from your mom? To keep it from hurting?"

# fifteen

Meg hoisted the suitcase out of the trunk of her mom's car, thankful for the muscles she'd gained hauling in traps. Without them, it might have toppled her.

"Okay there, kid?" her dad asked.

"Just fine," she said, settling the suitcase on the ground and pulling out the retractable handle. The wheels clicked and clacked over the cracks and bumps in the garage floor as she joined her dad at the passenger-side door, where he helped her mom out of the car.

"Hi, Mom." Meg leaned in and pressed a kiss to her pale cheek. "I'm glad you're home."

Her mom didn't give any indication that she'd heard the greeting. She simply slipped an arm around her husband's back and shuffled toward the door to the house.

Meg lagged behind, her smile fading and the pressure in her chest building. She'd been silly to hope for some improvement. Her mom wasn't going to change. She was only going to deteriorate. And all Meg would have to remember this time were hours of laundry and dishes and heavy rolling suitcases.

Oliver's words from nearly a week before still echoed in

her mind. Maybe she'd been a coward, but she'd changed the subject and refused to talk about her mom anymore that night. She hadn't let their conversations any night since circle into the same dangerous waters.

Yet she couldn't shut off the sound of his voice on repeat in her mind. She couldn't pretend she hadn't heard the questions that required answers.

Was she just keeping her distance, knowing what was to come?

She yanked the suitcase over a small cement step and past a perfectly organized set of metal shelves filled with plastic tubs of family history and Christmas decorations.

Oliver didn't know what it was like. He thought he understood loss—and maybe he did. But he only understood the surprise of it, the shock of everything changing. He knew nothing of preparing for it.

And Meg had to prepare. She had no other choice. If that meant protecting her own heart so she could care for her dad afterward, then that's what she'd do. She had to make sure her heart was ready to sustain the blow that was coming. It wasn't like she was purposefully building a wall between her and her mom. It wasn't even about her. It was about making sure she could be there for her dad.

*Telling yourself that doesn't make it true.*

It didn't make it not true either. She did care about her dad.

*But you're afraid of losing your mom.*

Who wouldn't be?

This was ridiculous. She was being ridiculous. Oliver wasn't right. He didn't understand. He may have known all the pressure points that hurt from lobster fishing, but he couldn't possibly know where this hurt.

And it did. It ached deep in her chest, stealing her breath and making her heart forget how to pump.

Her mom was home. Safe. Loved.

And she was just going to get worse.

Meg's breath caught on a sob, and she leaned against the closed door, pressing her forehead to the cool wood. Maybe it could soothe the burning in her lungs or the fire at her temples. Her pulse thudded in her ears. Just as Pastor Dell had described—the sound of pain.

"Meg, honey? Are you coming in?" Her dad's call came from the other side of the door, and she rushed to respond before he opened it.

"Yes. I'm on my way. Just . . . putting away some tools." She glanced at the pegboard, each of her dad's tools hanging in a penciled outline. Every one in place.

If he knew it was a lie, he didn't say. He only gave the door two quick taps before his footsteps shuffled away.

"Come on, Meg. Get it together." She wiped her hand down her face and sucked in three deep breaths. This was not the time for self-analysis. This was the time for service.

Plastering a smile into place, she pushed her way into the house. It smelled stale, like it had been shut up for two weeks, and she wanted to kick herself for not stopping by to air it out and open a few windows.

She rolled through the kitchen, left the suitcase by the hallway, and returned to stand in front of the sink. "What can I make you for supper?"

Her dad looked up from where he was settling her mom on the sofa. He tucked a blanket around her legs and propped a blue throw pillow beneath each arm. "You don't have to do that. You've been up since before the sun."

True. And she was not becoming a morning person. But that wasn't an excuse. "I don't mind." She ducked her head into the refrigerator. Nearly empty except a bottle of ketchup, a lone apple, and an open box of baking soda.

Right. They'd cleaned out the fridge because they were going to be gone. And—again—like an idiot, she hadn't thought to pick up a few things in anticipation of their return.

She tried the pantry, which was equally barren. "I'll just run out and pick something up for you at Carrie's. What would you like?"

Her dad strolled toward the suitcase and picked it up. But he didn't move down the hallway. "We're fine." Dropping the suitcase, he walked toward her and put his arm around her shoulders. "It's just so nice to see you again. I missed you."

Forcing a breath around the lump in her throat, she hugged him back. "I missed you too." Her words weren't quite as steady as she'd have liked them to be. Maybe that was why he changed the topic.

"How's the boat and the catch?"

"Fine. Good. We've brought in more than two hundred pounds of hard shell nearly every day." *And we've only had to replace one cluster of traps when someone cut our line.*

She couldn't say that last part. She couldn't let on that there had been hiccups. Or that in six nights on the *Pinch*, trading shifts sleeping, she and Oliver had seen nothing that pointed to the culprit.

"And Oliver?"

Every muscle in her body tensed. Was her dad reading her mind? Doubtful.

Thank goodness. Especially when memories of resting her head on Oliver's shoulder made her insides tingle in a way that could only mean one thing. One thing she was not going to name.

"He's fine. Good. Busy."

"You spending a lot of time together?" There was a note in his voice, a knowing flutter that she didn't like, and she pulled back, staring hard into his face.

"What's that supposed to mean?"

He shrugged, giving her shoulder one more squeeze before dropping his arms. "Nothing at all. Just hoping you haven't gotten into an argument that sank the boat."

"Of course not. He's good. I'm good. *Kyle* is good too."

"Glad to hear it." With a wink, he took off down the hallway toward the bedroom. But something didn't quite settle right in her stomach. He sounded like one of the gossips in front of the church on Sunday mornings, trying to drum up the latest scandal.

She wasn't a scandal. Neither was Oliver. But when their competition for the business became public knowledge, they would certainly be the talk of the town.

Shoving that thought aside, she walked across the living room and sank into the seat beside her mom. "Hi." She scooped up her hand and held it between her own. "I missed you."

Her mom squeezed her hand, and Meg jumped, clutching her weathered fingers even closer.

"I love you," Meg whispered.

Her mom's eyes didn't quite focus, but the corner of her mouth twitched. "Love you too."

Though Meg hadn't known it, that was all she needed to hear. For that moment, anyway.

They sat in silence. Together.

Oliver couldn't spend another night sleeping on the *Pinch*. Or—more accurately—not sleeping. Not that he minded the rocking motion or the fresh air or the company.

The company was pretty great—even if she'd kept their conversation safely away from her mom since he'd pushed. Maybe too hard.

He liked hearing about Meg's time in college, her love for all things mechanical, and even how much she missed her students. If he felt a little bit guilty about her missing out on the school year with them, he tried not to. She'd made her own choice. And if he'd been in her position, he'd probably have done the same thing.

Honestly, he was going to miss their nights under the stars.

However, he wasn't going to miss a foggy brain and lethargic body. He needed to sleep in his own bed for more than two hours at a time. He was young and resilient, but at the moment he felt like he was eighty-five and had lived hard every day of his life.

After church on Sunday, the congregation rushed outside to stand on the lawn in small pockets in their usual way. The kids played beneath the trees, and the women stood in front of the white chapel and talked of the latest play at the local theater and the state of tourism. The men discussed the falling price of lobster and the season's catch, as they always did.

Oliver broke away and strolled toward the parking lot, steeling himself for a conversation he didn't want to have. But it was the only one that might put an end to his sleepless nights.

"Oliver, what are you doing?"

His name on her tongue made him stop, and her hand on his arm made his stomach drop. He turned to face Meg.

"You look like a man on a mission. Where are you going?"

*To get some sleep.* Well, that wasn't entirely accurate. "I need some answers."

Her eyebrows dipped with concern. She knew. It was as clear as the Confederation Bridge, written in those beautiful blue eyes. "Do you want me to come with you?"

*Yes.* But only if she could be there and not hear any of what was about to be said.

He shook his head. "I'm good. I just can't go on like we have been."

Her lips pinched, and he felt her volt of keen disappointment.

"I just mean I need to get some sleep. Like real sleep in my own bed."

With a laugh, she pointed toward her eyes. "It takes a lot of makeup to cover these dark circles. Let me know if you ever want to borrow it."

He chuckled, lifting his eyes just as Jeffrey Druthers glanced his way. A subtle nod was all it took, and Druthers began to mosey in their direction.

Meg glanced over her shoulder. "You think Druthers has something to do with it?"

"I don't know, but . . . I need to talk with him. Alone."

"All right. Will I see you tonight?"

He wanted to confirm so desperately. But he wanted to be passed out with his own pillow more.

"I'll call you."

She nodded and gave Druthers one more glance before stalking toward her sedan.

Oliver stepped out of the way of a car pulling out of its spot. He crossed his arms and squinted at Druthers as he closed the gap.

"Ross." It wasn't much of a greeting, but Oliver had had worse. "You looking for something?"

"The truth."

"'Bout what?" Druthers was like flint, every stereotype of a crusty fisherman. His tousled gray hair and mustache would have been perfect on the box of those frozen fish sticks no one ever bought in the grocery store.

"I assume you're aware."

"I heard some things, like maybe you lost a cluster of traps." Druthers grunted. "Can't say I'm sorry."

There it was. The truth coming out. "Why's that?"

"Oh, you're not stupid enough to have to ask that. You know what your old man did to me—to my business."

"And you figured this was your chance to take it out on me?"

"Whoa." Druthers's face turned red, and he closed half the distance between them. Pointing a stern finger right at Oliver's chest, he said, "Just what are you accusing me of, b'y?"

It took everything inside him to keep his hands at his sides, but Oliver held his ground. "I'm asking you. Right now. Man-to-man. Do you know who sabotaged my traps?"

"Doesn't matter if I do or I don't. I wouldn't tell you either way." Druthers's lip curled in a sneer. "Besides, last I checked, those aren't your traps and the *Pinch* isn't your boat. And it's never going to be."

Oliver nearly bit off his own tongue spitting out another question. "What's that supposed to mean?"

"Only that Whitaker has better taste than to sell his family's name to a kid who's no better than his no-good thief father. It's in your blood. The lot of you boys. Eli's a liar and a cheat. Levi's slow—can't hardly speak. And you're every bit the swindler your dad was, sweet-talking Whitaker and his poor wife outta their business," he nearly snarled. "I'll make sure you never get his boat."

With that, Druthers stalked away.

Oliver let out a tight sigh and flexed his fingers, trying to ignore the kernel of truth in the man's words. His brothers weren't perfect, but they sure weren't what he'd called them. Levi wasn't slow. And Eli hadn't been a cheat either—last he'd seen him.

But the truth was that Oliver *was* the kid of a no-good thief. As for whether Whitaker would end up selling to him? That remained to be seen.

"He called you *what*?" Meg's words rose in volume until they echoed all the way to the red-and-white lighthouse and back. She scrambled to get to her feet.

Oliver laughed, holding on to her arm to keep her seated beside him on their stolen cushion. Back on the boat for another night. Pressing his finger to his lips, he reminded her that the cloak of darkness didn't make them invisible. He kept his voice low. "I told you that you didn't want to know what we talked about."

"Well, I didn't think I'd have to teach an old man some proper manners. But I will. I'm not afraid of him. I've taught ninth-year students. Nothing can scare me after that."

He laughed again, wrapping an arm around her shoulders and tucking her into his side. "You can't fight him tonight."

"But I would. I'd go knock some sense into him right this

minute." Every muscle in her trembled against him, so he pulled her closer. He threw a blanket over both of their outstretched legs.

"I know you would. And I appreciate it." He wasn't sure if she would feel the same way if he told her the rest of Druthers's accusations—about his brothers, about himself. Oliver had told her that Druthers had called him the son of a no-good thief. He had conveniently left out the part about being called a swindler. He knew it wasn't true. Whitaker had approached *him* about buying the business. But he also didn't want to plant a seed of doubt in Meg's mind.

And the part about his dad being terrible—that wasn't news to anyone. Least of all Oliver and his brothers.

"I mean, how could Druthers sit in church and listen to Pastor Dell preach about forgiveness and grace? We're supposed to forgive much because we've been forgiven much, right? And then he goes and holds on to all this hate for so long. I mean, it's been ten—aaaahhh!" She let out a breathy wail, pressing her face into her hands.

"What's wrong?" Shaking her shoulder, he tried to get her to look up at him, but she only buried her face deeper into her palms.

"I just heard myself." She groaned again. "Ten years. *Ten years.*"

"Well, I did ruin your future."

She looked up then, the moon shining right into her face, highlighting every line of regret. "No, you didn't. You might have changed it, but you didn't ruin it. I should have never carried that grudge for so long."

"I think we decided that sometimes you weren't really mad at me. Besides, you never insulted me."

She cringed.

"At least not to my face," he tacked on, unable to keep a grin from surfacing.

"Yeah, but I was mad at you a lot. And I'm so sorry. I didn't realize we could have been friends all this time."

He held out his hand. "Friends now?"

Nudging him with her elbow, she said, "Don't be so cheesy." And then, like she didn't want to let the moment pass, she slipped her hand into his as she added, "Yes, of course we're friends." She ducked her head, hiding the smile that played across her lips.

Sweet, pink lips. Sweet, kissable lips. Not that he was thinking about that. Much.

"So what are you going to say to Druthers?" she asked.

"Nothing."

She shifted to face him, her knee pressing against his, unmoving and far too familiar. "What do you mean? How can you just let that go? All those things he said about your dad."

He nodded slowly, wishing for the millionth time that he was someone else's son. But he couldn't deny them. "They're true."

She gasped like she didn't know. And maybe she'd truly never known. How could she? With a mom and a dad who loved her so much, doted on her, and praised her, how could she even fathom a childhood like his?

He tried for a soft laugh, but it came out dry and humorless. "Meg, it's my dad."

She shook her head. "I don't know what that means."

# sixteen

Oliver knew he had a choice, and everything inside of him wanted to choose the easy route—the one where he shrugged off what Druthers had said and pretended that Meg hadn't just asked him for the truth.

Those routes were easy for a reason, and he'd picked them most of his life. Anything to keep his dad from flying off the handle. Anything to keep his mom from hurting. Anything to keep from being reminded that Eli had chosen his skates and a sweet signing bonus over his own family.

Then again, he'd taken a hard stand with Eli, and the memory of that night and the following days lived in his dreams far more often than he'd like.

He wanted to laugh it off. But more than that, he wanted Meg to know, to really understand. Maybe then—well, she'd already told him she'd forgiven him. Still, maybe if she really knew what it had been like, she'd understand why he'd done such a terrible thing.

Maybe *he'd* understand why he'd done such a terrible thing.

Sinking his teeth into his lower lip, he bent one knee and rested his forearm on it. The blanket pooled in his lap, and he kept his eyes focused on the lines in the plaid, afraid of what he'd see in Meg's face if he looked her way.

"My dad wasn't a good man." The words came out on a croak. They were also the understatement of the century. "I guess you know that he was supposed to work for Druthers that season ten years ago."

Out of the corner of his eye, he saw her nod.

"Only he didn't. He took off without a word. And *with* a lot of Druthers's stuff."

He expected her to pull away. She leaned in, her breath warm on his cold cheek. "What do you mean? What stuff?"

"His hauler. His GPS. His trailer. His truck. Just about anything that wasn't nailed down. I figure he sold it all." Finally he risked a glance in her direction. Meg's eyes were rounder than the moon and twice as bright. And filled with what could only be labeled compassion.

"What happened to him? Was he arrested?"

"Maybe. But not this side of the border. He made it down to New York, and that's the last anyone I know has heard of him."

"He hasn't contacted you since? At all? No birthday cards or Christmas presents? Nothing?"

He did chuckle then. "He couldn't be bothered with those things when we lived under the same roof. No way he'd remember when we were out of sight."

"Oh, Oliver." Her hands slipped around his waist as she looked into his face. "I didn't realize."

"Yeah, well, that's not the worst part."

She let out a squeak as if to say it couldn't get worse.

"I was glad he left. I told him to go."

She didn't say anything, and the silence was somehow an invitation—not to fill it exactly, but to share the secrets he'd been carrying for so long. It was easier to find words when he was only competing with the low groans of the boats rocking in the water.

"My dad thought I was worthless."

She made a sound of protest, but a quick shake of his head silenced her.

"He ignored me for most of my childhood. When I was about fourteen, he told me it was time I started carrying my weight. Get a job, bring in some money. Eli was skating day and night by then, and it was pretty clear he had a future on the ice. But I was rotten at school and rotten at life. He made sure I never forgot that he thought I was a drain on our family."

She rested her head on his shoulder, squeezing her arms around him. And—if he knew her at all—biting her lips to keep from interrupting him.

"I thought it was just me. I thought he just hated me. He wasn't really violent—a smack on the head sometimes. But he never punched me. Until I was seventeen."

The memory washed over him like an icy shower, sending goose bumps down his arms and a shiver down his spine. The whole house had smelled like chicken and dumplings when he returned from mowing Benjamin Kirsley's back pasture. But when he stepped into the kitchen, he saw dinner splashed across the counters and cabinets. His mom cowered in front of the sink, her apron twisted and soiled, and his dad stood in the middle of the room, his hand raised.

"I don't know if he'd hit my mom before—she swears it

was the first time, the only time. But by the time I walked in on them that day, her cheek was already red. His lips were twisted. There was this evil inside him. Later, after, I found out that my mom had confronted him about drinking and gambling away their savings. And he was well beyond tipsy that day. But in the moment, I just knew I had to protect my mom. I'd never been in a fight before—you know, nothing more than scrapes with my brothers—but I shoved him, and his fist landed on my cheek so hard I thought I'd lose a molar."

He patted the cheek that had borne the scar, the eye that had swelled closed for days. "I missed a week of school afterward, but that day, I refused to go down. I hit him back as hard as I could over and over. Once he was down, he stayed down. Too drunk to stand back up. And then I dragged him outside, kicked his feet, and told him we'd be better off without him. I told him to never come back. The next morning all of his things were gone."

Letting out a tight sigh between his lips, he snuck a glance at Meg. She hadn't moved, but the moonlight turned the single tear track on her face to silver.

He brushed the streak away with his thumb, her skin like butter. "I didn't mean to make you cry."

"No." She sniffled and rubbed her cheek against his shoulder. "I didn't know."

"No one did. I didn't want anyone to. My dad was every bit the miscreant that Druthers called him, but I did everything I could to keep the rest of the island from knowing it."

"But you did such a good thing for your mom."

He grunted. "Maybe. But it wasn't enough."

"You *saved* her."

"No. I left her—I left us—broke and in debt and . . ."

His mouth opened, but it was dry and void of the words he wanted.

"That's not on you. You didn't do that."

"But I did."

*Dear Lord.*

The words were spilling out faster than he wanted them to. If only he could scoop them up and put them back into the hole in his chest where they'd come from. But now those empty spaces had filled with more words, more memories, more confessions. They knew that under this moonlight was a safe place to be laid bare. And oh, how they'd craved the light.

"I remember so clearly the day that we had to leave our house. Mom was crying but trying to hide it. Levi and I packed everything we owned into big black trash bags. He wanted to pack up Eli's stuff, and I told him to leave it because we were never going to see him again. He had left a couple weeks before. He'd been offered a tryout with a team that feeds into the Rangers, and it was his chance at the NHL. But we needed him. We were barely scraping by, and I told him we needed him to stay. He told me he was just going to go for the tryout." Oliver bent his head and scratched the top of it. "I yelled at him that if he was going, he might as well never come back, because I would never forgive him and we would be better off without him."

"Oh, Oliver. I don't even . . . What did your mom say?"

He let his chin fall forward, his shoulders hunching against a knot deep in his chest. But if he kept pulling at it, maybe the ache would ease. He didn't have to go all the way. He didn't have to tell her that he still wondered what Whitaker would think if he knew. He didn't have to put a doubt in her mind that he was worthy and deserving of the business.

"My mom doesn't know. She just knows he never came back, never got in touch. He followed his dream and left us to pack up our lives into . . . well, trash bags."

"But where did you go? I mean, I don't think anyone at school even knew."

"I certainly didn't go spreading it around. And by that point Levi was talking to exactly two people on the face of the planet—my mom and me. One of Mom's friends let us stay in her basement. It was fully finished—a studio apartment. When we got there, your mom was there."

Meg sat up like a shot, pulling away her warmth and leaving only the cold night air. Her question required no words.

"She had a bag of groceries for us and some homemade bread. She didn't say much except for us to let her know if we needed anything. Then she kissed my cheek and hugged my mom and squeezed Levi's hand. And the next day I broke your robot."

Meg wanted to hold Oliver, this big, hunched shadow of a man beside her. She wanted to cry for him some more. And mostly she wanted to erase all of those terrible memories for him.

Since the last was impossible, she threw her arms around his shoulders and pressed her face into his neck. He smelled of salt water and lavender lotion, and she couldn't help but smile at the contradiction.

He slowly wrapped an arm around her waist. "Did you hear what I said? That's why I broke your robot."

She rolled her eyes even though he couldn't see them and spoke into the point where his neck met his shoulder.

"I know. But if I'd been through all of that, *I'd* have broken my robot."

He held her tighter, pulling her closer, even though there was no space between them. "I doubt it. But I appreciate the thought all the same."

She had no more words after that, but she didn't move. She couldn't seem to let go. Pressing her face deeper into him, she savored the texture of his skin. It was somehow equally soft and weathered and scratchy where his beard started. But even that wasn't uncomfortable. Just a new sensation.

But that close, Meg knew the moment that he froze. Every muscle in him turned to stone, and even the rise and fall of his shoulders vanished for a split second.

Because of her.

The truth slammed into her, making her stomach drop through the bottom of the boat. What was she doing? They were just becoming friends.

No, that wasn't quite right. New friends didn't share family secrets or pour out their fears.

They were confidants. Secret safes. They were . . .

And then she couldn't think anymore about how to define their relationship, because his long fingers—slow and tentative—brushed up her spine, firing every nerve and setting her alight. His touch was gentle, but not even the extra sweatshirt she wore could hinder its warmth.

When he made it to her neck, he brushed her hair back, the very tips of his fingers sliding over her flying pulse and across her jawline. His hands, so big, moved with such grace.

All she could hear was the thundering of her own heart.

She knew what was going to happen next. She knew he was going to urge her to look at him. She just wasn't sure she could do it without falling apart.

His thumb ran the rim of her ear, pressing lightly just below the lobe and making her chest flutter. Pinching her eyes closed, she managed a stuttered breath.

"Meg?" The question in his voice rang through her. She had no answer for it.

But she could be brave. Pulling back just far enough to be able to look into his face, she met his shy smile with one of her own. Sucking in her bottom lip, she tilted her head and shrugged.

The moonlight over his face illuminated the shadows of his long dimples, his gaze so deep she was sure he could see all the way into her soul. And she let him look, staring back into his eyes. She'd long since memorized their color—the blue of the sky early in the morning, just before the sun broke the horizon—and she pretended for just a moment that she could really see them.

Reaching up, she brushed his hair from his forehead. Shaggy and dark as night. But soft and thick too. When she tucked it behind his ear, she remembered why he kept it long. His ears stuck out, cute and boyish.

She took her time running her fingers over his cheek, brushing his short whiskers, and curling into him.

All of a sudden, his hand braced around her wrist, and her gaze shot toward the place where his fingers met her skin. He held her gently, and she was quite sure he'd release her if she pulled away even a little bit. She didn't.

With his other hand, he swiped the line of her lower lip. Slow. Soft. Better than any kiss she'd ever had.

Leaning in, she turned up her face, closed her eyes, and prayed, *Lord, let him kiss me.*

Suddenly a light so bright it made her see white behind her eyelids flashed across the sky. Earth-shaking thunder followed only a split second later.

Before Meg could even get her eyes open, Oliver had hopped to his feet and pulled her with him. Pointing south toward a cloud of gray that seemed to connect the heavens and the earth, he said, "Look at that rain." Another flash of lightning zigzagged across the sky. "Come on. We should get out of here."

She took a step only to discover the boat was rocking side to side, the waves already picking up. Out of habit, she reached for the patch behind her ear. Still there. But it wasn't enough to keep her stomach from sloshing with the motion of the boat.

"I'm going to be sick," she moaned.

But then she was weightless, Oliver's arms about her as he carried her to the ladder, where he pushed her up to the dock. He followed right behind her.

"You okay?" He tucked her hair behind her ear, only to have the wind whip it free and back across her face.

"Yeah. Thanks." She cringed at the thought of getting back on the boat in a few hours. "Guess I better double up on my patch for the morning."

He shook his head. "Sleep in. This storm is coming in hard and strong. No one will be fishing in the morning."

Had anyone ever said such sweet words?

"All right. But . . . what are we going to do?"

He got close and whispered in her ear, "I'm going to sleep in too."

She playfully pushed his arm. "No, I mean what are we going to do about watching the boat?"

He shoved his hands into his pockets and lifted his shoulders high, staring out at the coming storm. His hair danced around his face as his lips pursed to the side. "Maybe it's time to move on. Let it go. We haven't had any trouble since that one line, and no one is interested in telling me anything. If it's about my dad, then maybe whoever's behind it feels like the debt has been repaid."

Oh, thank the good Lord.

Sleep. Precious sleep.

"Besides, there are other parts of the business we should be looking at—like the books."

Right. Of course. Because this was a business, and it had to make money to stay afloat—literally. She'd kind of forgotten that. Between learning how to fish and when to fish and where to fish and, well, Oliver, she hadn't thought too much about it.

"Yes. I'll do my part. Just . . . where are the books?"

"I'm going to the studio. Will you be here for supper?"

Oliver looked up from the accounting ledger spread out on the kitchen table before him. Mama Potts stood next to the counter, gathering her bag and apron, her jeans covered in colorful glazes. His eyes darted toward the window over the sink and the gray clouds sweeping across the sky. They had finally cleared away after two and a half days of pouring rain—three days without any income.

"Sure." He didn't have anywhere else to go. At least nowhere else he wanted to be.

His mom kissed his forehead. "Close these books and try to get into some trouble today. You've been so serious lately." With that, she disappeared out the kitchen door, slamming it closed behind her.

That was his mom's way of saying he'd been grumpy. And he had been, so he'd tried to keep to his apartment. But since he didn't have a table there where he could spread out the books and compare this year's numbers with last year's, he'd set up at his mom's kitchen table, trying to get his mind off of what had happened. More accurately, what *hadn't* happened.

It hadn't worked very well. Every time he closed his eyes—even to blink—he saw her face, saw her full lips. His fingers could still feel the silk of her skin, the way the muscles in her throat worked when she swallowed. And every breeze seemed to carry the smell of her shampoo.

He'd opened the books to try to be productive. But all he'd done was miss Meg Whitaker. He hadn't seen her in two days.

Maybe that was a good thing, because when he did see her, he wasn't sure he'd be able to stop from picking up right where they'd left off. She'd felt so good in his arms, the perfect fit, all softness and strength. And if he'd just moved a minute faster . . . but he hadn't wanted to. He'd savored every moment, every step closer.

Oh, they'd been so close.

What if he'd scared her off? What if all the things he'd confessed sunk in and she realized she was too good for him? He'd walked her home that night. He should have kissed her then. Given her a taste of what could be between them. He was pretty sure there was something.

He slammed a fist against the table. Stupid.

A deep chuckle behind him caught him off guard.

"What are you doing up?" he asked. "Isn't this usually your roosting time?"

Levi shuffled from the stairs to the table, his white socks flopping at the toes and nearly falling off. His black hair a wild mess, he rubbed his eyes. "Mom say something about supper?"

Oliver kicked his brother's foot. "It's barely noon."

Leaning crossed arms on the table, Levi nodded at the ledger. "Not good?"

"It's fine."

Over the years, Oliver had learned to read Levi's expressions. If he hadn't, they never would have talked. The one on his face now asked a question he didn't really want to answer. Then again, there were bonuses to having a brother who barely spoke. He wouldn't repeat what he heard.

"I may have almost kissed Meg the other night."

A smirk said he'd caught Levi's attention.

"Yes, Meg Whitaker. We were on the boat, and I don't know what happened, but I told her. Everything."

Levi raised his eyebrows, his forehead wrinkling.

"Yep. Told her about Dad leaving and Eli splitting and those stupid black trash bags."

A line formed above Levi's nose, and he rubbed at it.

"I guess . . . I thought . . . I don't know. It felt good to tell someone else. You know."

Levi let out a snort.

"Okay, maybe *you* don't know. But to a normal human being who's been carrying secrets for a long time, it was nice to just—it felt like I didn't have to carry it alone. Like she was willing to carry some of it with me." Oliver looked into his brother's face, which was twisted with confusion.

"You know she wants the same business you do."

Yes. He knew. He'd reminded himself of that over and over.

Levi took a breath. "You're never going to get both her and the boat."

That felt like a bee sting. Levi was right. There was no way he could win the boat and the girl at the same time. If Whitaker chose him, she'd hate him again for taking away the only part of her family not falling apart.

But if Whitaker chose her, Oliver would have nothing to offer. And there was no way he could work for someone he just wanted to kiss. She might not even deign to hire him.

The best outcome he could hope for was a boat and a fishing business. But was that enough?

"This isn't going to end well, is it?"

Levi chuckled and popped him on the back as he stood up. "Nope."

Oliver rested his elbows on the table and his face in his hands and called himself every kind of fool. Because he was.

He knew it for sure when his phone rang and Meg's name flashed across the screen.

"Hey, Meg. Ready to look at the books?"

"No." She laughed, the sound sweeter than the icing on a cinnamon roll. "I mean, I do want to look at them with you. But that's not why I called."

"Oh?" Hope bubbled in his chest, and he tried to keep it under control with a deep breath.

"I was thinking about what you said."

Well, that was an ominous start. He'd said a lot of things over the last month. Some he was proud of. Others might make her run screaming. But he bit his tongue to keep from blurting out a preemptive apology.

"About my mom. About making memories with her while I can." Her voice grew thick, but she powered on. "I had this idea. She's always liked the beach, and I wanted to take her. After all this rain, it'll be clean and beautiful."

"That sounds like a great idea. I'm sure she'll love it."

"It's just that . . . she's not very stable, and I'd rather not ask my dad. It would be nice to make a memory just with her." She paused for a second. "I was wondering—that is, if you're not busy—would you like to go with us?"

He was every kind of fool.

# seventeen

Meg opened the passenger door to Oliver's truck and turned to help her mom onto the bench seat. But Oliver was already there, picking her up by the waist and sliding her gently to just this side of the gearshift.

Her mom patted his cheek and offered a half smile. Meg moved to crawl up after her, and Oliver slipped his hands around her waist, boosting her in too. He winked at her as he closed them in. He was around the front of the truck and behind the steering wheel before she could get her mom buckled in.

When Oliver turned the key, the old truck rumbled to life, grumbling about being awakened.

Only then did her mom begin to look around, her hand grabbing Meg's thigh. "Where are we going?"

"It's okay, Mom. We're going to the beach. Remember? To splash in the ocean."

"Where's Walt?"

Meg grabbed her hand and held it firmly. "He's at home." They'd left him sitting down with the latest spy thriller from his favorite author just a few moments before. He'd kissed his wife's cheek and then let Meg lead her out the door.

"Ready, ladies?" Oliver asked.

Meg nodded, and her mom did too, if cautiously.

Oliver stretched his arm across the back of the seat and turned to look over his shoulder as he backed out of the driveway. His fingers brushed Meg's shoulder, and she froze, trying not to relive every moment of their last interaction. Every moment on the boat beneath the moon and stars. In his arms.

But the memory swept over her, like she was swimming in a sea of seltzer.

He pulled his hand away as though he hadn't even realized they'd made contact. She forced herself to let it go, focusing on her mom's bouncing knee.

"It's nice to get out of the house, isn't it, Mom? After being cooped up for a few days."

Her mom nodded, but her gaze was pointed toward one of the air vents. Meg followed the line and then expanded her focus from the vents to the entire black dashboard—clean and nearly shining in the September sun.

She'd only been in Oliver's truck once before, and she'd been so distracted on the trip to the hospital that she hadn't paid any attention. Now she looked her fill. She didn't know what she'd expected, but this wasn't it. The floorboards were as neat as the seat, every dashboard crevice free of dust. Even a glance into the truck's bed revealed only a chipped red toolbox and nothing more.

"What's your favorite part of the beach, Mrs. Whitaker?"

Meg jumped at his question, but her mom didn't seem surprised.

"The waves. When the sand disappears."

Meg knew that moment well, the feeling when the outgoing waves pulled the sand beneath her toes back out to sea. It felt like she was going to be dragged right along with it out to the deep. She had to fight to stay standing despite the longing to see where the tides would take her.

But her mom wouldn't ever know that surging joy again. There was no way she could stand on the shifting sand without falling, let alone hold her own against the rolling water.

Maybe this had been a terrible idea. Maybe Meg would only be making memories she'd rather forget. She wanted to remember her mom as strong and shining and filled with joy. But would she only regret this later?

The realization came too late as Oliver pulled into a parking spot beside a short boardwalk through tall grass that led to the sand. At least they were only minutes from home. If this went south, they'd just go back to the house.

Meg opened her door, and the smell of freshness, of water and earth and sky baked in warm sunshine, flowed in. Her mom immediately lifted her nose and inhaled, a lazy smile following.

"Sit tight," Oliver said. "I'll help you down."

Meg decided that the offer wasn't for her, so she hopped down on her own, nearly landing on his bare toes.

He was wearing thongs. She was too, but this was the first time she could remember seeing so much of him—from his knees down his hairy calves and well-shaped ankles to his solid feet.

"I'd have helped you down too," he whispered, leaning past her to lift her mom to the ground.

Positioning himself on her mom's other side, he looped his arm through hers. "Ready?"

Her mom nodded, and they took off for the bridge, Meg slamming the truck door behind them and scrambling to catch up. As they reached the wooden walkway, the sounds of life disappeared, fading into the gentle clapping of the water. Slow. Steady. Inviting.

At the far end of the bridge, her mom stopped, her foot raised but not ready to step into the shifting dry sand.

A few kilometers down the shore, there was a beach of red clay, rippled and rocky. The water had packed it tight. It might have been so much safer.

"Whoa, whoa." Oliver held her back. "Bare feet only." He knelt before her mom and slipped off her sandals. Looking up with a wink, he said, "Now don't go running off without me."

Meg's insides turned into spaghetti, her chest expanding with something even bigger than she'd felt that night on the boat. His smile was for her mom, but it filled her like it was just for her. Like he'd come to this beach with her in mind. Planned this moment for her alone.

Meg wrapped her arm about her mom's waist, and they took a careful step. And another. Then they paused to squish their toes in the sand. Her mom lifted her face to the sky, the afternoon sunshine enveloping them.

It took nearly twenty minutes to make it to the water, and her mom took the last steps faster, her toe catching on the sand. She jerked forward, but Oliver was right there, his arms looping around her shoulders and pulling her to safety even as Meg clung to her arm.

"All right there?" Oliver said.

"The . . . um . . . the . . . in."

Meg froze. Her mom wanted to put her feet—or more—in

the water. She began to shake her head, but Oliver was already there. "All right. But you have to hold on tight."

Meg caught his eye and tried to wave him off.

"We've got this." He motioned Meg to the other side, and they each wrapped an arm around her waist. Then they held on to her hands.

Her mom stepped forward slowly. When the water nipped at her toes, her eyes went wide and bright. Another wave caught them off guard, splashing cool water up to their knees and getting the hem of her pink Bermuda shorts wet. Then came the tug of the receding wave.

Meg felt the pull but fought it. Her mom didn't have the same strength, and her feet began to slip.

"Mom!"

Oliver moved so quickly she didn't even realize what he was doing, until he scooped her mom into his arms. Her chirp of laughter reached the tops of the trees in the parking lot.

Every worry melted away with that sound, and Meg reached up on her tiptoes to kiss her mom's cheek. "I love you."

"Me too," she said.

Oliver caught her eye, his smile filled with joy and only a brief touch of sadness.

"Thank you." She mouthed the words just as her mom wiggled to be put down.

They returned to playing in the surf, splashing each other, laughter abundant, joy even more so. The sun had almost reached the western horizon by the time her mom sagged into Oliver's arms. Meg motioned to the truck, and Oliver scooped her mom back up.

They rode back in contented silence, her mom's head lolling. Oliver parked by the side door and carried her back inside, where her eager husband was waiting.

Meg kissed his cheek, squeezed his hand, and then led Oliver back outside. Her cheeks still hurt from smiling as she closed the door behind them.

"That was brilliant," he said, a near skip in his step into the side yard. "I had no idea she loved the water so much."

"Honestly, I think she's missed it." Meg lifted her face, closed her eyes, and let the moment wash over her.

"You did a good thing today, kid."

She nodded as she opened her eyes, her smile tilting as something new took hold of her. "You were right."

He slapped a hand to his chest, his face contorting in comical surprise. "Who, me? Right? Who'd have guessed it?"

She shoved his shoulder, and he swayed away before coming back close to her, his dimples cutting laugh lines on either side of his mouth. A light in his eyes that she'd missed before outshone the orange sun.

Suddenly she lost all control of her faculties. It was the only explanation for why she shot to her tiptoes, grabbed either side of his face, and pressed her lips to his.

Oh dear. That was not what she'd meant to do. Certainly not part of the day's plan.

No. No. No. Not good.

He froze, his lips warm but unmoving.

She thought they'd been on the same page on the boat, but he hated this. He didn't respond at all. Nothing. Limp noodle.

Despite the flash mob destroying her insides.

She jumped back, eyes wide—but they couldn't be any wider than his. He was still as stone, and she prayed for a tidal wave that would wash her away before he pulled himself from whatever trance she'd caused.

She'd meant to say thanks and wish him a good day. Instead, she'd lost her mind.

She'd meant to tell him he was a good friend. Instead, she'd thrown herself at him.

And he was not interested.

*Idiot.* There weren't enough words in the English language to describe how foolish that had been, so in the absence of said tidal wave, she turned to bolt.

She didn't even get two steps. His hand, so coarse yet gentle, gripped her wrist and spun her right back around to him. She would have slammed into his chest except that she pressed her free hand over his heart. His other hand snaked around her waist, pulling her in closer, deeper.

Breath catching in the back of her throat, she tried to look away, but all she could see was the strong column of his neck and the bob of his Adam's apple. In all honesty, she wanted to flee the scene of the crime. But that didn't seem a real possibility given the vise around her waist and the wall in front of her.

Then he took a breath. Closed his eyes. And kissed her.

She squeaked in response, but there was nowhere to go. Nowhere she wanted to go either, at least not anymore. So she sank into him.

He was an expert at this, his lips firm and urgent, drawing her into something unexpected and wild. He was a riptide pulling her out to sea, and she couldn't fight it. Not that she wanted to. It was the sweetest tide she'd ever known.

Releasing her arm, he cupped her cheek, his thumb gliding below her closed lashes, leaving a trail of electricity in its wake. It crackled and sparked, but she refused to open her eyes, only leaning further into his embrace.

Her pulse skittered, the rhythm strange and new. Only when she'd learned it did she realize that, beneath her palm, his heartbeat matched her own. He was lightning and she thunder, their stories so long intertwined.

Her legs turned to pudding, and she grabbed his shoulders, holding herself up even as he scooped her into his arms and up against the side of the house. They crashed into the wall hard enough to rattle a window. He gasped. She laughed. They both gulped in air.

His forehead pressed to hers, he whispered, "Tell me to stop."

Eyes still pinched closed, she gave the only response that came to mind. "Why?"

Oh dear. At this rate she'd become a scandal in no time. She was kissing her former nemesis against the side of her parents' house, in view of God and anyone who happened to be driving by.

And she couldn't make herself care.

"Because . . . I don't want you to regret this."

"Not going to be a problem."

Hands on either side of her waist, he stepped closer, leaving not even a breath between them. Walking his fingers up her arm, he shot fireworks down to her toes. His hands were magic. She should have known it wasn't Mama Potts's cream that was so special. It was him.

For her, it was him.

"How do you do that?"

"Hmm?" His breath was at her ear, and she sighed as his nose pressed into her hair.

*Make me feel like I'm going to melt and I don't even care.*

But she couldn't get her tongue to form the words, not with him surrounding her. The smell of wood and salt and the sea clung to him.

"You smell like my face cream," he growled into her neck.

"It was mine first." Her words were muffled against his shoulder, but she could feel the shaking of his laughter.

"Fine. But it smells better on you."

"Agree to disagree," she whispered.

Then she couldn't disagree about anything as his lips dragged from her ear to her chin, his whiskers prickly, sending all of her focus there. To the point where they connected. To the point of fire. And oh, such sweet fire.

When his lips finally found hers again, she was lost. Adrift in the sea without a lighthouse. Except for him.

Because somehow he'd become that steady, faithful beam across the rolling waves.

Oliver needed to stop. He had to pull away. If he kept this up, he'd be addicted. And there was no endgame that saw them happy—saw them together.

But the more he drank from her lips—her sweet strawberry lips—the more he craved.

She sighed into him, and he was lost. He couldn't care about the future or think past the moment. He could only hold on to her, enjoy every second for as long as it lasted.

Dragging his fingers down the bare line of her arm, he savored the silk of her skin. She shivered, and he did it again, remembering the whimper she'd made when he'd massaged Mama Potts's miracle cream into her sore muscles. He'd give anything to hear her make that sound again.

Instead, she nearly purred, wiggling against him like she wanted to get beneath his skin.

She was already there. Already so much a part of him that he couldn't imagine a morning without her.

It wasn't the coffee she brought or the way her nose wrinkled when he scooped out bait from the bucket. It wasn't the way she worked as hard as Kyle or refused to leave any part of the business to him alone. It wasn't anything but her. Just Meg. Just who she was. The way she fiercely loved her mom and cared for her dad. The way she gave him a safe place to spill his secrets.

When the season was over, he'd have to settle for sitting behind her every Sunday, leaning forward, praying for just a whiff of her shampoo, a sniff of the woman she was.

It wasn't going to be enough. It never would be.

As much as he wanted to hold on to her forever, to pretend they could go on just like this, he had to put some space between them.

As he pulled away, he caught sight of her shy smile, lower lip caught between her teeth. All he could say was, "Meg Whitaker, you've been holding out on me."

She laughed—the rich, sweet sound he always had to work so hard for. If this was work, he'd sign up for a lifetime of it.

No. That was future thinking. He could think only of the present.

"You're one to talk, Ross. If I'd known you could kiss like that, I'd have made you make up for my robot years ago."

"Gladly." He shoved a hand through his hair and tried not to stare at her. Long, tanned limbs in jean shorts and tank top, leaning against the house with one knee bent and a foot pressed to the wall behind her. Her long blonde hair, which he'd grown accustomed to seeing confined to a tight bun, hung loose over her shoulders. She looked just like she had in high school, relaxed and peaceful, all the world for her taking.

She could do anything. Why would she settle for the life of a fisherman? He knew why she wanted the business at that moment. But how long would she want it after her mom was gone? Maybe she was chaining herself to something she didn't want for the sake of a legacy. Maybe she wasn't being fair to herself.

"We'll be back on the water in the morning."

With a nod, she pushed away from the wall. "Thank you, Oliver. For what you did for my mom—and for me—today."

"Anytime." He hated that he meant it.

# eighteen

Meg hadn't been on a date since her last semester at school. Charlie Bunting had been a graduate student too. Philosophy. He'd taken her to a poetry reading where they'd sipped bitter tea, and she'd said exactly six words. "Thank you for a lovely evening."

He hadn't called her for a second date. Thank goodness. Dating wasn't exactly her forte. Which was fine, since this was most definitely not a date.

But as she pushed open the white door of Carrie's, the two-story blue home that had been converted into a restaurant, her stomach swarmed with butterflies.

"Hey, Meg," Carrie called, her hands filled with dirty dishes. She huffed a strand of curly brown hair out of her eyes. "Come on in. Sit anywhere."

Meg scanned the tables, looking for a familiar face. They were all familiar—neighbors and church members, store owners and actors she'd seen on the little community theater stage her whole life. All finally taking a breath and a break after a busy tourist season. And most treating themselves to Carrie's famous pot roast.

But she didn't see shaggy black hair and bright blue eyes among them, so she slipped into the far seat at the nearest empty table and watched the door. The steady buzz of conversation rose and fell as she tapped the toe of her sandal against the center pole of the square table.

Carrie reappeared, dishes gone and a washrag in hand. "You haven't been here in ages. How you been?"

She scrambled for a response that didn't include falling asleep on the sofa because she was so tired. Or skipping meals because procuring food was harder than being hungry. So she went with simple. "Really busy."

"But you're not at the school anymore? Jenna said she has Mr. Wilkey for science. She said he's terrible, and they really miss you."

Meg tried for a smile. "Oh, I'm sure he's doing his best." But even she knew that wouldn't be enough. Jenna had been one of her prize pupils the year before. Her love of physics and calculus was unmatched by her peers. Though Jenna was teased by her classmates, Meg had always encouraged her to do what she enjoyed.

But she'd closed the door on that. She'd chosen her family's legacy. She'd made the right choice.

She was pretty sure.

"Jenna is a very smart girl—she'll do fine."

Carrie offered a curt nod, but even the freckles that covered her cheeks looked sad. "Can I get you something to drink?"

"Um, I'm waiting for—"

The bell over the front door jingled, and they both turned

toward it. A pretty woman entered on a cloud, floating across the floor. Back straight, nose high, she could have been one of the new generation of princesses. It wasn't unheard of for British royals to make their way to the Maritimes. Even Kate and William had visited the island once on their Canadian tour.

But when the woman turned, Meg recognized her. Not royalty. Violet Donaghy. She wasn't related to Oliver's family, but she might as well have been. Her past was certainly a question. One the old biddies in town wanted answered, and one they'd never been able to.

All that was truly known was that she was a talented artist, her pottery some of the best on the island. Mama Potts had taken her in as her own, and together they'd built a blooming little tourist shop along the highway. But Violet had never blended into little Victoria by the Sea.

Violet's gaze landed on her, and Meg waved. It seemed to be the invitation she needed to glide in Meg's direction. "I'm looking for Oliver. Have you seen him?"

"Um, no. I'm supposed to meet him here."

Carrie raised her eyebrows. "I'll come back?"

"Yes, thanks," Meg said. Turning back to Violet, she asked, "Is everything all right? Is Mama Potts—"

"No, no. Nothing like that. Everyone is fine. Well, nearly fine. No one is . . . injured, exactly."

"Levi?"

"Is at the school."

Precisely where he was every weeknight. Cleaning up after rowdy students, working quietly away. A few times she'd worked late grading exams and surprised him when he came in to empty the garbage bins. He'd mumbled an apology and scooted backward into the hallway. He didn't say much, but the floors of their school shined. The walls received regular coats of fresh paint, and the pipes never froze in the winter. His name wasn't on the building, but everyone knew that it belonged to Levi.

"Wait." Violet's gaze swept over her, precise and assessing as she slid into the opposite chair.

Meg ran a hand over her ponytail, taming any flyaways. She pressed her lips together, smoothing the pink gloss she'd applied before leaving her apartment. "What?"

"Are you and Oliver on a date?"

"No. Of course not." Her cheeks heated, and to keep from covering them she tucked her hands under her legs. Maybe Violet would just think it was warm inside. Which was partially true.

"I saw him earlier." Violet's smile grew wide, delight in her eyes. "He was shaving. He's so lazy about it most of the time."

Meg couldn't help it. Her hand shot to her neck, to the place that had been red after they'd kissed. It wasn't even noticeable after a week. But Violet didn't seem to miss anything.

"It's you. Have you and he been . . . ?" Violet's fingers bounced back and forth. Meg didn't even know what that meant.

"Working together? Yes. A lot. And we're talking tonight about more work things."

"Ri-ight." Her singsong would have fit right in on a school-yard, followed by a song about kissing in a tree. But there was genuine joy painted across her face. "He's such a—"

"You're in my seat."

Both women looked up, and Meg had never been so thankful to see her coworker. Oliver towered above them, broad and imposing except for the gentle smile across his clean-shaven face. He looked younger, softer. She wondered what his skin felt like.

She sat on her hands again.

Violet got up slowly. "I thought you were having dinner with a friend."

He looked at Meg, then back at Violet. "I am."

"Uh-huh." Violet's gaze swung back and forth between them. "You kids have fun now." She turned to go but stopped short. "And Oliver, call me later."

"Doubtful," he said, falling into her vacated seat. "Sorry about that. She thinks she's my big sister."

"Did you"—she gave the room another quick survey for familiar faces—"tell her about what happened?" How he'd kissed her silly and made her doubt everything she'd ever thought she wanted.

"What? No." His denial came out louder than her question, and he immediately dropped his volume. "I wouldn't. I didn't tell anyone."

She nodded silently, taking in the new lines of his face, crisp and even.

"What about you? Did you tell your dad?"

Chewing on her fingernail, she shook her head. "That's not exactly the kind of thing we talk about."

He rubbed a hand down his face, and she could tell he wasn't used to the smooth parts as his fingers slowed down, following the new shape to his chin. "I just meant, maybe it would be best if we don't tell him—or anyone. At least not until . . ."

His voice fell away, but she understood completely. It would do them no favors to confuse her dad about their relationship—whatever it was. A decision still had to be made. Besides, the extent of their relationship was an axis-tilting kiss. Nothing more.

*Yeah, right. Keep telling yourself that.*

No. They'd had exactly one kiss and one almost-kiss. That did not make a relationship.

*What about the way he is with your mom?*

Irrelevant.

*And the way he held you when you cried?*

Those were extenuating circumstances.

*And how he's safe and strong and way more handsome than you thought?*

Pipe down.

This was no time for her inner voice to decide it had an opinion. A wrong one at that.

In the end, she simply nodded her understanding to him and pointed to the books he'd brought with him. "Want to look at those or eat first?"

He responded before she'd even finished her question. "Eat."

———

Oliver scooped up the last bite of Carrie's famous pot roast and let it melt in his mouth. So tender and filled with rich flavor, its spices subtle and inviting. And so filling. He set his fork down, leaned back, and rubbed his stomach.

Across the table, Meg looked down at her plate, still half full. Then she looked at his empty one. "Feel better now?"

"I do, thanks." He stretched from side to side. "But I'll be ready for second dinner in a couple of hours."

Her forehead wrinkled. "*Second* dinner?"

"Follow-up food. You know, that meal you have before bed so you don't wake up in the middle of the night because your stomach is trying to eat itself."

The corners of her mouth twitched, and he knew she was fighting a smile. Still, she managed a benign question. "Is that a problem you normally have?"

He shrugged. He was a big guy with a big appetite, and he worked hard every single day. His peewee hockey coach had always yelled something about feeding the beast. And his beast liked protein. Lots of it.

But for Meg, he said, "At least I share my snacks."

"Yes, you do. And it's greatly appreciated."

They fell into silence, but without the clinking of their forks against plates and quiet chewing, it was louder than before. Before, he'd been able to focus on his meal. Now he could only stare at her and notice subtle things, like how her eyelashes swept across her cheeks when she looked down. How her honey-colored hair curled as it fell over her shoulder.

How if he kept looking at her that way, someone was bound to notice. Bound to tell the whole town. And it was bound to get to Whitaker.

That was the unknown.

Whitaker could be overjoyed. Or he could decide he didn't have to wait the four weeks until the end of the season to send Oliver on his way.

Oliver couldn't take that risk. Not when he already knew how he and Meg would end up.

"So, the books?" Meg reached for the ledger at the same time he did, their fingers connecting, pausing. For just a moment, he let his touch linger on her hand, felt her curl into him, only their pinkies touching.

He heard her breath catch and felt the sting in his chest, the desire to pull her into his arms in front of half the town.

Instead, he slid his chair around to the side of the table, pushed the salt and pepper shakers out of the way, and opened the black book. Its fake leather cover gave way easily as the pages fell open to the latest entries in his own hand.

Meg leaned in, squinting at the narrow lines.

"How much do you know about keeping the books?"

She looked up at him, her nose wrinkled and lips pinched. "Let's pretend there were no accounting classes in my engineering degree."

"Sure." He pointed at a column on the far right. "So the simple explanation—at least the way Whitaker explained it to me—is that this column is for expenses and this one is for income. Every business expense, from paychecks to fuel for the boat, gets recorded here."

Pointing a long finger at a line item, she nodded. "You made new traps to replace the cluster we lost."

He nodded. "That's the wood I bought for them. And these"—he pointed to the other column—"are income. Every time we deliver crates of lobster, the shore buyer pays us by the pound for hard shell based on the going rate."

"How come the numbers are going down? We've been catching more."

"The prices are fluctuating. They usually even out over the course of the season, but they've taken a hit for whatever reason. Could be a big supply from Nova Scotia or Maine. Or maybe the demand is just down right now."

Her lips pursed to the side, pinched together as she tapped a finger next to each of the income numbers. "There's one for every day of the season so far, except the three days we couldn't fish."

"No fishing, no income."

She nodded, her gaze devouring the numbers, probably seeing patterns and sequences that he never could. "And if we keep going in this direction, we're barely going to break even for the season."

His gut twisted hard, but not from shock. He'd figured out the same thing. Sitting at his mom's kitchen table on those rainy days, he'd seen the same trajectory. If the fisheries didn't raise their prices or the catches didn't increase, he and Meg would end the season with not much more than a handful of two-dollar toonies to split between them.

Sure, they'd each been taking home a paycheck every week. Enough to get them by. But he'd been counting on an end-of-the-season bonus—the money that fishermen used to get them through the rest of the year. Only his wasn't to hold him over for the rest of the year. It was to set him up for the rest of his life.

As the owner, Whitaker would take home a hefty chunk. But without a decent paycheck at the end of the season, Oliver would never be able to afford his first payment on the business. He'd been saving for more than a year, socking away every nickel and dime he'd made the season before and every extra penny from the odd jobs he'd worked through the winter, spring, and summer. He was so close to having the first payment—but he'd been counting on making up the rest at the end of this season. He was determined not to be disqualified on a technicality.

Okay, it was more than a technicality. No one would give a loan to someone who couldn't pay them back. And at the moment, even paying Whitaker the first payment would be more than a stretch.

It would all be different when he owned the business. At that point, he'd be the one taking home everything off the top. He might have to pinch pennies for a few more years, but he'd make enough for the next four payments. If he couldn't come up with the first payment, though, he wouldn't have to worry about making any of the others.

Meg leaned in closer, her shoulder brushing against his, her gaze zipping back and forth over the lines. "Are there expenses we can cut?"

He pointed at six lines. "These are all from having to replace the traps that were cut. Those others are bait and fuel." He indicated another three lines. "These are our paychecks."

She tapped the largest number. "And what's this one?"

"Your dad's cut."

She grinned at him. "I guess it's good to be the boss."

He chuckled, but it didn't really feel like a laughing matter. Of all the years for the market to tank.

Her finger found its way back to the income lines, each day steadily lower. "So how much did we start at?"

"Nearly eight dollars a pound."

"So we're at a little more than half that now?"

"A little better than five."

She closed her eyes, but he could see them shifting back and forth as she worked the numbers. "So if we stay at five, we'll more than break even. But if the prices keep dropping, we're going to be in serious trouble."

"Or if we have more unexpected expenses. Or if we can't fish for some reason."

Her face filled with concern, she asked, "What do we do?"

"Same thing fishermen have been doing for hundreds of years. Pray for good weather, floating boats, and a big catch."

That made her smile as he'd hoped, but he could still read the fear in her eyes.

"Nothing about this job is stable," he said. "None of it's a guarantee."

"So why do you want it so much?"

Her question pushed him back in his chair, and he crossed his arms, his mind playing over the right answer. This was his chance to convince her that fishing wasn't the job for her, that this wasn't a business she wanted to take on. But she had something he didn't—a heritage of lobstermen who had weathered the storms of the industry a lot longer than he had.

His legacy wasn't anything to be proud of, but he could change it for the next generation. He didn't have to leave the same for them. The sins of his father didn't need to become the sins of his children.

"It's a chance I'll never get anywhere else. I never went to uni—I never really wanted to. But the lobsters make sense to me. And if I want to pass anything down to my children, then this is my chance."

Her cheeks turned pink, as they often did. Cute and sweet. "You've thought about having kids?"

"Sure. I guess. I mean, it's hard not to when you think about buying a license that's been one family's heirloom for three generations. I see why your dad wants you to have it."

He could cut his own tongue off. He had no business blurting out things like that. Reminding her why she should care about something she hadn't until a couple months before.

But it was the truth. No matter how much leverage it gave her in this competition.

That didn't mean he was giving in. Not until Whitaker announced his decision. And that meant one thing. Oliver had to figure out a way to come up with the gap in his first payment. Fast.

No problem. Five thousand dollars grew on trees. He hoped.

# nineteen

After another week of sunshine, the storm clouds rolled in thick and heavy once again. The weatherman said that the rain wouldn't stick around for long.

Meg stuck another motion sickness patch behind her ear before she left the house. Just to be safe. Based on the numbers she and Oliver had looked at the week before, they couldn't afford to miss even a day's catch. Unless the waves were bigger than the boat or lightning was striking the water, they were going out.

When she arrived at the dock, there was a chill in the air, which felt thick and wet. The leggings that had kept her warm and dry all season suddenly felt thinner than linen. She snuggled deeper into her hoodie, wishing she'd added a fourth layer. Once they were out on the water working, she'd warm up.

She grabbed the paper tray of coffee cups from the passenger seat and held it close, breathing in the rich aroma and steam.

Oliver and Kyle were already aboard the *Pinch*, and she

handed them the coffee before crawling down the ladder. Kyle's was gone before her feet landed on the deck. He raised his cup in a silent toast of appreciation.

Oliver savored his, but his gaze never drifted from the horizon and the coming storm.

"You worried?" she asked softly.

He took another sip. "Don't suppose that would help anything. Let's get in and get out as fast as we can today."

She nodded and set about doing her part to get them on their way. In a few minutes they were chugging through the water, rolling with the waves. Her stomach took a roll too, and she pressed at her extra patch. It hadn't been on long enough to do much, so she just had to fight through.

Ignoring the rise and fall of her stomach, she pulled the hauler from its below-deck storage spot and wrestled it into place on its base. While she held it still, Kyle secured it to the footing with a metal pin. She extended the arm, adjusted the angle, and plugged it into the water-tight socket. As they approached the first green buoy, she gave Oliver a thumbs-up.

But when she hooked the line and fed it through the wheels, the machine didn't turn on. She flipped the switch again. Nothing.

"Something's wrong," she called to Oliver, who was almost immediately by her side.

"What is it?" His eyebrows came together in a deep *V*, his arms crossed over his chest.

They couldn't afford this. Not any day. Especially not today, with the wind picking up and the storm brewing.

"I don't know. Either it's not getting power or the motor is broken. But the rest of the boat has power, right?"

"Yes. The GPS and everything else are plugged in and working."

Kyle stepped to her other side, silent, his face shadowed by uncertainty.

"Maybe the motor snapped."

Oliver sighed, scrubbing a hand down his face. "We're going to have to pull this in on our own. We've got a backup hand crank." He didn't say it, but they all knew that would take longer. So much longer.

Meg unplugged the hauler and plugged it back in, praying to hear the subtle whirring. But there was nothing. She left it unplugged, lifting her face into the drizzle. Not the ideal place to work on anything electrical, but she had to try. "Do you have a screwdriver and needle-nose pliers?"

Oliver pointed toward the wheel. "In the cabinet on the lower left."

"Okay, you set up the hand crank. I'll see if I can fix this."

She immediately found the tools she needed in Oliver's organized kit. It was sparse, but it reminded her of her dad's garage with every tool in its place. She threw a clear tarp over the hauler and knelt under it. With a few quick twists of the Phillips-head screwdriver, she removed the cover from the little motor. Shining a flashlight around it, she looked for anything that might have caused it to stop working. It had worked just as it should the day before, and all the pieces of the motor seemed to be in place. She pressed her nose right up to the metal. No burning smell or strange odor.

She couldn't very well take all the pieces apart in this situation. But there had to be a Band-Aid. A patch. Something to get them through this day.

The beam of her flashlight bounced, and then she saw it.

A red wire, severed. The power supply couldn't get to the motor if the wires weren't connected. She clipped the red outer protector and peeled it back to reveal the tip of the loose wire. Crisp. Sharp. Cut.

This wasn't an accident. In fact, it was clearly sabotage. But why so subtle? Last time it had been blatant. This was hidden inside and covered back up with the motor's casing. Someone had wanted them not to find it or to discover it far from shore.

Well, she wasn't going to let them win.

With the pliers, she unwound the short end of the cut wire, careful not to jostle any of the other small pieces.

The tarp over her head rustled, and a pair of broad shoulders wedged their way into her cocoon. "Find anything?"

She held up the ends of the wire. "Someone didn't want us to be able to use our hauler." She kept her voice low, her gaze darting toward Kyle, who was baiting a cluster of traps.

A shadow fell across Oliver's face. "You're saying someone broke onto the boat last night, took apart the hauler's engine, clipped one little wire, and then put it back so we wouldn't notice?"

"I know it sounds ridiculous, but I don't see any other explanation."

"But who knew we weren't staying on the boat anymore?" He pinched his eyes closed and sighed. "If this is really about my dad . . ." He didn't finish his thought. He didn't need to.

But no one had confessed. No one would own up to anything.

She cocked her head as she stared into the distance through the clear tarp. There wasn't much to see but gray skies and clouds so low they covered the bridge. So she tried to conjure memories of her dad telling stories at the dinner table. Tales of the water and sailors and the rules.

"My dad told me a story once about a guy who fished out of his area. He was technically in his zone, but he set his traps in another fisherman's spot. His line was cut, and no one fessed up to the actual act. But his sins were made clear, and he never made that mistake again. Last time, you said someone thought we broke a rule. That means you thought someone was trying to punish us. But that doesn't work if you don't know what you're being punished for. You can't change your ways if you don't know what you've done wrong."

He grunted in agreement.

"This isn't punishment. They're trying to scare us off."

His eyes narrowed. "Can you fix this?"

"I just need a spool of wire."

He disappeared, the tarp flapping in the wind and letting in a gust of cold air, and returned before she'd warmed her little shelter back up. Bending on one knee, he presented the gray wire to her as a knight to his princess.

Chuckling, she snipped and twisted the wires together. In two minutes she had the motor humming and the wheels spinning, pulling in the catch. Kyle cheered and Oliver bestowed a broad smile, and they fell back into the rhythm of their routine.

With every buoy she caught and every haul she made, Meg couldn't help but wonder just who wanted them to give up. Who would benefit if she and Oliver backed out? Was there another buyer interested in the business? Or was it all about Oliver's dad?

She had so many questions. And the only person who might have some answers was the one person she couldn't ask. Talking to her dad would mean revealing the trouble they'd encountered, adding a weight to his shoulders. He'd told them he didn't want to be bothered by phone calls and negotiations. He didn't want to deal with questions and problems. He just wanted to take care of her mom.

Besides, if she asked what he knew, she'd be compelled to share what she knew—or at least what they assumed. And if she shared their assumptions about Druthers, she'd have to reveal what she knew about Oliver's dad.

Her own dad knew what had happened—at least the part about Oliver's father leaving town. But something in her gut told her that a reminder of Oliver's father's theft wouldn't reflect well on the man he wanted to sell his business to. Dean Ross's reputation couldn't sink any lower, but Oliver's would take a hit too.

And Oliver didn't deserve that.

———

That evening, Oliver slammed the door of his truck below the stairs to his apartment. He eyed the kitchen window on the house, the light shining bright even in the twilight. Mama Potts had surely made something delicious, but darkness would come soon. And with it, a return to the *Pinch*.

Whoever was sabotaging them was brazen and fearless, and apparently nothing short of sleeping on the boat was going to protect her, protect their business.

Meg had taken the hauler home for the night to give it a more permanent fix. But what else could be—would be—taken or broken?

He'd hoped his days of sleeping on the boat were over, but he didn't have much of a choice. Even if he'd miss his night-watch partner. Meg could probably use the sleep, and he wasn't about to guilt her into another night under the stars. Or another three weeks under the stars, as the case was likely to be.

A hearty meal would hit the spot. An hour in his own bed would be even better.

As he reached the foot of the stairs, his phone rang. Violet. Again. She'd called him nearly every day for a week, but she hadn't left him a message. If it was important, she'd tell his mom, who would pass along the news. Not that he'd seen his mom much lately either.

He sent her call to voicemail and slid his phone back into his pocket. It immediately rang again. He yanked it back out, prepared to give Violet a piece of his mind. Only it wasn't her number. It wasn't one he had saved in his phone.

"Hello?"

"Oliver Ross? This is Chad Stein. I'm the sales manager at South Shore Auto."

"Mr. Stein." Oliver dropped to sit on the third step, resting his arm across his bent knees. "Thank you for calling me back."

"What can I do for you?"

Oliver stared over the grass to his truck parked at the end of the gravel drive. She was faded and weathered and nearly as old as he was. And he'd owned her since he was eighteen. She was also the only thing of any value that he owned.

"Yes, sir. I was wondering if you might be interested in purchasing a 1999 Ford F-150."

Chad coughed. "A '99, you say?"

"Yes. But she runs great and has less than a hundred thousand kilometers on her."

"I'm sure it's a great vehicle, but we don't keep anything

that old on our lot. Now, if you were looking to trade it in on a new model, I'd be happy to make a deal for you." His tone turned salesy, something he probably didn't even notice.

But Oliver scowled as it grated on him, a reminder that he couldn't afford a new truck. He couldn't afford a used truck. He couldn't afford anything—including a dream that was almost in his grasp.

"Thank you," he forced out. "I'm not looking for a new vehicle. Just looking to unload the one I have."

"Ah, well, good luck with that," Chad said before ending the call.

Oliver held his phone, resting his forehead against his hands. He tried to pray for wisdom, for the right next step, but his mind was a jumbled mess of boats and traps and a beautiful blonde and kisses—such perfect kisses.

Once, he had been focused. He'd known what he wanted and gone after it. He still wanted that boat, that license, that life. But he was afraid it wasn't enough anymore. Even if he managed to scrape up enough money for that first payment, then what?

*God, what am I supposed to do?*

"Why aren't you answering my calls?" A shrill voice carried across the lawn, jerking him out of his prayers.

"Violet? Were you calling me from inside the house?"

She shrugged, marching through the grass. "So what if I was? You're the one not picking up."

"I know." He waved his phone. "I've had a few things going on lately. Some of us work for a living instead of playing with clay all day."

She clucked her tongue. "You better not let Mama Potts hear you talking like that."

With a shake of his head, he said, "Never." He meant it. His mom had worked endless hours to build Mama Potts's Red Clay Shoppe, her artsy studio and boutique, from nothing. Literally. She'd squared his dad's debts and then started at zero, working three jobs. She'd refused to let him drop out of school to work full-time. "What's so urgent that you keep calling but can't leave a message?"

Some of the fire left her eyes, and her shoulders stooped a little bit. Pushing at his shoulder, she squeezed onto the step beside him, the holes in her jeans splitting at the knees, revealing pale skin. "I heard something the other day, and I figured you'd want to know." Her tone carried the weight of the world in it, and his stomach clenched tighter than a fist.

"What is it?"

"Your brother—"

"Levi," he clarified, no doubt in his tone.

When she shook her head, her dark hair fell from one shoulder down her back. "Eli."

The fist moved from his stomach to his chest, squeezing his heart, shutting down his lungs. He opened his mouth, but nothing came out. He didn't know what had overtaken him. Fear? Dread? Hope? He nodded for her to keep going.

"Well . . . he's been in the news lately. He was released from his contract with the Rangers."

Oliver let out a loud breath. "Is that all? Players get released all the time. He'll get picked up."

Her back hunched and her face fell forward. "I don't think so."

Something in her tone made that stupid fist bear down even harder until his breaths were shaky and uncertain. "Why?" was all he could croak out.

"There's a lot of speculation right now. The sports shows are all trying to figure out what happened, but no one's talking. Not your brother. Not the Rangers' front office. Not the coaches. No one." She took a little breath, peeking at him from the side. "But he wasn't suspended. He's been blacklisted from the NHL."

Oliver didn't know how to respond. The NHL had been his brother's dream. Shoot, it was the dream of every little boy who grew up on skates.

Gretzky. Howe. Messier. They were legends, household names. And Eli Ross had wanted his name to be among them. He'd deemed it worth turning his back on everyone else in his life. He'd walked away and never looked back. Never reached out. Never cared what became of his family. All for the NHL.

And now the NHL had turned its back on him.

For the last ten years, Oliver had avoided the sports channels, given up watching hockey games, and ignored every insinuation from his neighbors that he must be so proud. After a few months, they'd gotten the hint that he didn't want to talk about Eli. Now it took every bit of strength inside him to ask, "What's the media saying?"

She shook her head again. "It's all speculation."

He nearly growled. "But what are they saying?"

"Drugs, mostly. They're blaming it on performance-enhancing drugs."

"No. It's not drugs. Even if he was on them, he wouldn't get kicked out of the league. He'd get a slap on the wrist, a fine. He'd lose his spot on the Rangers' bench. He wouldn't be kicked out of the NHL."

"What could it have been then?"

Shrugging one shoulder, he kept his gaze on the cement step between his feet. He could think of only one thing that would get a good player banished. Eli was selfish and arrogant, but he wasn't stupid enough to do that. Or at least the Eli he'd known ten years before wasn't.

"Have you told my mom?"

She snorted. "Why do you think I've been trying to get ahold of you all week? This is something that should come from a beloved son."

"Then you should have gone to Levi."

Crashing her shoulder into his, she chuckled. "I couldn't get Levi to sit in the same room with me long enough to tell him. So you're up. She's still in the living room. She was reading when I left."

"Sorry, not tonight." He had other things that had to be done, like watching a boat that wouldn't watch itself.

"But soon?" Violet made him promise before she wandered toward the road. She strolled toward the studio and her attached apartment as the sun made its last hurrah before turning in for the night.

Oliver watched her go for a long moment, wishing he could go to sleep, knowing he'd missed his chance. Instead, he trudged up the stairs, grabbed his pillow and an old sleeping bag, and walked toward the harbor. He wasn't shooting for covert any longer—let whoever was messing with his stuff know he was coming. He'd meet them gladly. But it seemed a waste to drive a kilometer when he had energy to spare. Well, it wasn't exactly energy. More like anger, a raging fire. And every step stoked it. Every step reminded him of his brother's choice, his selfish, hurtful choice.

Yeah, maybe he'd told his brother to go. Maybe he'd

screamed at him to never come back. But that had been ten years ago, and every single day Eli had made the choice not to call. Every single day he'd made the choice not to think about them.

And every single day he had left Oliver to care for their mom and little brother. He'd left their family a little more sad. A little more broken.

The more he thought about it, the more he wanted to kick something. Hard. Kicking a robot hadn't helped the last time his brother broke his heart. But his toe caught a small rock, and he sent it flying in an arc toward the moon, then clattering against the pavement as it rolled away.

If only it were that easy to get rid of the memories. To get rid of his brother.

He marched down the pier toward the Lobster Barn, the gray building closed for the night, its windows dark. One car was parked down the way, but he didn't recognize it in the shadow. When he reached the *Pinch*, he leaned over to toss his sleeping bag down.

His heart jumped into his throat, and he shouted as a dark shadow ran across the boat's deck.

"Stop!"

# twenty

Meg screamed and nearly dropped the hauler in her arms, her heart slamming against her rib cage. "Oliver?" It came out barely a squeak, and in the darkness she couldn't be sure just who had joined her.

"Meg?" He tossed something fluffy aboard and scrambled down the ladder and onto the deck. "What are you doing here?"

"Returning this." She lifted the machine higher in the air. "What are *you* doing here?"

He stepped closer, relieving her of her burden and carrying it to the compartment hidden in the stern. "Making sure nothing else happens on this boat."

"Me too."

He closed and locked the trap, pocketed the key, and looked back up at her. "I thought you were returning the hauler."

"Yes. And . . ." Her gaze darted to the outline of blankets stacked on the port side. The storms had swept in more than rain and wind. They'd ushered in fall, and with it a drop in temperatures. She'd been chilled before, so she'd come prepared to stay warm. "I didn't want to have to fix the hauler on the fly again."

"You were pretty good at it this morning."

"Thanks." Her shoulders bounced. "It's much better now, and I even gave it a little extra boost. It should work like a charm tomorrow."

His chuckle was low and warmed her from her chest to her toes. "The morning's going to get here soon. You don't have to stay, you know."

"I want to."

White teeth flashed through the night, and she couldn't help but smile in kind. "Mind if I join you?" he asked.

They set about making up pallets for themselves, Meg using thick comforters and even an electric blanket that she'd converted to plug into a battery. Oliver had a sleeping bag and a lumpy pillow. When he'd unrolled it, he stood back to admire his handiwork.

Meg laughed and threw an old quilt at him. "At least wrap up in this before you get in that thing."

He wrapped it around the shoulders of his coat like a cape and swished side to side beneath it. "Am I doing it right?"

Rolling her eyes in his general direction, she shook her head. She couldn't afford to throw anything else at him, so she peeled back a few layers and crawled into her nest, then pulled the covers up to her nose. But her teeth still rattled, the tips of her nose and ears stinging in the wind.

"Here." Oliver knelt beside her pallet, pulling a toque from his pocket. He slid it onto her head and over her ears. "Better?"

She nodded. "But you'll be cold."

He flapped up the hood from his sweatshirt and yanked on the strings until all but his nose disappeared. Laughter spilled out of her in waves. How could he do that? Make her forget her worries and just enjoy a silly moment.

She'd forgotten how to do that. After her mom got sick and her dad started worrying and she had to leave school, it had become easier to be serious, to think serious. But Oliver had been right about making memories with her mom. Memories filled with laughter and joy and sweet moments together.

And he was right to make her laugh tonight.

As he settled into his sleeping bag, she whispered, "Thank you."

"What's that? Can't hear you through my super-warm hoodie."

"Maybe it's because you're five kilometers away," she yelled. The distance between them was rather ridiculous. When they'd stayed on the boat before, they'd shared a cushion and a blanket and plenty of body heat. But they'd both been expecting to spend tonight alone.

She didn't want to. And she didn't want to feel the two meters between them so acutely.

"Come closer," she whispered.

He didn't pretend he couldn't hear her that time. Instead, he stared at her for a long moment, then—still zipped up in his sleeping bag—he rolled over twice until his body was pressed against the side of her pallet, his face only inches from hers.

"Hey," he whispered, his breath warm and minty like he'd brushed his teeth before walking this way.

"Hi. How was your night?"

He wiggled his hoodie loose and met her gaze. In the light of the moon, she could make out his features and even the shadow of the divot beside his mouth. If it wouldn't have opened her up to all sorts of cold air, she might have pressed her finger to it just because.

"Pretty terrible," he said, keeping his voice low. "How about yours?"

Suddenly she didn't care about the cold air or freezing her fingers. She slipped her hand out from her cocoon and reached for his, finding it wrapped in the silky lining of his sleeping bag. "What happened?"

His bag swished and hissed, and his hand disappeared beneath her grip only to reappear a moment later, his long fingers twining with hers. She gave him a soft squeeze, and he met her gaze.

"Something's going on with my brother."

"Levi?"

"Everyone forgets I have another one."

Her forehead wrinkled beneath the soft wool of his cap. "Eli?"

He nodded slowly, his face twisting with grief and uncertainty as the story spilled out. Expelled from the NHL. Everyone keeping silent. And Oliver was worried it might mean the worst.

"Professional athletes get a pass at most things. Steroids? Oh, he made a mistake. Make him sit out a few games." His tone made it clear that he didn't agree with such leniency. "Hit your spouse? We forgive you. You can still be a role model to kids. Whatever he did was worse. So much worse. And there's not a thing I can do about it."

"Would you?" she asked. "If you could?"

He sighed, rolling onto his back and staring into the starry night. He never let go of her hand. "I know I told him to never come back, but what I really wanted was for him to want to stay."

"I know. And it's all right."

He leaned toward her, turning his head to look right into her face. "What if he's lost everything and still doesn't come home?"

"What if he does?"

He flopped his free arm over his face. "Oh, man. How am I going to tell my mom?"

"You don't have to tell her tonight."

~~~~~

Oliver took a deep breath, the first in hours. He didn't have to tell his mom right away. There was no deadline, no fire under him that said it had to be done immediately. Timetables and calendars had no part in this. He'd tell his mom when the time was right. And at the moment, he'd just lie next to Meg under a sea of starlight.

"When'd you get so smart?" he asked.

"I came by it naturally." The sweetness in her voice was better than honey on a homemade biscuit. And almost as good as her kiss.

He hated that he knew that. He loved that he was certain of it. When he closed his eyes, he saw only the image of her against the side of the house, hair tousled and face glowing. He could nearly feel her against him, taste the strawberry of her lip balm.

And he wanted more. He didn't care how it would end. If there was a chance for them, he would make all the memories he could. That was what she was doing with her mom, and it was what he'd do with her.

"Meg?"

"Uh-huh?"

"I've missed you."

Her nose wrinkled, but not in the way it did when she smelled bait or heard something she didn't like. It was cute and sincere and completely adorable. "You saw me this morning."

"I know. It wasn't enough."

She tugged on his hand, pulling it under her blankets as a shiver shook her. "I've missed you too."

Suddenly his free hand was in her hair, his lips crashing into hers. She whimpered, and he almost pulled back, except her hand was fisted into his hoodie and wouldn't let him go. She smelled of moonlight and fresh air, and her skin was intoxicating.

This moment. He wanted to cling to this moment for the rest of his life. If this was the only memory he had of her, it would be enough.

*Liar.*

It wouldn't be enough. It would never be enough. He wanted more. More memories. More days. More kisses. Mostly, he didn't want to waste a single day. And the truth crushed him, stealing his breath.

He was in love with Meg Whitaker.

He couldn't put his finger on the moment it happened, only that it had. If love meant comforting and trusting and caring for the other person, he was in it. Neck deep.

Other guys groused about women crying, but Oliver didn't mind Meg's tears. So long as she came to him to dry them. He loved that she shared her worries and fears with him and invited him to tell her his secrets.

And he certainly didn't mind the sweet moments locked in her embrace. When he pulled back, he rested his head against hers, his arms around her back. She snuggled against him through layers and layers of blankets and bedding. But he could feel warmth radiating from deep in his own chest.

"Oliver?"

"Hmm?" He felt too lazy to form a full response.

"Can I ask you a favor?"

"Anything." He meant it. Literally whatever she asked for.

"I need the boat."

All his relaxed, languid thoughts spun into a sharp blade that sliced straight through his belly. The reminder that they couldn't be together. That they weren't meant for forever. That no matter what, the boat would always come between them.

"I want to take my mom to see the bridge at sunrise."

His breath came out choppy with relief. "But you don't have a license."

She ducked her head, chewing on her lip and wrinkling her nose. "I know. It'll just be for one morning. But it would mean a late start one day."

He opened his mouth to say she could wait until after the season—they only had a few more weeks left. But in her eyes, he saw the fear that her last chance would be soon. She didn't know when her mom would no longer be able to make such an outing. She was getting worse, and no one knew how fast. If he were Meg, he wouldn't want any regrets either.

Smoothing his thumb over her cheek, he said, "Sure. I'll take you and your mom out. Whenever you want to go."

Her smile could have lit up the night sky.

———

Meg woke slowly at first and then all of a sudden when she squeezed her empty hand. Every time she'd woken through-out the night, his hand had been locked in hers. But when she looked over, he was gone, his sleeping bag rolled and stored.

Movement along the dock meant the day had started, and she scratched her head, wishing she could scratch her fuzzy brain awake too.

"Morning, Sleeping Beauty." Oliver squatted beside her, a tall cup of coffee in his outstretched hand.

She took a long sip. "Thank you. Isn't this my job?"

"You just looked so cute all curled up this morning. I didn't want to wake you." In the barely-there light of dawn, his smile showed off his teeth. He looked boyish and free, like the weight he'd been carrying the night before was gone.

With a glance over his shoulder, he said, "Kyle will be here soon. Let's get this cleaned up."

They made quick work of folding and storing her blankets just in time for Kyle's arrival. In no time they were out on the water, the hauler reeling in the catch better than ever.

Kyle thumped her on the back, his mustache twitching in the wind. "Nice work, Meg. I haven't seen it move this fast since your dad bought it."

Her chest filled at the praise, warming her from the inside out. She loved fixing motors and making machines work. She loved tinkering and playing around with gadgets. But when she took a deep breath through her nose, she caught a whiff of the bait, and her stomach heaved. She did not love fishing.

The motions had become habit over nearly six weeks. Snagging the buoy with the gaff, feeding the vinyl line through the hauler, setting the traps on the counter for Oliver and Kyle to empty and then reset before throwing them back into the water. She'd emptied a fair number of traps too. But the strength it took to put the rubber bands around the lobster claws still made her hands ache. And no amount of Mama Potts's magic cream soothed it away.

Oliver's big paws made it easy. He didn't flinch when the lobsters snapped at him. He gave an easy toss back to the water for the mama lobsters flush with eggs and the little babies and crabs that had lost their way.

He made it look effortless. It wasn't.

Teaching wasn't effortless either. It was just a different kind of effort—a kind she genuinely liked. She liked watching her students grasp a tricky concept or see their pride in making an A on a difficult test. Jenna had been one of her favorites—a student who genuinely loved the formulas and the math. Her big brown eyes had lit up, her smile radiating to every corner of the classroom as she waved her returned test with a red 100 circled at the top.

But this was Meg's family history. And if she wanted it to be her family's future, she had to keep going. Maybe she could learn to love the work. Maybe it was in her blood. It was just hidden.

After dropping off three crates of live lobster at the shore, Oliver steered them back into the harbor, gliding them right against the wharf. Kyle tied them off, and Meg pulled out her mop and bucket.

A phone rang, and it sounded like the corded green one her dad had had on the wall up until a year before. Oliver dug into his pocket. He pressed the phone to his ear and strode toward the far end of the boat. "Hello." He dropped his voice, but it still carried over the calling gulls. "Thanks for calling me back."

Meg didn't try to eavesdrop, but after everything he'd shared about his brother the night before, she couldn't help but wonder if the call held some sort of news. With one ear toward Oliver, she turned back to her task, her mop sloshing across the deck.

Oliver turned his back, his shoulders hunching and his voice dropping even lower. She could only make out about half his words. "It's a ninety-nine . . . Right . . . As possible." He paused for a long moment. "Is that all? . . . To get three."

Her stomach rocked with the boat, and she gave up all pretense of actual mopping. The call wasn't about Eli. It almost sounded like Oliver wanted to sell something.

What did he have to sell? And why did he want to unload it as soon as possible? Or maybe she'd misunderstood that. Except she was pretty sure she hadn't.

He turned toward her, his voice returning to normal. "Let me know if you change your mind." Slipping his phone back into his pocket, he sighed.

"Everything okay?"

He nodded, but the tight line of his lips told a different story.

She wanted to sidle up next to him and ask him for the truth, but she wasn't privy to all of his secrets. Just because he'd shared some didn't mean she had a right to the others.

Resting her hands on the mop handle and her chin on top of them, she gave him what she hoped was a soothing smile. "You want to talk about it?"

He gave her a quick shake of his head, then paused. She could see the battle in his eyes between a desire to share and needing to hold close whatever was bothering him.

His phone rang again. He stared at the screen for a brief minute, then pointed toward the ladder up to the dock. "I'm going to take this over there."

# twenty-one

When Oliver pulled up to the Whitakers' home a few days later, Meg's car was already parked in front of the garage. Darkness blanketed the house, save for one window alight with life and the moon's glow from above.

That boded well for their outing. Clear skies and perfect weather. So it did not explain why his insides were tied so tight he could hardly breathe.

He wasn't nervous about seeing Meg or upset about starting their fishing day later than usual. Kyle had had another commitment and decided to take the day off, but he and Meg would have no problem pulling in the catch on their own. As long as he could keep from pulling her into his arms and kissing her soundly between reeling in every trap.

Just imagining that made him smile. But it didn't remove the snarled mess in his belly.

He wasn't upset about spending time with Mrs. Whitaker. In fact, he was looking forward to it. He knew his feelings couldn't be compared with Meg's, but he would savor every minute he got to spend with the sweet woman before they couldn't make any more memories. The adventures might be for Meg, but he didn't mind taking advantage of them too.

That left only one thing responsible for the writhing in his guts. Seeing Whitaker.

Oliver hadn't said more than a brief greeting in passing at church the day before. Certainly not since he'd gotten that strange call.

Everything he knew told him he needed to tell Whitaker about the call, about the offer. But telling him that a broker had another interested buyer—a cash buyer at that—when Oliver wasn't sure he was going to be able to scrape together the down payment did not bode well. In fact, it spelled devastation.

For him, at least. For Whitaker, it might be the good news he'd been hoping for. He'd make a pretty penny before the falling industry prices tanked the market. They'd swing back up. They always did. But it would certainly drop the going rate on a boat and a license. And right now was the best Whitaker could ask for.

The call had been cursory at best. The broker from Charlottetown had heard from his friend Jeffrey Druthers that Whitaker was looking to sell. And he knew someone looking to buy. The buyer would pay up front as soon as the season was over. Oliver was privy to all of that information because the business number had been forwarded to his phone.

He should have expected something like this—after all, Druthers had warned him—but it had knocked Oliver back, knocked him clear to the ground. He'd mumbled something about passing the message on to Whitaker and then hung up.

Why hadn't he told Whitaker already? Why hadn't he at least told Meg?

He hung his head and slammed his fist against his steering wheel. This was not the man he wanted to be. But apparently it was the man he was.

Suddenly the side door swung open, framing two silhouettes in bright light. Oliver jumped from the truck and ran up to them, reaching for Mrs. Whitaker's hand. "Good morning."

Her forehead wrinkled. "Are you coming with us?"

"Yes, ma'am." He held on to her elbow as she took the three steps down, her foot reaching and retreating with uncertainty. She was bundled up in a heavy parka, her joints frail and thin.

Meg stood on the far side of her, and Whitaker was at the threshold, watching his wife like an eagle watching her chicks. "You sure you have to go out this early?" he asked.

With a reassuring smile in her dad's direction, Meg waved off his worry. "We'll be back before you know it. This is an adventure that Mom needs to have. Oliver will take good care of us, won't you?"

He nodded, a lump in his throat leaving no room for words. Whitaker and Meg trusted him with their most important things. Loves and legacies. And he was keeping a secret that could change both of their lives.

Whitaker looked at him hard. "Take care." It wasn't an admonition to care for himself but a warning to bring back the women he loved unscathed.

Oliver nodded. He could do that.

Mrs. Whitaker sat tense, shaking on the bench seat beside him as they rolled down the deserted street toward the marina.

Meg grabbed her hand. "You're going to love this, Mom."

Such a small reassurance was all it took for her to relax. "Water?"

"Yes. We're going out on the water. On the *Pinch*."

Her body grew stiff again. "I don't want to . . . don't want to . . ." Her lips moved and closed and opened again, searching for a word.

"Don't worry, Mom. We're not fishing." Meg's thumb made a slow sweeping circle over the back of her mom's hand, her voice even and mellow. "You don't have to fish."

Mrs. Whitaker let out a pent-up breath between trembling lips.

Oliver caught Meg's gaze over the top of her mom's head. He tried to give her an encouraging smile, but her lip quivered too.

How he wished he could tell her it was all going to be all right.

───

By the time they reached the boat, Meg decided she'd made a terrible mistake. Her mom's mood had swung from excitement to fear to wide-eyed anticipation to hand-wringing anxiety in only a few short minutes.

She tried to picture her mom's smile as she splashed in the ocean and to imagine how she would respond to the splendor that was coming. But all she could think about was how this disease was changing her mom. How she was no longer the woman who delivered groceries to Oliver's family all those years ago, who comforted Meg after her robot had been destroyed, her chance at the scholarship shredded.

This PSP was turning her mom into someone Meg barely recognized. It was stealing her away.

Maybe it would be better to just turn around and take her home. Tuck her back into bed, keep her in familiar surroundings.

And miss out on the chance to see her face glow.

Nope. She wasn't going to miss out on this. Maybe her mom wouldn't always remember, but for as long as she did, she'd remember that Meg had brought her to see this.

After Oliver set her mom on the ground and made sure she was steady, he plucked three long canvas bags from the bed of his truck. Slinging their black straps over his shoulder, he linked arms with her mom and strolled toward the big gray pub.

"You haven't been on the *Pinch* in a while, have you?"

Mom shook her head. "Can't remember the last time. Walt . . . took me dancing once."

Oliver nodded, shooting a questioning gaze over her head.

"For their anniversary one year, he strung white lights around the boat and took her out on the water," Meg said. "They had dinner and danced under the stars." She had thought it was maybe the most romantic thing in the world. How much her dad loved her mom.

"That must have been quite a night."

Mom mumbled in agreement as they reached the boat. But she froze above the ladder, refusing to climb down. "I can't."

"It's okay," Meg said, wrapping her arms around her mom's shoulders. "I'll go first."

Oliver stopped her, his big hand on her shoulder. "Let me." He nearly leapt onto the deck, tossing his cargo down, and then reached back and lifted her mom in some sort of eighties-movie dance move. He even added a spin at the end that made her giggle.

Meg scrambled down after them and held her mom steady as Oliver set up cushions for them to sit on. After she was comfortable and secure, they headed into the darkness. The boat purred and trembled beneath them for ten minutes until Oliver maneuvered it into position only seconds before the growing dawn split the sky from the earth.

He grabbed the totes he'd brought, pulled out contractible

camping chairs, and set them up. "I thought these might be more comfortable."

Her mom sank into hers, and Meg tucked a blanket around her legs before falling into her own seat just as the show began. The base of the giant gray bridge exploded with color, and her mom leaned forward, almost bent in half to see it more clearly, more closely. She gasped a breath of pure joy, lost in the moment.

At a gentle tap on her shoulder, Meg glanced to her left. Oliver sat in his own camping chair on the other side of her mom, his legs outstretched, ankles crossed. He was staring at her, a gentle smile telegraphing exactly what she was thinking.

It was worth it.

His fingers dipped from her shoulder toward her elbow, hooking her arm and pulling it free until his fingers locked with hers behind her mom's back. The touch of his hand was familiar now, but his gentleness never ceased to surprise her. He was so tender. Unhurried. Cherishing. He squeezed her hand once, and she squeezed back twice. *Thank you.*

"Anytime." He mouthed the word, but she felt it vibrate deep inside her as she held his gaze, his blue eyes as deep as the ocean.

This. This was romantic. It wasn't dancing under the stars, it was doing whatever it took to help her fulfill her dreams. It was caring for her mom, carrying her mom. It was making memories possible. Meg couldn't have—*wouldn't* have—done any of this without him. She didn't want to do it without him either.

The truth rose in her like the sun rising on the bridge, steady and then overwhelming.

This was love.

She had to look down as her throat closed. How had she

ever thought him selfish or unkind? How could he be when he loved her so well?

When the light reached the top and flashed its brightest, Oliver whispered, "So what do you think, Mrs. Whitaker?"

"Gold and fire and . . . and . . . and light." Her words were hushed with awe, her face open and bright. "Again?"

Meg laughed back a trembling sob. "Yeah, Mom. We can come again."

—

Oliver shoved open the door of the studio with a little more force than necessary. It slammed against the adjacent wall, rattling a window.

"Well, hello to you too." Violet looked up from the rotating wheel before holding her red clay–caked hands off to each side. "To what do I owe such a genteel arrival?"

"Is my mom around?" His voice was more growl than he wanted, but his insides had been eating him up all day, and he needed some advice. Worse, he wanted to go to Meg for it, and he couldn't.

"Nope. You just missed her. She's headed to the women's Bible study at church."

He sighed, leaning his head on his arm against the open door frame. His mom would be unavailable until after he had to be back to the boat, where he'd likely spend another evening talking with Meg. Which was normally one of his favorite things to do.

Except when it wasn't. Like that very moment.

Violet rubbed her sticky hands together over an oddly shaped bowl in the center of her wheel. "Something I can help you with?"

He squinted at her with one eye. "Doubtful. Unless you can turn back time?"

She sat up a little straighter, shifting the skirt of her apron to fall between the legs of her jeans as she spun her stool in his direction. "Interesting. And exactly what part of history are you interested in rewriting?"

"All of it." The words came out on a groan, and he thumped the frame with his fist, shaking a nearby shelf.

"Hey, careful now. Those haven't been fired yet."

He jumped back. His mom would send him packing if he toppled a vase or ruined one of her signature pieces before it made it into the kiln. "I'm sorry. I just needed to talk with my mom. I'll go."

"I didn't say you had to go." Violet walked over to the sink at the back of the room and turned on the faucet. "I'm not your mom, but maybe I can help. Tell old Aunt Violet what's going on. Have a seat on my sofa."

Right. Because "old Aunt Violet" was about a year younger than he was. And the "sofa" she pointed at was the stool in front of an empty wheel, the one his mom generally occupied. The rest of her office consisted of wooden worktables lined with benches down each side, six-foot wooden shelves that housed pottery in various stages, and trays upon trays of ceramic glazes. A wooden staircase over the sink led to the loft apartment where Violet lived, and in good weather, the enormous garage door on the adjacent wall let in the sun and birdsong.

Nothing was pristine, but it was clean and tidy and inspiring. Maybe it would inspire some answers for him. He sank onto the stool she'd indicated, pumping the pedal with his foot and making the empty gray wheel spin.

"You want me to throw down a hunk of clay on that thing, or you want to tell me what's going on with you lately?"

"I haven't told my mom about Eli."

"I figured as much. She hasn't said anything to me." With the back of her hand, she brushed a strand of hair out of her face. It was already coated with red, and she had a matching streak down her face. "I guess there's no rush—except that the rest of the town knows. Your mom will hear sooner or later."

Yeah. He knew that too. But he was hoping it would be later. After all, the rest of the town had learned not to say anything about Eli to anyone in his family for years. Why should this change anything?

"Is that what this"—she waved a hand to encompass all of him as she dropped to her own stool—"is all about? Your brother?"

"Not exactly." Clapping a hand on the back of his neck, he pumped the pedal even faster.

"Then what's this—" She sucked in a quick breath, her voice dancing. "Is this about Meg?"

"I might have . . ." He held up a finger to correct himself. "I may have sort of . . . you know. I kissed her."

Violet clapped her hands and stamped the toes of her once-white sneakers. "Tell me everything."

He scowled. "No. This is not a slumber party, and we are not girlfriends."

She frowned. "Okay. Tell me something, at least. What happened? How did you get there? How was it?"

Great. Fantastic. Amazing.

But he was not going to tell Violet that. "We . . . we had this moment. See, there's been something strange happening on the boat. Someone cut one of our lines and broke our hauler. Not enough to really damage the business, but enough that I've been sleeping on the boat—*we've* been sleeping on the boat."

"You and Meg?"

He nodded.

"Tell me more."

"There was this . . ." Maybe he'd already said too much. "Never mind. I changed my mind. I don't want to talk about it."

"Come on, Oliver. I'd tell you if I was kissing someone."

"I wouldn't want to hear about it," he grumbled, meaning every word.

"Too bad," she singsonged. "I'm like the sister you never wanted. If I'm going to bestow my wisdom on you, you also have to listen when I want to share. Now keep talking. You and Meg have been spending extracurricular time together."

Wiping damp palms down his jeans, he sighed. "Her mom is sick."

The glee in Violet's eyes went out like a flame. "I heard that. I'm so sorry. I know how much you like Walt and Sandra."

He nodded. "I suggested to Meg that she might want to make some memories with her mom. Sandra loves the beach, but it's not a great place if you're not so stable, so Meg asked me if I'd go along. We had such a good time, and Sandra just—it was like she was a kid seeing the ocean for the first time. She was splashing and kicking at the waves, and we were laughing. It was such an amazing afternoon. We took her home, and then Meg kissed me. Out of the blue. She just kissed me, and I swear, I wasn't going to kiss her back or anything." He held his face in his hands. "Then she started to walk away, and I thought, if that was the only kiss I ever got with Meg Whitaker, I didn't want that to be how she remembered me. So I kissed her. For real."

"And?" Violet pumped her eyebrows.

Heat rushed down his neck, and he ducked his head, wrapping his hands around the parts surely turning red.

"That good, huh? So why is this such a terrible thing? It seems like she liked it. And you *really* liked it."

"Shut up."

"Well, why is this making you stomp around like a moose in a bear trap?"

He wasn't. Okay, maybe he was a little bit. But he had reasons.

When he was silent too long, Violet nudged his shin with her foot.

"Because one of us is going to get the business, and the other one is going to be devastated. Either way, there's no future that ends with Meg and me together."

"Why not?"

He scoffed. He couldn't help it. He didn't think Violet should need it spelled out. "If her dad gives me the business she wants, she won't forgive me. She's got nothing to fall back on. No job. No prospects. No stability. The only thing in her life that's stable right now is the legacy of that fishing license. But if he gives her the business, I've got nothing to offer her. I have no job, no money, and no future."

"You think you'd lose your job? Walt wouldn't do that."

Oliver shook his head. "He wouldn't, but he won't be in charge for long. And I can't work for Meg."

Violet pursed her lips. "I'm going to bite my tongue and assume that you have reasons other than not wanting to work for a woman."

"No, it's not about her being a woman. It's about—how do you work for someone you want to hold tight every day and whisper all your secrets to every night? How do you keep it professional knowing that you want more but don't have anything else to offer?"

"Okay. That would be hard. But what makes you think the business is all you'd have to offer?"

Oliver groaned. "She wants stability. Her life is changing faster than she can come to terms with it. And the life of a fisherman isn't exactly what I'd call steady. The price per pound is tanking, and I'm going to have to sell my truck just to even get close to being able to make the first payment I promised Whitaker."

At least he'd found a buyer, a dad who wanted an old beat-up truck for his sixteen-year-old son. Oliver didn't know what it said about him that he was having to sell that old beat-up truck—and that it was the most valuable thing he owned. But in a day or two, the money would be in his account. Ready for Whitaker. Just in case.

"And then there's this little matter of another buyer."

"What do you mean?"

"I got a call the other day from a broker who has an interested buyer ready to pay cash up front. Whitaker always said it wasn't about the money, but who would turn down that kind of offer? He'll pay more than what I can. Even over five years."

Violet's features had grown increasingly taut, her grimace clearly from pain. "What did Walt say when you told him?"

Oliver peeked out from between fingers covering his face. "I haven't told him."

"Well, what did Meg say?"

He only shook his head.

"Oh, Oliver. You have to tell them."

"I know I do. But how? Casually knock myself out of the game? 'Oh, by the way, there's another offer I really think you should see, but don't forget the great deal you promised me.'"

"Maybe he wouldn't take it."

"I don't know if I can risk it. But every day I don't tell them, I feel sick. Worse than seasick. Like something inside me is trying to claw its way out."

"Then you know what you have to do. Tell Walt the truth. You want to stop feeling sick? Be honest. Leave the rest up to God."

Argh. She was right and he knew it. He'd thought the same thing a million times, but he still hated her for making it sound so simple. Yes, he needed to confess the truth, lay it bare. Hidden secrets only ever festered. God would do what he would do, and it would be what was best.

But knowing that and acting on it were different. Yet if he didn't act on what he believed, did he really believe it at all?

"And what about Meg?"

He scratched his nails down his face. "What about her?"

"What are you going to do?"

"I don't know." He'd never been more honest in his life.

"What would it take for you to have a chance with her?"

His throat tried to close around the words, but he pushed them out. "I'd have to walk away from the business. She'd have to know that what I feel for her has nothing at all to do with the *Pinch*."

"And would it be worth it? Would she be worth it?"

Such a hard question. Such an easy answer.

# twenty-two

Meg flew through the door at Carrie's, her money already in hand. The small café was busier than at the height of tourist season. Every table was filled with grown men and women whispering with their heads together. One name seemed to be on everyone's lips. Eli Ross.

Carrie caught her eye from across the room, a full busing tub in her hands. "Your order isn't quite ready. Give me a few more minutes?"

Meg nodded, looking for an empty chair. But there were none.

"Hey, Miss Whitaker." Jenna flew by, carrying a tray of drinks.

"Hi, Jenna. Good to see you. Tell your mom I'm going to wait outside."

Jenna nodded, and Meg slipped onto the front deck, its wooden beams sporting a fresh coat of white paint. There were no chairs, so she leaned her arms against the rail, staring off into the row of homes beneath the outstretched arms of big oak trees. The leaves were only just beginning to change, sparks of gold and amber dotting the green landscape, reminding her of a childhood spent raking piles of leaves only to run and jump in them. Her mom had laughed, raked them again, and fallen right back into them with her.

"Hey, Meg."

She turned at the sound of her name to see Violet and offered a smile.

"I always seem to run into you here."

"Just picking up dinner for my parents."

Violet gave her a knowing smile. "And then back to the boat?"

Meg paused, not sure how to respond. "Um, how did you know that?"

"Oh, you know Oliver. He let it slip that you've been spending a bit of time together. I'm sorry to hear about the issues on the boat, but it sounds like it's all going to work out."

"What do you—" Meg wasn't quite sure what she wanted to ask. "I'm sorry, what's going to work out?"

Violet's face turned blank, a flash of uncertainty in her eyes. She flipped her hair over her shoulder and bit her lip. "Just, you know. I told him to be friendly. I knew it would all work out if he was . . . It seems like you're getting along."

Meg nodded slowly, her brain trying to register exactly what Violet wasn't saying. "You told him to be friendly?"

Violet dismissed her own words with a flippant wave. "You know how it was at first, back before the season started. Well, you both would have had a terrible season working together. And neither of you would have gotten—"

The door flew open, and Carrie shoved a plastic bag with three trays in it in her direction. "Meg, I'm so sorry about the wait."

Meg held out the colorful twenties in numb fingers and mumbled, "Keep the change" before flying down the steps.

Violet called after her, "I'm sorry. I shouldn't have said anything."

Meg could barely hear her for the ringing in her ears and the thunder of her own footsteps as she marched toward her parents' home.

Be friendly. Violet had told Oliver to be friendly. She'd told him to become her friend. Was that why he had apologized? Why he'd been so nice to her? Except for that whole pretending to drown when she'd pushed him off the *Pinch*, he'd gone out of his way to show how nice of a guy he could be. But how far had it extended?

She understood wanting peace between coworkers. But Violet had admitted there was more—a bigger reason.

What about all of the things he'd done for her? No one was that good of an actor.

The way he'd held her when she cried. Cared for her mom. Kissed her until she was breathless. No one did those things unless they were real.

Unless . . .

Unless it was all part of some scheme. But it wasn't. It couldn't be. Nothing was worth all that. Except . . .

The business.

Her stomach heaved, and she thought she was going to be sick on the side of the road. This was ridiculous. She just needed to talk with him. Oliver would clear everything up. Of course he would. He wasn't pulling some scam to steal the business out from under her. Besides, it was her dad's decision, and he hadn't made one yet.

No. Just no.

She was letting her imagination get the better of her.

By the time she got to her parents' home, barely a kilometer from Carrie's, she'd worked herself into a fine lather, teeth grinding and sweat dripping down her forehead. Rushing inside, she dropped the bag on the counter and took two deep breaths.

*You're overreacting, Meg. Pull yourself together.*

She took another breath. Then another. She walked over to her mother and sat down next to her on the couch. "Hey, Mom."

Her mom rested her hand on top of hers. "Honey."

A moment later her dad appeared from the back room. "Thought I heard you come in. Glad you're here." He pulled three plates from the cabinet beside the refrigerator. "Has Oliver said anything about talking to a broker?"

Her stomach took another roll, and it was worse than being on a boat without her patch. "What kind of broker?" Her voice was dry and little more than a whisper. She shouldn't have bothered asking because she already knew.

"The kind who arranges buyers for lobster fishing fleets. I got an email from one today. He said he spoke to Oliver." Her dad sounded more puzzled than concerned, but Meg couldn't shut off the alarm bells fast enough.

She'd heard him on the phone trying to sell something. She'd heard him making arrangements, looking for a better deal.

Had he been so certain he was going to win her dad's favor that he was already . . .

The truth slammed into her heart, stopping it for one endless beat. She couldn't breathe. She couldn't move. All she could feel was the searing agony of her own foolishness.

Oliver hadn't only been trying to win her dad's favor. He'd been trying to win hers too. This whole time. Either way, he thought he'd end up with the business. Either her dad would give it to him or she would.

But he'd never intended to keep it. He'd thought he would get her legacy at a cheap price and then sell it at a profit.

No. No. No. It couldn't be. He would have to be the world's greatest actor to pull that off. Everything he'd said. Everything he'd done . . .

She needed answers, and there was only one person who could provide them.

———

Oliver was pretty sure Meg's car was the one kicking up a trail of dust as it spun out of her dad's driveway and fishtailed onto the road. He wanted to follow her, to see what had her all riled up—and also to avoid the conversation he needed to have with Whitaker. But it wouldn't wait any longer. His gut had felt a lot better after he'd decided what he was going to do. But there was an aching nerve that spit fire every time he played the conversation out in his mind. It was well past time to shut it down.

He rapped twice on the window of the Whitakers' side door and then shoved his hands into his pockets. His phone buzzed, but he ignored it. Probably Violet calling again to ask why he hadn't talked to his mom about Eli. But he could only handle one crisis at a time, and he was going after the big one first.

Whitaker answered within seconds. "Oliver. Didn't expect you tonight. Come on in."

The kitchen smelled like meat loaf, and Mrs. Whitaker

sat at the snug dining room table, hands in her lap, a plate in front of her and a takeout container beside her.

"We were just sitting down to supper. Care to join us?"

Oliver swallowed, and it felt loud enough to ring through the whole house. "No, sir. I'm sorry to interrupt, but I need to have a word with you. Alone."

Whitaker's gaze darted to his wife. "Sandy? Are you okay?"

She nodded and took a sip from the straw in her plastic cup.

"I'll be right back." Whitaker led the way down a short hall to the office where he'd run his business for years. The single desk held an enormous monitor, as deep as it was wide. On the floor beside it, a computer tower whirred away. When everyone else had upgraded and downsized, Whitaker had kept what still worked. No need to upgrade when the old motherboard still worked fine.

The last time Oliver had been in the room, the desktop had been piled with paper and receipts and check stubs. Now it was mostly clean, save for a few receipts from the nearest grocery store.

Of course, the last time he'd been in the room, Whitaker had offered to sell him the business.

Whitaker pointed to the empty folding chair. Hard and cold, it wouldn't be comfortable for long. At least Oliver wouldn't be staying.

Whitaker lowered himself into the ergonomic desk chair, propping his elbows on the armrests and folding his hands in front of him. Leaning forward, he said, "What can I do for you?"

"Sir." Oliver took a deep breath when the rest of the words didn't come. He'd practiced them, but they were suddenly elusive. "I . . . um . . . I can't buy your business."

Whitaker's mouth dipped in an offended frown. "You don't want it?"

"Oh, no. It's not that I don't want it. I want it very much."

Whitaker's weathered features wrinkled more than usual, his gaze narrowing. With a slow nod, he said, "Yeah, the market's been a tough one this season. You having a hard time coming up with the down payment?"

"You've been watching it?" Oliver couldn't keep the surprise out of his voice.

"'Course I have. Forty years fishing, watching those numbers every day, first with my dad, then by myself. It's a hard habit to break. I wondered why you kids didn't tell me about it though."

"We didn't want to add any worries." Oliver dropped his gaze to his own folded hands before him. "Seems like you've got plenty of other things to think about."

Whitaker nodded again. "I suppose. So, this is about the money?"

"Um . . . not exactly. I mean, it would be close, but I have what we talked about."

With a grunt, Whitaker leaned even further forward. "Is this about the outside buyer you didn't tell me about?"

His gut clenched, and he had to bite his tongue to keep from asking how Whitaker had found out about it. "I didn't tell you about him because I hoped you'd choose me. I was afraid that a cash offer might look pretty appealing, and I knew I couldn't compete with it. But I was coming here today to tell you the truth."

"His email sure made it sound like you told him I would be selling soon."

Oliver's head snapped up. "No, sir. I didn't say anything

like that. I told him he'd have to talk with you. I just . . ." His voice trailed off as he fought the weight on his chest.

Whitaker was the closest thing he'd ever had to a real father, and he'd rather kick himself in the pants than ruin that relationship. But all those things Meg had thought about him at the beginning of the season, all the things Druthers had accused him of . . . well, maybe they had been right. He'd hidden what he should have confessed. He'd taken the easy road instead of the honest one.

"I should have told you right away. But I was afraid he'd make you an offer better than I ever could."

Whitaker leaned back in his chair, his hands folded over his stomach and his jaw shifting back and forth. "What has ever made you think I cared about the money? You think Meg has more than a couple of loonies to rub together if I give it to her?"

"But this is her legacy, her heritage. I can't take that from her. Not with everything else she's losing."

"So." Whitaker's voice did a little jig. "This is about more than the *Pinch*, eh?"

"I don't know what you mean." That wasn't entirely truthful, but it wasn't going to hurt anyone either.

"This is about Meg."

Of course it was about Meg. Everything from the moment she'd said she wanted Whitaker Fishing until now had been about her. It wasn't about teaching her the ropes or getting her to like him so she'd consent to selling to him. Not anymore. Not for a while.

Whitaker's smile twitched, and Oliver leaned forward. He felt like he was missing something, but he wasn't going to talk about Meg. Not until he'd talked with her.

"Well, I guess that's all I have to say. I'll finish out the season, and then I'll be moving on."

The smile that had barely been there fell away, and Whitaker scowled. "Where are you going to go?"

Someplace where no one had ever heard of Dean Ross. Someplace where his heart wouldn't be pummeled every time he saw Meg around town. Someplace where he could forget just how much he loved her. "I'm not sure yet."

"And you'd just give up on the chance to own my business."

"You're the first person to ever believe in me, to trust me, to take a chance on me." Oliver looked him squarely in the eye. "I'm grateful. But I don't have another choice."

"But you still work for me?"

"Of course I do."

Whitaker leaned forward again. "Good. I want you to take the *Pinch* out tonight. Go over to that favorite spot of yours. Feel the wind on your face. Remind yourself why you love this job."

It wasn't going to change his mind. He didn't need to be reminded why he loved fishing. He'd never forgotten. But he nodded anyway.

Meg rubbed her eyes, praying the twilight and exhaustion weren't playing tricks on her. But there was no mistaking Oliver's form standing at the helm, the hum of the *Pinch*'s motor filling the marina.

She'd run all over town looking for him—at his place, at his mom's studio, and even at Carrie's. But of course he was aboard the boat. She bypassed the ladder and jumped right onto the deck with a thud. Immediately she realized she'd taken off her patch from that morning and hadn't yet put on a replacement.

Her stomach dropped and then did a full barrel roll, and she staggered toward the wall, leaning on the cement with one hand.

"Meg? Did you hurt yourself?" Oliver ran to her, reaching out both hands, but she couldn't stand for him to touch her.

"What are you . . ." She swallowed against the bile in the back of her throat. "What are you doing?"

"Taking the boat out. Your dad asked me to."

"He asked you to sell his business too?" Her head started spinning in time with her rolling stomach, and she didn't know if she needed to sit down or get to dry land immediately.

"No, Meg. That's not—"

She waved her finger in his direction. She didn't have the strength to listen to him try to explain away his sins. "Just like Violet told you to be nice to me."

His face went white, his eyes unblinking. He'd been caught, and he knew it. Guilt was written across every feature and printed in his gaze. "It wasn't like that."

"You thought you'd get me to just give you the business. You thought you'd make it so hard I wouldn't want it. You thought you'd make me look incompetent and ridiculous."

A sudden realization made her face flush. It couldn't be true.

But the pieces lined up like railroad tracks, every one fitting into place. The damages to the business had been relatively small and inexpensive to repair. They hadn't stopped the catch or made a significant financial impact. And they'd been done by someone who knew when she and Oliver weren't watching the *Pinch*.

It had all been to scare her off or make her look a fool without hurting the business. And he'd succeeded.

Staring him down, she said, "You sabotaged us." A knife sliced through her middle, and she bent over.

Suddenly his hand was on her back. "Let me take you somewhere."

"No." She whipped back up, cracking his nose with her skull and setting off another bout of vertigo. Fire shot up the back of her head as she lumbered forward. "Just tell me the truth—you've been pretending this whole time. Everything with my mom was just so I'd think you were a good guy, so I'd think you deserved it. So *my dad* would think you deserved it."

"No." His eyes flashed brighter than the setting sun as he pressed a hand to his nose. "It wasn't like that."

"That's not what Violet said." She spit out the words. "She told me all about how she coached you. How she encouraged you to be my friend. Why?"

He scrubbed a hand down his face, his lips tight, pained. "All right, maybe it started like that, with me trying to be your friend. But we had to work together. I thought it would make things easier. I thought, yeah, okay, there was no way your dad would sell to me if you still hated me. But I swear, I never sabotaged anything."

"You manipulated me," she said between clenched teeth. "You purposefully pretended to be my—" Her voice caught and she couldn't go on. She didn't know how she wanted to finish. Her friend? Her confidant? Her love?

Oh, she'd been so stupid to open her heart.

"I swear, I didn't know I could feel this away about anyone— let alone you." His voice was so deep, thoroughly sincere, just like when he'd apologized that first time. "But I wasn't lying when I kissed you. I wasn't pretending to care. Meg, I love you."

If that first apology had been a lie, then this could be one too.

Except part of her heart begged for it to be true. The very deepest parts of her soul had longed to hear him say those words.

Now they rang hollow, bitter, and stale.

"Not nearly as much as you love this boat."

"How can you say that?"

A wave hit the boat, and her knees nearly buckled. She clawed at the wall of the wharf next to the ladder to keep herself standing. Her stomach ached, but her chest burned, her heart beaten and bloodied. "It's not like you have a glowing list of recommendations."

He jerked back, and she knew he'd heard exactly what she hadn't said, Druthers's words echoing between them.

"Just tell me one thing." She took another stabilizing breath. "Was it *all* for show? All to win the business?"

His face turned to stone, and he crossed his arms. "If you have to ask that, then maybe we both know the answer."

Well, give him the starring role in the next production at the Victoria Playhouse. Because he'd fooled her. And ripped her heart out along the way.

# twenty-three

Meg didn't get out of bed the next morning or the next. She didn't go to the wharf, didn't catch buoys, and didn't haul in traps. She didn't pick up coffee for the guys or laugh as Kyle downed his like a shot. She didn't see Oliver's dimples or the light in his eyes. Not that she was thinking about him.

She turned off the sound on her phone, ignored its buzzing, and wrapped herself in her quilted cocoon, praying something would sew all the broken pieces of her heart back together.

Nothing did.

"Meg, you home?" Her dad's voice cut through the silence of her apartment, his steps into her living room loud as though announcing himself. "Honey? I'm worried about you. Kyle called. He said you didn't go out this morning." His voice drew closer.

Meg buried deeper. "Not today, Dad," she mumbled into her pillow. The case was covered in damp spots, wicked reminders of the crying jags that had robbed her of sleep.

"Sorry, honey. Today is all we've got. Debi Ross is staying with your mom, and I'm here to check on you."

She burrowed out from under her down comforter, peeking over the edge. Her dad stood next to her white dresser, running a finger over one of the necklaces on the metal tree stand. "Guess you don't have much call to wear these in my line of work."

Her eyes burned and she rubbed them, but they only felt like sandpaper. So she closed them and dropped her head. "Did you come here to talk about my jewelry?"

"No." He plopped onto the edge of her queen-size bed, tugging on the corner of her blanket until her whole face was free. "I came here because I'm worried about you. Because I care about you. Because I know you're hurting, and I didn't want you to be alone."

Tears rushed to her eyes, and she fisted them away. "What makes you think that? I'm fine."

He let out a pop of laughter, running a big hand across her cheek and catching a few teardrops along the way. "Nice try. This"—he held up a damp thumb—"doesn't look like fine to me. Want to tell me about it?"

"No." Even that was hard to get out without her lower lip trembling.

"That's all right. Can I sit with you?"

She wanted to shake her head. She wanted to tell him to go home to be with her mom. But mostly she wanted him to sit right where he was and hold her close. She nodded and then sat up, scooting to his side and letting him wrap his arm around her shoulders. They sat in silence for several long minutes.

"That must have been some fight," he said.

She nodded again.

"You must have really cared about him."

Another nod.

"What did you fight about?"

She couldn't respond, her lower lip quivering at just the thought.

"From what Kyle said, I get the feeling that Oliver's about as friendly as a mama moose."

She stiffened at the use of his name, pulling her blankets tighter around her, holding them closed beneath her chin, and curling deeper into her dad's side. She didn't care how Oliver was. She didn't.

Except that she did. Everything inside of her ached at what she'd said to him. At how she'd treated him.

She didn't know the truth, and she hadn't listened to a thing he said. She'd lashed out with all of her anger targeted at him.

Oh, how the tables had turned.

Maybe he hadn't been an innocent bystander like she had been all those years ago, but he'd certainly taken the brunt of her unleashed anger. And he probably didn't deserve half of it.

"I think Oliver's been sabotaging the business," she whispered through cracked lips.

"Oh, really? What makes you say that?"

She swallowed thickly and sniffed back a sob. "We ran into some trouble. A cut line. Someone tampered with the hauler."

"And what makes you think Oliver is responsible?"

She stared at her legs dangling over the side of the bed, trying to remember how it had all seemed so plausible. Hating the memory at the same time. "It was all blatant, but it was fixable. It didn't really set us back too much financially.

It was more of a nuisance—like he was trying to make things harder. Like he wanted me to fail or to get discouraged."

"And did you—fail, I mean?"

"No. I mean, we're going to break even and then a little. And we got the lobsters in."

"And were you discouraged?"

She closed her eyes, feeling once again the disappointment, but also the moment when she'd been able to fix the hauler. And all those nights on the boat. All those nights they'd shared together. "Not for very long."

"Why'd it take you so long to tell me about the sabotage?"

She looked up, her dad's sweet face blurring before her eyes. "I didn't want to add anything more to your plate. I just wanted you to be able to focus on Mom."

He sighed, patting the leg of her fuzzy pajama pants and then picking up her hand in both of his. "You know, Oliver said something similar to me the other day."

She nearly choked at just hearing his name again. "Yeah, well . . ." She'd told him that. She'd told him they had to protect her dad. She hadn't expected him to tell on her.

"Is that why you've been trying to be so strong all this time? Never showing your emotions?"

"I haven't—" A squeeze of his hand cut her off. He knew it wasn't the truth, and she did too. "I just didn't want you to think you had to take care of me too."

"Sweetie." He pushed her blanket back from where it framed her face, brushed her hair behind her ears, and looked right into her eyes. "I want to take care of you. You're my little girl."

"I'm almost as tall as you are."

His chin dropped, his serious eyebrows coming together.

"Megan, you will always be my little girl. And I'm here for you. I know all of this with your mom is hard. I know the answers we got weren't what we hoped for. But we're promised storms in this life. We're also promised that our hope in God is an anchor in those storms. He'll hold us steady even in the wind and the waves."

"Yes, but—"

"It's been scary for you, all this change and all the unknowns." There was no question in his words.

She nodded.

"I'm scared too sometimes. But I know that God gave me you and your mom, and there's no one I'd rather go through this storm with than my two girls."

She couldn't blink back the tears fast enough, and they escaped, rolling down her face, spilling onto her chest.

"I'd worry more about you if I never saw you cry. You think I haven't had a few moments myself?"

She shook her head. The very thought of her rough and steady dad breaking down made her chest jerk on a silent sob and the tears press harder.

He flicked his thumb over her cheek, catching a few strays. "I don't need you to be strong for me—or your mom. I just need you to be here with us. Your mom has had more fun going out with you and Oliver than I've seen her have in years. You did that for her, and I can't tell you how much I've loved watching you both together lately. Something's changed."

"It was *his* idea." She still couldn't say his name. "He said maybe we should make memories while we could." Her gaze dropped to her hands, and she bit her trembling lip to hold it still. "I don't want to have any regrets."

"Then let's not." He pressed a gentle kiss to her cheek,

and she sank into his shoulder, free for the first time in years to just sit and be sad. To simply hug her dad and not have to hold him up.

He was stronger than she'd given him credit for. Or maybe he knew how to lean into the One even stronger than him.

Maybe Pastor Dell had been right about the sound of tears being the sound of love. Her mom and dad didn't need her to pretend, they just needed her to be with them. When the time was right, there would be words of truth and hope. But in the sorrow, in the cacophony of pain, all she could hear was her dad's slow and steady heartbeat.

The hole in her heart hadn't changed. It was the place where all of Oliver's kindness, all of his understanding had been. Those were gone now, but she heard her dad's love echoing in the vacant corners of her soul.

When her breathing gradually calmed from the erratic half sobs to an even pace, her eyes beginning to dry, her dad patted her leg once more. "What did Oliver say when you told him you thought he'd been sabotaging your work?"

She took one more steadying breath. "He said he didn't do it."

"And do you believe him?"

"I think I want to," she whispered.

He chuckled, his shoulders shaking so much that she had to sit up and give him her best teacher look.

"Then why don't you? The Scriptures say that love bears all things, but also that it believes all things. Love lets you see the best in Oliver, even when it might not look like he deserves it."

"But it all started off as a lie. He was just trying to make me like him so he could get the *Pinch*. Violet told me."

"Hmm." He hummed low in his throat. "Is it possible that he's not the same man he was on the wharf that morning all those weeks ago?"

"Maybe."

"I think you might be surprised."

Narrowing her gaze, she nudged her dad's leg with her toe. "What do you know?"

"A great many things, my dear. Chief among them—love is worth the sacrifice."

She wanted to scoff and roll her eyes but couldn't. If anyone knew the cost of love, her dad did. He'd given up everything—his livelihood, his legacy, his life—to serve her mom. Because love was worth it. "And you think I'm in love with Oliver Ross?"

"I think love grows in unexpected ground. And I think it looks a lot more like caring for the things you care about than boxed chocolates and red roses." He stood then, kissing her squarely on her forehead. "I love you, kid. And I'll come cry with you anytime."

Her throat closed, and she managed only a wobbly nod as he walked away.

———

"You practicing to face down a bear or something?"

Oliver slammed the trap down, shoving a fistful of bait into the netted kitchen. "I have no idea what you're talking about." But his growl was on par with a grizzly's.

Kyle chuckled dryly. "You want to talk about it?"

"Nope."

"This have something to do with Eli?"

Oliver shook his head hard. But it didn't do a thing to dislodge the memory of his mom's silent tears the night before, when he'd told her as much as he knew about his brother's situation. He'd read in her face the same question he'd asked. What if Eli still didn't come home? It was a question he couldn't answer, and one he refused to dwell on.

"It's not Eli." But he almost wished it was.

"I get it. You and Meg break up?"

"Hard to break up when you were never together." Oliver shoved a cluster of traps back into the water, watching the line disappear into the blue bay and wishing that this conversation would go with it.

"Coulda fooled me. You seemed like you were getting pretty close there. Thought I didn't notice. Pah." Kyle leaned back as Oliver set the boat toward the next buoy. "All those covert glances. Rubbing the tip of her hair with your fingers. Watching her every move."

"It wasn't like that," Oliver nearly snarled, not bothering to turn from his place at the helm.

"Either you liked her a whole lot or you thought she was up to no good. No one watches anyone that way without a reason."

Oliver liked the older man, always had. Kyle had had every right to push back when Whitaker said he was going to sell to Oliver, but he hadn't. That didn't mean Oliver was going to stand around and listen to his nonsense or willingly let memories of Meg sneak back into his mind.

"I didn't—"

"You can keep lying to yourself all you want, but that don't make it true. And it wasn't like it was just you. Her eyes lit up whenever she saw you."

"Ha." It was his turn to laugh, even if it held no humor.

If what Kyle said was true, Meg had sure done a good job of hiding it. "She hated me." Oliver pulled up to their next stop and turned to face Kyle, who was already working Meg's job at the hauler.

Kyle shrugged. "Maybe. Early on. But that lasted all of three seconds."

"Coulda fooled me," he mimicked Kyle. "She laid into me last week pretty good. Told me I'm about as trustworthy as my dad. Accused me of being the one to cut the line and break the hauler."

Kyle's snort rippled like the waves. "That's pretty funny."

"She said I was trying to make her quit, trying to make it hard and scare her off so I'd get the license. So I could sell it."

Kyle let out a belly laugh then, his shoulders shaking so hard that he missed the table and dropped a trap back into the water. Oliver pulled it back up, lined it up, and extracted a perfect brown hard shell. With a quick flick, he measured it, then put rubber bands on its claws.

When he finally caught his breath, Kyle tucked the catch into its cubicle within the plastic crate, his eyes glistening. "Well, why'd she do that?"

Oliver chewed on his lips. "I may have failed to tell her and Whitaker that some big-shot broker had an interested buyer. But only because I was so close to making the down payment, and I just needed a few more days to get it together."

Kyle whistled low and serious.

"And there was this thing about how Violet told me I should be nice to Meg. How it was the only way I'd have a chance to walk away with the *Pinch* at the end of the season." Oliver wanted to scrub a hand down his face, but his gloves were covered in seawater and herring, so he settled for hanging his head and taking a deep breath. "Meg found out, and now she thinks I was just trying to manipulate her."

"So, her pride is hurt because she thinks she fell for a charade."

"But I wasn't pretending. I mean, maybe it started out a little bit like that. But I genuinely . . ." He squeezed his glove into a fist to keep from running it through his hair. "Meg is amazing—she's smart and strong. She cares so much about her parents. She's never complained—not once—about having to leave uOttawa. I don't think she's ever regretted that choice. And even though it scared her to get closer to her mom, knowing she's going to lose her . . . Meg's face when she made her mom smile—making her mom laugh is her joy. And I understand." He shook his head. "The first time I made Meg laugh, it was like I'd invented the lightbulb and was looking for the chance to flip the switch again and again."

Kyle closed up the last of the traps on the line and gave them a push back overboard. "Sounds a lot like love to me."

"Well, it's too late." Oliver slid off his gloves and tossed them down, sitting on a plastic crate as he dug into his pocket. He held out a protein bar, but Kyle shook his head and pulled out his own snack. "She made her choice. And it wasn't me."

"Or you need a second chance. Seems to me she gave you one awhile back."

"Yeah, and then she took it back."

"Is that the truth, or is that your wounded pride talking?"

Oliver crunched into the peanut butter and chocolate bar, usually his favorite flavor. It tasted like sawdust.

"I'm just saying—pride'll get you. Look what it did to your dad."

He snapped to attention, his gaze narrowing onto Kyle's

face. The man's features were relaxed, but there was a calm certainty to his voice that couldn't be ignored.

"Your dad wasn't always a thief. Your mom never would have married him if he had been."

That was true. Mama Potts wouldn't have put up with that. And Oliver had a feeling that if he hadn't told his dad to get out and never come back, his mom would have. Nineteen years of marriage was gone with one fist to his face.

Kyle shoved another bite of his bar into his mouth and spoke around it. "Your dad thought he'd beat the odds, thought his bets couldn't lose. And with every loss, he thought one more would be enough to win it all back, to make up for all the savings he'd burned through. He had a choice. Own his sins and change or leave. At the end of the day, he couldn't face the mistakes he'd made. And here's what I know—he may have left, but he took his pride and his sins with him."

Oliver had never thought of it like that. He'd only ever thought about the mayhem his dad had left behind. What chaos had he taken with him? Aside from all he'd stolen from Druthers, he'd carried a weight that he wouldn't be free of until he faced it.

"You know Whitaker cares about who takes over his namesake."

Oliver nodded, his eyes drifting into the *Pinch*'s corners and shadows.

Kyle shook his head. "I'm not talking about this boat or the license. I'm talking about what he leaves behind. We're all going to shuffle off this mortal coil and meet our Maker at some point. When we do, what will we leave behind? Whitaker loves fishing, and I'd never seen anyone who loves it as much until I met you. I think when Whitaker met you, he saw a chance to help you leave your own legacy—by passing down the boat to you, he'd give you a chance to change your course. He'd give you a chance to choose a different path than your own father."

The protein bar turned to solid rock in his stomach. If Kyle was right, Oliver was Whitaker's legacy. Meg too, of course. But he'd *chosen* Oliver. He had chosen to pour himself into a twenty-one-year-old kid, to pass down his love of the sea and his love for people.

The weight of that honor pushed Oliver's shoulders forward as his arms rested on his knees.

"Seems like a waste if it's pride keeping you and Meg from being together. I'm pretty sure that's not what Whitaker wanted for you."

"It's too late." Oliver pressed his hands to his face. "We've tried, and there's too much history between us, too many reminders of past hurts that make us jump to the worst conclusions. We tried to forgive, but . . ."

"That's the thing about forgiveness—it's a renewable resource. The act of giving it fills you up to give it again. The more you practice forgiveness, the more you have to give." Kyle swiped his hand down his pants. "And trust me, when you're married as long as I've been, you'll be glad of that fact."

"Married?" Oliver swallowed thickly.

Kyle shrugged. "Seems to me that when a man loves a woman, he wants to share his life with her, even if it starts out a little bit rocky. When you know you can get through the rough patches and still choose the other person—well, that's a good start."

Oliver heaved a sigh, knowing he should return to the wheel and get them to the next buoy. But all he could think about was having Meg in his life. Forever.

Except at the moment, he didn't have Meg at all, which pretty much explained his more bearish qualities of late. And when he saw his future stretched out ahead of him without her in it, he felt seasick. Pressing his hand to his stomach, he scowled. He hadn't been looking for her. He hadn't been looking for anyone, really. He'd been working toward building a future. And then, after his debt was repaid, he would have thought about a family.

Only now his dreams weren't about a boat and a good price per pound. They were little girls with their mom's blonde hair and shining blue eyes. They were making Meg laugh every day. They were caring for each other when the two of them were weathered and worn.

"I don't know how to fix it," Oliver said. "How do I make it right?"

"Well, maybe start by showing her you're not like your dad."

"And how would I . . ." But the truth was already there. "I could tell her why I told Whitaker I couldn't take the business."

Kyle's jaw dropped almost comically low, his eyes nearly popping out of his head. "You did what?"

Oliver pushed against his knees, already turning toward the helm. "I couldn't take it from her."

"Does she know that?"

"I have no idea. But she's going to know it as soon as we finish up." With that, he launched the boat toward the next buoy and the chance at the dreams that mattered.

———

Meg squeezed her mom's hand and squatted down before her spot on the sofa. "Can I get you anything?"

Her mom began to shake her head but stopped. "Where's Oliver?"

Meg's heart thumped a little harder. She hadn't talked about him since her dad had come to see her four days before. She wished she hadn't thought about him either, but he'd taken a seat in the front of her mind and wouldn't give it up.

With a glance at the clock on the wall, she said, "I guess he's probably on the boat."

"Why aren't you . . . there?"

Her tongue felt thick and useless. Taking a deep breath, Meg searched for her voice. When it finally came, it was scratchy and unfamiliar. "We had a fight, Mom."

For the briefest fragment of time, her mom's eyes focused. Meg could physically feel the intensity of her gaze, leaving a trail of goose bumps across her skin. "Then make up. Apologize."

It was so simple but so terribly complex. Her mom made it sound like one small word would change everything. But in her experience, "sorry" wasn't always enough. It wouldn't wash away the wrongs that had been done on either side.

But neither had her anger changed all the wonderful things Oliver had done for her. All the times he'd held her. All the times he'd let her cry on his shoulder. All the times he'd dropped everything to care about the things she cared about. If that's what love looked like, love looked like Oliver Ross.

"He's a good boy." Her mom reached out and cupped her cheek, and Meg held her hand there, the frail fingers so soft. "He'd do anything for you."

And he had. He'd forgiven her awful grudge. He'd taught her how to fish—even when that meant he could lose it all. And he'd shown her a better way to grieve her mom's condition.

She'd never regret investing in her relationship with her mom. But she would have missed out on all of it without him.

"Mom, I don't know how to make it right. I don't know—"

Only she did know. She knew exactly what he wanted most in the world. Exactly what she could offer him.

Kissing her mom's hand, she said, "Thanks. I'll be back later." She raced down the hall to her dad's office, where he sat in his desk chair staring at the ancient computer. Mouse clicks echoed their sharp staccato, and she recognized an industry news report on the screen.

"Dad?"

He spun around, a wide grin in place.

Before he could speak, she said, "I want you to give the business to Oliver."

"You don't want it?" He sounded a little bit disappointed, a little bit sad, but not at all surprised.

She snuck across the room and pulled the folding chair closer to him, leaning forward so she could look directly into his eyes. "Come on. You had to know. The mornings are killing me. And the bait—oh, man. It smells like leftovers that have been in the fridge for years. And if I ever forget my patch, I can barely stand on the boat. I'm so grateful that you want me to want to take it over, but Oliver deserves it. I made him promise me that he'd split the responsibilities evenly—but it was never even. It was never going to be. He loves the business in a way I never can. And he's worked so hard, given it everything. If I step back, he'll have everything he wants."

"Everything he wants?" There was a knowing undertone to his words that made her skin tingle.

"It's his dream, right?"

Her dad pursed his lips to the side and smoothed down his whiskers with two fingers. "Maybe. Once."

Her skin began to crawl, and a stone settled in the pit of her stomach. "Dad, you're not making any sense. He loves the *Pinch*. I understand now why you chose him."

He cocked his head and scratched his chin, his bushy eyebrows pulling tightly together. "Well, that'll be a bit of a problem. He told me he doesn't want it anymore."

She shot to her feet, staring down at him. "What do you mean? When did he say that?"

Her dad closed one eye and stared toward the ceiling with an exaggerated thinking face. "About a week ago, I suppose."

"Why would he say something like that?"

"Well, now, I'm not quoting him, but I think he figured if there was a boat between you two, there couldn't be anything else."

"Da-ad!" She slapped his arm. "Why didn't you tell me sooner?"

He chuckled. "I wanted to see if you felt the same."

"Don't wait on me for dinner," she cried as she raced out of the room, her dad's laughter following close behind.

# twenty-four

"Mom, I'll be back later," Oliver hollered over his shoulder as he slammed the kitchen door behind him, racing for his truck. Which wasn't there.

Didn't matter. He would run to her apartment. Or her parents' place. Or wherever she was.

He looked down at his clean jeans and tucked-in button-up. Okay, he'd walk. Briskly.

He hadn't gotten a step past the paved driveway when tires squealed on the road, then kicked up a red cloud of dust into the lane. He knew the car but couldn't comprehend what Meg was doing at his place.

She skidded to a stop a few feet in front of him, flew out from behind the wheel, and marched toward him like the queen had personally called her to battle. He couldn't tell from her stern teacher face if she was still upset with him or just upset at the world.

"Meg, what's wrong?"

She stabbed him in the chest with her finger, and he rubbed at the sting. But he couldn't stop staring at her. Her blazing eyes and fierce features. Her hair wild about her shoulders.

"What was that for?"

"You told my dad you didn't want the *Pinch* and the license and everything he's worked his whole life for." It wasn't a question but an accusation.

He wasn't going to let her walk all over him this time. "Yes, I did. And I'd do it again."

She blinked twice, and the corner of her mouth gave the smallest twitch. "Why would you do that?"

"Because." He stabbed his hand through his hair, still damp from his shower. "Because I love you. Because I wanted you to know that I love you more than any boat. More than any job. More than any future. Because without you, I don't have a future."

There. That had shut her up. But it might have also terrified her.

Meg froze, her perfect pink lips slightly open, her eyes wide and unblinking. Her lightning tongue seemed to have vanished—at least for the moment. He took the opportunity to say what he wanted to.

"Meg Whitaker, you amaze me. You are stubborn and loyal and strong, and I thought I was just going to have to put up with you this season. Then, out of nowhere, you showed up. And your pain was so familiar I couldn't ignore it. Then I didn't want to ignore it because I didn't want to ignore you."

He let out a short breath, turned his head, and clapped a hand to the back of his neck, ruffling the hair hanging over his collar. "I was not expecting you. I was expecting the girl you were ten years ago. The one who still hated me. But then you weren't. You were this." He waved his hand at all of her.

"You worked just as hard as Kyle and me, and you were so set on proving yourself.

"Then one morning I realized I was looking forward to seeing you. Every day I tried to make you laugh. I wanted to watch your face light up with the sunrise. I wanted to tell you my secrets. I've never told a soul about my dad and Eli and all of that. But you were my shelter in the storm. I loved every night we spent on that boat, every minute we spent with your mom. And I love you. So there you go. I didn't sabotage the boat. I didn't set out to manipulate you. I was never going to sell to some buyer. I wanted to buy Whitaker Fishing for myself. But then all of my plans didn't mean anything. Not without you. And I wasn't expecting it. I just fell in love. All right?"

Meg gasped a small breath but still didn't move except for a little quiver in her lower lip.

A possibility that he hadn't considered before slammed through him, a punch to the ribs. Maybe she didn't love him. Maybe she wouldn't forgive him. That made his heart physically ache. But he'd done his part. If she didn't feel the same, well, he'd be right back where he'd been that morning, practicing his best grizzly impression.

"Listen, it's okay if you don't—you know." He had to force the words out. "If you don't feel the—"

Then she was in his arms, hers tangled around him, pulling him closer, her lips on his. She wasn't frozen anymore. Melting into him, she clung to his shoulders and sighed. He scooped her closer until there was nothing between them.

Brushing her hair from her face, he let his thumb trace the smooth lines of her cheekbone and then dip to the hollow behind her ear. The sweet scent of lavender followed her every movement as she shivered all over and buried her face into his neck. Her breath was warm and comforting against his skin, sending lightning down his spine and all the way to the tips of his toes.

"Meg." Her name came out on a growl from deep in his chest. Right where he held her.

She finally pulled back just far enough to meet his gaze. "Oliver?"

"May I assume that means . . ."

"That I'm a little bit in love with you?" She nodded, and his arm around her waist tightened. "And that I'm so sorry I said such awful things to you?" Again she nodded. "I can't believe you would give up all of your dreams for me." Her words came out hushed, awed, and he dragged a hand down her arm until their fingers met. They brushed briefly at first, tentative, uncertain. Then she slipped her fingers between his, locking them together, holding on tight.

He held on too as he searched for the words. "It turns out it was an easy choice. You or the boat. I'll choose you every time."

Meg nearly melted into a puddle on the ground. How could he say such wonderful things and expect her to remain upright, expect her to keep her wits and her senses about her? And then she didn't need to as he tugged her toward the stairs by the garage. They sat on the third step, shoulder to shoulder, hip to hip, fingers still locked. Right there she could tell him anything.

"I was scared. Before the season started, I was scared of losing my mom, scared of change. Somehow the *Pinch* became this familiar thing I could hang on to."

He nodded a silent encouragement.

"And then you came along." She motioned at him with her free hand. "You were not what I expected either. Somehow you became the anchor I needed—more than the business. It was you. You pointed me to hope even when I couldn't hear it."

He grunted softly, a question of clarification.

"Just something that Pastor Dell told me." She stared off toward the setting sun, the bridge a gray blur against the pink-and-purple sky. "I can't imagine all the things I would have missed with my mom if not for you. Thank you."

He squeezed her hand.

"I told my dad today that I don't want the business."

He swung his whole body toward her, his shoulders blocking her view of the tree in the yard and the kitchen window across from them. "What? Why did you do that?"

"I guess probably for the same reason you did." She lifted a shoulder. "And I *really* hate the early mornings."

His laugh broke across his face in waves, first splitting his mouth with a grin and then diving into his dimples. "What are we going to do?"

"I want you to take it."

"I can't do that."

"No, I think you should work the *Pinch*, carry on my family's legacy. And maybe sometimes I could help. You know, with . . . not early-morning things. And no bait."

He opened his mouth, but no sound came out, so he threw his arms around her, crushing her to him. When he pressed his face to her hair, she couldn't stop a little hiccup of joy.

He held her for a long time, his heart a steady rhythm, pacing her own. The sun sank lower beneath the horizon, crickets chirping their evening song. When she couldn't contain it any longer, she whispered, "I might be more than a little bit in love with you."

"Right back at you, kid."

"And you kids are sure about this?"

Meg glanced down to where her hand rested on her parents' dining room table as Oliver reached over to hold it, passing his strength to her. "Yeah, we're sure. I want Oliver to take over the business." When she looked back up, her dad's face seemed to reflect the sun. Her mom's thin lips held a distinct smile.

Her dad let out a soft chuckle. "I've got to say, you took long enough getting here."

Meg darted a glance in Oliver's direction, but his furrowed brows said he understood about as much as she did. "What's that supposed to mean?"

"Only that I knew you didn't really want to be a lobsterman. But I also knew if you could just get past your history with Oliver, you two would make a fine couple. He's the kind of guy I always prayed you'd find."

"Da-ad," Meg said, covering her face with her free hand as her cheeks burned.

Oliver laughed, picking up her hand and carrying it to his lips. "Well, he's not wrong."

The corners of her dad's eyes crinkled, his smile wide enough to span the bridge. "I just thought maybe if you spent some time together, you'd see it for yourself. But Kyle reminded me that fishing isn't very romantic work."

"Kyle was in on this?" Oliver nearly growled. "I thought

he was sure quick to share all his romantic advice with me. Pushing me to patch things up." He shot Meg a quick glance, his eyes filled with a tenderness she had only recently recognized he saved just for her.

"You won't fire him, will you, Oliver?"

He shook his head. "No. I'm glad he pushed me when he did."

"Me too," she whispered.

When she glanced back across the table, something in her dad's smug look made her breath catch. Her stomach dropped, and she closed her eyes as her head spun, connecting memories with scenes she hadn't before. The back of her neck tingled as she thought about all of their struggles—and how the culprit hadn't really harmed them but had forced them together.

Her eyes flew open, and she pointed at her dad. "It was you. You sabotaged our season."

Oliver's mouth dropped open as he turned toward her dad, questions written all over his face.

Her dad held up his hands in surrender, but his smile didn't diminish. "You got me."

"But you were in Toronto when our line was cut," Oliver argued.

"True. I had an accomplice."

"Kyle," she and Oliver said at the same time.

"I can't believe you would cut your own traps and leave them on the bottom of the bay," Meg said.

Her dad looked like she'd personally offended him, pressing a hand to his chest. "I did no such thing. *Kyle* took the *Pinch* out the night before, hauled in the traps, and cut the line. They're in his garage."

Oliver shook his head and laughed in disbelief. "Of course they are. And the hauler?"

"I knew Meg could fix it in a minute. I just wanted to remind you what a good team you are, what special skills you each bring."

Meg sat back in her chair, her shoulders shaking with mirth, her head still spinning. She waited for that feeling of being duped, the reminder that she'd been manipulated. But it wasn't there. Not when she knew how much her dad loved her. Not when it was so clear that what he wanted for her was no less than what he shared with her mom. He wanted her to know a true partnership and a lifetime of sharing with Oliver the very best she had. Because it was worth it.

"I can't believe you'd do all of that just to get us on the boat together."

Holding up a finger, her dad added a clarification. "To get you on the boat together *alone*."

Oliver squeezed her hand still cradled in his. "Well, sir, I'm awfully glad you did."

"I'm glad you're worth it," her dad said.

Meg saw Oliver's Adam's apple bob and a subtle tremble in his lips. And she knew without a doubt that Oliver was the son her dad had never had, and her dad was the father Oliver had always wanted.

"So about the business . . ."

Oliver leaned forward, resting his elbows on the table. "I have the down payment. I can pay you the first installment we agreed on."

Her dad scratched his chin, his white whiskers rustling. "Well, now, it seems to me that that money might be better used on a new truck. You're going to have a hard time hauling the *Pinch* out of the marina before it freezes over without one."

"But . . ." Oliver's single word held a world of questions. Probably the same ones flying through Meg's mind.

"I didn't buy the license from my dad, and I'd never sell it to family." Her dad's knowing look made her entire face burn. Subtle he was not. Because it was written somewhere that fathers had to embarrass their daughters.

She and Oliver hadn't talked much about their future beyond the business. They were just enjoying the present. Assuming that he would propose anytime soon was presumptuous at best.

Oliver leaned further across the table. "I just want to make it clear that I love your daughter, and it has nothing to do with your license. If you want me to have it, I'll be grateful. If you'd rather keep it and just have me run the business, then I'll do that. But at the end of the day, I'll do whatever it takes to care for her. Always."

Somewhere between "whatever" and "always," Meg lost her breath and her patience. Pushing back her chair, she said their goodbyes. Then she rushed around the table to give her parents quick hugs and pulled Oliver through the kitchen and out the door with her.

The midday sun was bright and the air filled with a touch of autumn. She tugged on Oliver's hand, spinning him toward her before she backed him up against the yellow wall. Memories of the time he'd pressed her against it made the butterflies in her stomach take off, and she laid her hands against the soft blue flannel on his chest.

"Always, huh?"

He shrugged. "We've been through too much to let it go

to waste. And I kind of like the sound of Whitaker-Ross Fishing."

Her stomach took flight, but not the way it did when she stepped aboard a boat. The way that only Oliver and his kindness could make it fly. "Whitaker-Ross, eh?"

His smile turned nervous, the corner of his lip disappearing beneath his tooth. "Yeah. It has a nice ring, don't you think? And won't Little Tommy and Druthers spit out their coffee when they hear it?"

Pressing up on her toes, she kissed the angle of his jaw. He stiffened, his breathing shallow. She kissed the other side.

"I wasn't thinking right away or anything." His words came out in a rush, probably because she hadn't answered his questions. But she was having too much fun.

Sliding closer, she whispered into his ear, "What *were* you thinking?"

"That I love you a little bit."

She tickled his sides, and he yelped.

"Okay, a lot. I love you a lot. Besides . . ." His voice dropped away.

She pressed her lips to his chin and then to his nose. He groaned, and she knew exactly what he wanted. She wanted it too. But torturing him was too fun. She walked her fingers up to his neck, sliding her nails around to the back, getting lost in his silky hair.

"You know all my secrets. Can't risk letting you get away."

"Hmm? Really?"

Wrapping his arms around her waist, he didn't let her go. Which worked out well because she didn't want to be anywhere else. Especially not when he pressed his lips to hers and held on with everything he had.

She held on right back.

This time she really didn't care that God and anyone driving by could see them. Because she wanted to kiss him in front of the world for the rest of her life.

After a long while, she snuggled beneath his chin, her nose pressed into his neck. He was warm and familiar and so stable. Exactly what God knew she needed.

Looping a strand of his hair around her finger, she whispered, "You smell like my face cream."

"No, you smell like mine." And then he kissed her again, long and slow and so, so sweet.

# LOVED THIS BOOK FROM
# LIZ JOHNSON?

## DON'T MISS THE NEXT BOOK IN THE SERIES!

Turn the page for a special

sneak peek of book 2.

**COMING SUMMER 2022!**

# *one*

Eli Ross had a black eye, a fractured wrist, and nothing else to his name. It was not the way he'd planned to come home.

Then again, he hadn't planned to come home at all. He hadn't planned a lot of things. Didn't mean they hadn't happened. So here he was. Standing in front of the little green house he'd called home until he was nineteen. It had been repainted—at least, the chipped paint on the side facing the bay had been scraped and replaced. The house nearly gleamed in the morning sun.

It still made him feel a little seasick, the memories from the other side of the white door just as fresh as they had been more than a decade before. His father's empty closet. His mom's pinched features. His brother's face twisted with rage.

He shouldn't be here. There was a reason he hadn't been back in eleven years. A reason he'd kept his distance. A reason he'd never settled down and made a home of his own.

He didn't need a home. But at the moment, he needed a *place*. Somewhere to rest his head, to regroup, to be still.

If they would take him back.

He stabbed the fingers of his good hand through his short hair and flexed his other hand beneath the black wrist brace.

The breeze off the bay carried the almost forgotten scent of salt water and sunshine, setting the clay wind chime on the house's white wooden porch singing. His mom had made that when he was seven or eight. She'd been inordinately proud of it, hanging it where all the neighbors could easily see it.

The other houses on the small block gleamed just as bright, the sunshine filtering through towering trees and dancing across two-story roofs. Lacy white curtains hung in kitchen windows, and bright welcome mats sat before front doors.

It would be better if he walked away. No uncovering of old sins or confessing new ones. No need for apologies and atonement. No fear that they might send him right back where he came from.

After all, Oliver had told him in no uncertain terms that he wouldn't be welcome back.

Leaving had been his choice. Returning, less so. He had nowhere else to go. And he'd spent his last loonie on the bus ride over the Confederation Bridge that had dropped him off along Route 1. He'd walked to Victoria by the Sea without the aid of a map, his feet sure of the way before his mind could be. They'd carried him past the white theater and Carrie's Café, unchanged by time. And they'd taken him down the old paved street, the center line long faded.

He'd been standing in front of the old house for going on thirty minutes, and if he didn't make a move, one of his mom's neighbors was likely to report him for suspicious activity. Although if the neighbor recognized him, he might be asked for an autograph—which would be so much worse.

"They're not there."

Eli jumped, stumbling off the sidewalk and into the street, his gaze swinging toward a sprite of a woman who had snuck up on him. The top of her dark head didn't quite reach his shoulder, but the angle of her sharp chin and the power of her gaze made her appear to take up more space than her slender frame actually did.

"Excuse me?" He glanced around, because surely she couldn't be speaking to him. But they were the only two people here.

"They're. Not. There." She overly enunciated each word, her eyebrows raising higher on her forehead with each syllable.

"Who?" But his sinking stomach suggested he already knew. He just didn't know how she did.

He hadn't seen her before in his life. He was pretty sure. He squinted at her, studying the smooth lines of her fair cheeks, the button nose, and the plump pink lips set in a frown. Unfamiliar. He was almost certain. But it was her eyes that convinced him. He'd have remembered that strange shade of blue—half intensity, half serenity, nearly royal.

"You're Eli Ross, aren't you?"

His entire body went rigid except for his hand, which ran down his face and over the early beard he'd hoped would mask his identity. "Have we met?"

She crossed her arms. "I know who you are."

Was he supposed to know her too? He scratched his chin and offered a fake smile, the one the team publicist had coached him to give until it was second nature. Maybe they'd gone to high school together. Truthfully, he hadn't paid much attention to anything beyond the ice. And the girls in the stands at every game.

"Good to see you again," he said.

Her frown turned into a smirk. "Again?"

He swallowed thickly. "For the first time?"

She nodded, quick and sure.

He turned toward her, facing her fully. "Then you seem to have the advantage. How do you know me?"

"Oh, I don't assume that I know you. I just recognize your face."

She was talking in riddles that made him want to shake some truth out of her. "But you assume that you know who—or what—I'm looking for." He nodded toward the house.

Her smirk turned sheepish, her nose flaring. "I suppose I do. Only because if I hadn't been home in more than ten years, I'd probably be looking for my family too."

He nearly growled at her. "There you go again, making assumptions about my life. What makes you think I haven't been back in ten years?"

"Because your mom misses you."

Her soft comment hit him harder than any opposing player checking him against the boards ever had, and he clenched his teeth, using everything inside him to keep from showing how much he hated those words.

And how much he'd longed for them too.

Maybe he'd succeeded in keeping his face from reflecting his reaction. Or maybe he hadn't. Her lips twitched, and then her whole face softened.

"I guess it's really none of my business," she said and turned to walk away.

His hand shot out to catch her elbow, and she spun easily on the uneven sidewalk. "Who are you? How do you know so much about my family?"

Eyes turning serious, she glanced down to where his hand was wrapped around her arm. Her pointed glance back up at him made him drop his grip, and the intensity in her eyes dimmed a fraction. "I don't like seeing my friends hurt."

And he definitely wasn't one of her friends.

When she stepped away again, he didn't try to stop her. Instead, he watched her stroll past the deep purple house with the white porch and lots of gingerbread at the end of the block. Mrs. Dunwitty used to live there—back when the house was brown and Oliver had mowed the old woman's lawn every other week.

She turned the corner and disappeared, and only then did he ask the question he should have from the start. "If they're not here, where's my family?"

By the time Violet Donaghy returned to Mama Potts's Red Clay Shoppe from her midmorning walk, her pulse was racing, her head spinning. She slammed the front door and sank against the wall beside a six-foot wooden shelf. Rows of mugs made from the island's famous red clay rattled in their places, and she reached out to still them.

"Vi? Is that you?" Mama Potts's voice rang through the open door to the studio in the back. It carried a touch of worry, and Violet's heart pounded even harder.

Did Mama Potts know already? Maybe she'd heard the news. Maybe Victoria by the Sea's gossip mill had been hard at work, spreading the word, ringing the church bells. Kill the fattened calf. Prepare the family signet ring. The prodigal son had returned.

Eli Ross was back in town.

"Yes." Violet's voice cracked, and she cleared her throat to try again. "It's me." She wanted to ask what Mama Potts had already heard, but she could manage only silence. Something Mama Potts knew well. After all, they'd heard exactly nothing from Eli in the more than seven months since every sports reporter on the continent had announced that he'd been let go by the Rangers and ejected from the entire National Hockey League.

Not that silence was unusual from him. It was all that Mama Potts, Oliver, and Levi had known since Eli took off for his chance at a career in the pros. Therefore it was all that Violet had ever known from him. Well, silence and the aftermath of heartbreak.

But he was every bit flesh and blood. And piercing blue eyes—despite an impressive shiner. And unruly black hair. And more than a five-o'clock shadow at ten in the morning. And broad shoulders.

Not that she'd noticed. Much.

She scowled at herself.

Okay, so he was a broader, handsomer version of his brothers. He was also a selfish, thoughtless—

"I think there's something wrong." Mama Potts had rarely raised her voice in the nine years Violet had known her, but there was an edge to it now, an urgency that sent Violet pushing off the wall.

She weaved between the rows of waist-high wooden bookshelves that displayed countless pieces glazed in bright blues and greens and every other color of the rainbow. She whipped past a stack of purple platters, rattling them as her hip bumped the corner of the shelf. Pain shot toward her knee, but she didn't stop until she'd raced past the built-in counter and through the open door off to the left.

"Are you—" Violet's question and feet both stopped when she saw Mama Potts standing on the far side of their studio.

The older woman looked just fine, small but strong. Her fists were pushed against her hips, and her pretty features pinched as she glared at the large round kiln in the corner.

Violet pressed a hand to the thudding in her chest and tried for a smile. Whatever had made Mama Potts call out couldn't be that concerning. And most likely it did not involve any knowledge of Eli. She hoped.

Then again, that did leave her to share the news—the beans she was not eager to spill. These were family beans, and despite nearly a decade of mentorship and business partnership, Mama Potts wasn't her mom, and Oliver and Levi weren't her brothers.

"What's wrong?" Violet finally asked.

Mama Potts shook her head and kicked the front of the metal kiln. "Something's off. It's—" She stopped at the exact moment the room filled with the acrid scent of burning rubber.

Violet twisted her neck, looking for the source, and shrieked as sparks jumped from the wall beside Mama Potts. Racing across the room, Violet had nearly reached her side when the socket kicked out another round of fireworks and the white wall around the plastic plate turned black and charred.

"It's in the wall!" Mama Potts shrieked, grabbing Violet's arm and tugging her back.

But the fire didn't stay there. Flames suddenly burst from the electrical panel on the kiln and lit up the whole room. The morning sun shining through the open garage door made the flames disappear except for the blue at the center, which flickered in the wind.

Mama Potts's hand beat on her shoulder. "Get the—get the—get the—"

Violet ran for the red fire extinguisher mounted below the wooden steps that led to her apartment on the second floor. She fumbled with the release, and when she finally got it open, she spun around just in time to see the flames jump to the wooden shelves that held pieces waiting for their turn to be fired.

Right beside the shelves sat a pile of rags atop a small pallet holding metal cans of glaze mixed with solvents. And all with plastic lids.

Her stomach hit the cement slab floor. She tried to scream, but her throat closed.

The wind whipped the fire across the pallet, igniting the rags and melting the lids.

The explosion wasn't like in the movies. Shrapnel didn't go flying. The roof stayed firmly in place.

And the fire was manageable. Until it wasn't. The blaze went from blue to towering orange flames in an instant, consuming everything in its path. The heat weighed on Violet's shoulders, dozens of kilos pressing her arms to her sides. She couldn't even lift the extinguisher in her hands. Not that it would have helped.

Mama Potts scrambled back from the flames, her heel catching on a worktable and sending her sprawling on the ground.

Violet screamed, trying to warn Mama Potts, but her words were lost. She glanced at the extinguisher again but set it aside without any real consideration. The spray it held wouldn't stop the inferno devouring their studio. But at least she could get Mama Potts out safely.

Rushing toward the heat, she squinted into the light as sweat poured down her back. When she reached Mama Potts, she squatted next to her, bracing an arm behind her back. "Here. Get up. Come on."

But when the older woman braced her foot against the floor and began to push herself upright, she cried out.

Violet gasped, immediately choking on the smoke and chemicals filling the air. Her lungs burned, and tears rushed to her eyes. "Come on. You have to help me."

Mama Potts coughed, doing her best to scoot across the floor. She cringed with each inch, and Violet turned to see how far they had yet to go to reach the sunshine-covered yard.

*Please, let us make it.*

She didn't pray as often as she had as a child, but if ever there was an occasion, this was it. She hoped God heard even the desperate cries of those who had almost forgotten how to pray.

Then there wasn't time to think about it. There was only a massive black silhouette in the open door, his arms pumping and his feet swallowing up the ground.

"Oliver!" Violet couldn't help the tremor in her voice as relief rushed through her. His dark head bowed over his mom, and he scooped her into his strong arms. Mama Potts rested her head against his shoulder, linking her hands about his neck as he cleared the fire.

Free of the building and the suffocating smoke, Violet pressed her hands to her knees, savoring the salty tang of the fresh air. The wind dried her tears to her cheeks as she looked back at the building, half of their studio already consumed.

The metal buckets flickered among the flames near the kiln. Right where she knew better than to leave flammable solvents. Right where she'd left them anyway.

This was her fault.

Her stomach heaved, and she gasped for more air as sirens split the air. They were still a kilometer or more away, but they were on their way. She hadn't called. Neither had Mama Potts. They hadn't had time.

Oliver. He must have called for firefighters. When she turned to thank him, her insides twisted again. This time she really was going to be sick.

Because the man gently setting his mom on the ground wasn't Oliver Ross. Or even his little brother, Levi.

In the sunlight and free of the shadows, there was no denying the way his mom cupped his cheek and whispered his name with pure love.

"Eli."

# Acknowledgments

I had hoped to go back to Prince Edward Island while writing this book, but a global pandemic changed my plans. So, like you, my reader friends, I'm thankful for the chance to visit it once again on the page. And I couldn't have done so without an incredible group of people.

Rachel Kent and Books & Such Literary Management, thank you for believing in my stories. Thank you for believing in me. Thank you for your steady guidance and calm assurance for more than a decade.

The amazing team at Revell makes every one of my books better and each publishing journey more fun. Thank you, Vicki, Jessica, Michele, Karen, and the rest of the team. Thank you for helping me tell my stories well.

The writing journey can be a lonely one. I'm beyond grateful that God brought a special group of writers into my life. Thank you, Lindsay Harrel, Sara Carrington, Jennifer Deibel, Sarah Popovich, and Erin McFarland, for your brainstorming and your input, your kindness and your encouragement. This group has been one of the joys of my life.

The earliest seeds of this story began to bloom on a sweet

writing retreat in the mountains of Southern California with Joanne Bischof and Melissa Tagg. I'm forever grateful to have spent a long weekend with such amazing writers and stellar women.

A special thank-you to reader and friend Debi Hodam, who suggested the name Mama Potts.

While I was writing this book, my family weathered a terrible storm, an awful blow. There's no doubt that I could not have written these words without their love and support. God gave me an extra blessing when he made me a Johnson. Being a part of this family is the best.

Finally, I owe all my gratitude and all my joy to the Miracle Maker, my good, good Father, who has showed up and showed off more times than I can count.

**Liz Johnson** is the author of more than a dozen novels, including *A Sparkle of Silver*, *A Glitter of Gold*, *A Dazzle of Diamonds*, *The Red Door Inn*, *Where Two Hearts Meet*, and *On Love's Gentle Shore*, as well as a *New York Times* best-selling novella and a handful of short stories. She works in marketing and makes her home in Phoenix, Arizona. But she wishes she could live on Prince Edward Island.

# Escape to
# PRINCE EDWARD ISLAND . . .

"A charming inn in need of restoration, Prince Edward Island, and a love story? Yes, please! I thoroughly enjoyed the vicarious visit to the Canadian Maritime Province of Prince Edward Island. I could almost feel the sea breeze!"

**—BECKY WADE,**
**ECPA bestselling author of the Porter Family series**

# Meet
# LIZ JOHNSON

## LizJohnsonBooks.com

Read her
BLOG

Follow her
SPEAKING
SCHEDULE

Connect
with her on
SOCIAL
MEDIA